CONTENTS

A
LOUISA MAY ALCOTT
CHRISTMAS

Selected Holiday Stories
and Poems

LOUISA MAY ALCOTT
Edited by Raina Moore

HarperFestival®
A Division of HarperCollins*Publishers*

The editor would like to thank Pat Pflieger
at West Chester University in Pennsylvania and
the reference librarians of the Central Children's Room
at the Donnell Library Center in New York City.

HarperCollins®, ☷®, and HarperFestival® are registered trademarks of
HarperCollins Publishers Inc.

A Louisa May Alcott Christmas: Selected Holiday Stories and Poems
© 2004 by HarperCollins Publishers.
For information address HarperCollins Children's Books,
a division of HarperCollins Publishers, 1350 Avenue of the Americas,
New York, NY 10019.
www.harperchildrens.com

Library of Congress catalog card number: 2003115276

Typography by Fritz Metsch
1 2 3 4 5 6 7 8 9 10
❖
First HarperFestival edition, 2004.

A
LOUISA MAY ALCOTT
CHRISTMAS

Selected Holiday Stories
and Poems

LOUISA MAY ALCOTT
Edited by Raina Moore

HarperFestival®
A Division of HarperCollins*Publishers*

The editor would like to thank Pat Pflieger
at West Chester University in Pennsylvania and
the reference librarians of the Central Children's Room
at the Donnell Library Center in New York City.

A Louisa May Alcott Christmas: Selected Holiday Stories and Poems
© 2004 by HarperCollins Publishers.
All rights reserved. Printed in the United States of America.
For information address HarperCollins Children's Books,
a division of HarperCollins Publishers, 1350 Avenue of the Americas,
New York, NY 10019.
www.harperchildrens.com

Library of Congress catalog card number: 2003115276

Typography by Fritz Metsch
1 2 3 4 5 6 7 8 9 10
❖
First HarperFestival edition, 2004.

1
An Old Fashioned Thanksgiving

November, 1881

SIXTY YEARS AGO, up among the New Hampshire hills, lived Farmer Bassett, with a houseful of sturdy sons and daughters growing up about him. They were poor in money, but rich in land and love, for the wide acres of wood, corn, and pasture land fed, warmed, and clothed the flock, while mutual patience, affection, and courage made the old farmhouse a very happy home.

November had come; the crops were in, and barn, buttery, and bin were overflowing with the harvest that rewarded the summer's hard work. The big kitchen was a jolly place just now, for in the great fireplace roared a cheerful fire; on the walls hung garlands of dried apples, onions, and corn; up aloft from the beams shone crook-necked squashes, juicy hams, and dried venison—for in those days deer still haunted the deep forests, and hunters flourished. Savory smells were in the air; on the crane hung steaming kettles, and down among the red embers copper saucepans simmered, all suggestive of some approaching feast.

A white-headed baby lay in the old blue cradle that had

rocked six other babies, now and then lifting his head to look out, like a round, full moon, then subsided to kick and crow contentedly, and suck the rosy apple he had no teeth to bite. Two small boys sat on the wooden settle shelling corn for popping, and picking out the biggest nuts from the goodly store their own hands had gathered in October. Four young girls stood at the long dresser, busily chopping meat, pounding spice, and slicing apples; and the tongues of Tilly, Prue, Roxy, and Rhody went as fast as their hands. Farmer Bassett, and Eph, the oldest boy, were "chorin' 'round" outside, for Thanksgiving was at hand, and all must be in order for that time-honored day.

To and fro, from table to hearth, bustled buxom Mrs. Bassett, flushed and floury, but busy and blithe as the queen bee of this busy little hive should be.

"I do like to begin seasonable and have things to my mind. Thanksgivin' dinners can't be drove, and it does take a sight of victuals to fill all these hungry stomicks," said the good woman, as she gave a vigorous stir to the great kettle of cider applesauce, and cast a glance of housewifely pride at the fine array of pies set forth on the buttery shelves.

"Only one more day and then it will be the time to eat. I didn't take but one bowl of hasty pudding this morning, so I shall have plenty of room when the nice things come," confided Seth to Sol, as he cracked a large hazelnut as easily as a squirrel.

"No need of my starvin' beforehand. *I always* have room enough, and I'd like to have Thanksgiving every day," answered Solomon, gloating like a young ogre over the little pig that lay near by, ready for roasting.

"Sakes alive, I don't, boys! It's a marcy it don't come but once a year. I should be worn to a thread paper with all this extra work atop of my winter weavin' and spinnin'," laughed their mother, as she plunged her plump arms into the long bread trough and began to knead the dough as if a famine were at hand.

Tilly, the oldest girl, a red-cheeked, black-eyed lass of fourteen, was grinding briskly at the mortar, for spices were costly, and not a grain must be wasted. Prue kept time with the chopper, and the twins sliced away at the apples till their little brown arms ached, for all knew how to work, and did so now with a will.

"I think it's real fun to have Thanksgiving at home. I'm sorry Gran'ma is sick, so we can't go there as usual, but I like to mess 'round here, don't you, girls?" asked Tilly, pausing to take a sniff at the spicy pestle.

"It will be kind of lonesome with only our own folks." "I like to see all the cousins and aunts, and have games, and sing," cried the twins, who were regular little romps, and could run, swim, coast, and shout as well as their brothers.

"I don't care a mite for all that. It will be so nice to eat dinner together, warm and comfortable at home," said quiet Prue, who loved her own cozy nooks like a cat.

"Come, girls, fly 'round and get your chores done, so we can clear away for dinner jest as soon as I clap my bread into the oven," called Mrs. Bassett presently, as she rounded off the last loaf of brown bread which was to feed the hungry mouths that seldom tasted any other.

"Here's a man comin' up the hill lively!" "Guess it's Gad Hopkins. Pa told him to bring a dezzen oranges, if they warn't too high!" shouted Sol and Seth, running to the door, while the girls smacked their lips at the thought of this rare treat, and Baby threw his apple overboard, as if getting ready for a new cargo.

But all were doomed to disappointment, for it was not Gad, with the much-desired fruit. It was a stranger, who threw himself off his horse and hurried up to Mr. Bassett in the yard, with some brief message that made the farmer drop his ax and look so sober that his wife guessed at once some bad news had come; and crying, "Mother's wuss! I know she is!" Out ran the good woman, forgetful of the flour on her arms and the oven waiting for its most important batch.

The man said old Mr. Chadwick, down to Keene, stopped him as he passed, and told him to tell Mrs. Bassett her mother was failin' fast, and she'd better come today. He knew no more, and having delivered his errand he rode away, saying it looked like snow and he must be jogging, or he wouldn't get home till night.

"We must go right off, Eldad. Hitch up, and I'll be ready in less'n no time," said Mrs. Bassett, wasting not a minute in tears and lamentations, but pulling off her apron as she went in, with her head in a sad-jumble of bread, anxiety, turkey, sorrow, haste, and cider applesauce.

A few words told the story, and the children left their work to help her get ready, mingling their grief for "Gran'ma" with regrets for the lost dinner.

"I'm dreadful sorry, dears, but it can't be helped. I couldn't cook nor eat no way now, and if that blessed woman gets better sudden, as she has before, we'll have cause for thanksgivin', and I'll give you a dinner you won't forget in a hurry," said Mrs. Bassett, as she tied on her brown silk pumpkin-hood, with a sob for the good old mother who had made it for her.

Not a child complained after that, but ran about helpfully, bringing moccasins, heating the footstone, and getting ready for a long drive, because Gran'ma lived twenty miles away, and there were no railroads in those parts to whisk people to and fro like magic. By the time the old yellow sleigh was at the door, the bread was in the oven, and Mrs. Bassett was waiting, with her camlet cloak on, and the baby done up like a small bale of blankets.

"Now, Eph, you must look after the cattle like a man, and keep up the fires, for there's a storm brewin', and neither the children nor dumb critters must suffer," said Mr. Bassett, as he turned up the collar of his rough coat and put on his blue mittens, while the old mare shook her bells as if she preferred a trip to Keene to hauling wood all day.

"Tilly, put extry comfortables on the beds to-night, the wind is so searchin' up chamber. Have the baked beans and Indian-puddin' for dinner, and whatever you do, don't let the boys get at the mince-pies, or you'll have them down sick. I shall come back the minute I can leave Mother. Pa will come to-morrer anyway, so keep snug and be good. I depend on you, my darter; use your jedgment, and don't let nothin' happen while Mother's away."

"Yes'm, yes'm—good-bye, good-bye!" called the children, as Mrs. Bassett was packed into the sleigh and driven away, leaving a stream of directions behind her.

Eph, the sixteen-year-old boy, immediately put on his biggest boots, assumed a sober, responsible manner, and surveyed his little responsibilities with a paternal air, drolly like his father's. Tilly tied on her mother's bunch of keys, rolled up the sleeves of her homespun gown, and began to order about the younger girls. They soon forgot poor Granny, and found it great fun to keep house all alone, for Mother seldom left home, but ruled her family in the good old-fashioned way. There were no servants, for the little daughters were Mrs. Bassett's only maids, and the stout boys helped their father, all working happily together with no wages but love; learning in the best manner the use of the heads and hands with which they were to make their own way in the world.

The few flakes that caused the farmer to predict bad weather soon increased to a regular snowstorm, with gusts of wind, for up among the hills winter came early and lingered long. But the children were busy, gay, and warm indoors, and never minded the rising gale nor the whirling white storm outside.

Tilly got them a good dinner, and when it was over the two elder girls went to their spinning, for in the kitchen stood the big and little wheels, and baskets of wool rolls, ready to be twisted into yarn for the winter's knitting, and each day brought its stint of work to the daughters, who hoped to be as thrifty as their mother.

Eph kept up a glorious fire, and superintended the small boys, who popped corn and whittled boats on the hearth; while Roxy and Rhody dressed corncob dolls in the settle corner, and Bose, the brindled mastiff, lay on the braided mat, luxuriously warming his old legs. Thus employed, they made a pretty picture, these rosy boys and girls, in their homespun suits, with the rustic toys or tasks which most children nowadays would find very poor or tiresome.

Tilly and Prue sang, as they stepped to and fro, drawing out the smoothly twisted threads to the musical hum of the great spinning wheels. The little girls chattered like magpies over their dolls and the new bedspread they were planning to make, all white dimity stars on a blue calico ground, as a Christmas present to Ma. The boys roared at Eph's jokes, and had rough and tumble games over Bose, who didn't mind them in the least; and so the afternoon wore pleasantly away.

At sunset the boys went out to feed the cattle, bring in

heaps of wood, and lock up for the night, as the lonely farmhouse seldom had visitors after dark. The girls got the simple supper of brown bread and milk, baked apples, and a doughnut all 'round as a treat. Then they sat before the fire, the sisters knitting, the brothers with books or games, for Eph loved reading, and Sol and Seth never failed to play a few games of Morris with barley corns, on the little board they had themselves at one corner of the dresser.

"Read out a piece," said Tilly from Mother's chair, where she sat in state, finishing off the sixth woolen sock she had knit that month.

"It's the old history book, but here's a bit you may like, since it's about our folks," answered Eph, turning the yellow page to look at a picture of two quaintly dressed children in some ancient castle.

"Yes, read that. I always like to hear about the Lady Matildy I was named for, and Lord Bassett, Pa's great-great-great grandpa. He's only a farmer now, but it's nice to know we were somebody two or three hundred years ago," said Tilly, bridling and tossing her curly head as she fancied the Lady Matilda might have done.

"Don't read the queer words, 'cause we don't understand 'em. Tell it," commanded Roxy, from the cradle, where she was drowsily cuddled with Rhody.

"Well, a long time ago, when Charles the First was in prison, Lord Bassett was a true friend to him," began Eph, plunging into his story without delay. "The lord had some papers that would have hung a lot of people if the king's enemies got hold of 'em, so when he heard one day, all of a sudden, that soldiers were at the castle gate to carry him off, he had just time to call his girl to him, and say: 'I may be going to my death, but I won't betray my master. There is no time to burn the papers, and I can not take them with me; they are hidden in the old leathern chair where I sit. No one knows this but you, and you must guard them till I come or send you a safe messenger to take them away. Promise me to be brave and silent, and I can go without fear.' You see, he wasn't afraid to die, but he *was* to seem a traitor. Lady Matildy promised solemnly, and the words were hardly out of her mouth when the men came in, and her father was carried away a prisoner and sent off to the Tower."

"But she didn't cry; she just called her brother, and sat down in that chair, with her head leaning back on those papers, like a queen, and waited while the soldiers hunted the house over for 'em: wasn't that a smart girl?" cried Tilly, beaming with pride, for she was named for this ancestress, and knew the story by heart.

"I reckon she was scared, though, when the men came swearin' in and asked her if she knew anything about it. The boy did his part then, for *he* didn't know, and fired up and stood before his sister; and he says, says he, as bold as a lion: 'If my lord had told us where the papers be, we would die before we would betray him. But we are children and know nothing, and it is cowardly of you to try to fight us with oaths and drawn swords!'"

As Eph quoted from the book, Seth planted himself before Tilly, with the long poker in his hand, saying, as he flourished it valiantly:

"Why didn't the boy take his father's sword and lay about him? I would, if any one was ha'sh to Tilly."

"You bantam! He was only a bit of a boy, and couldn't do anything. Sit down and hear the rest of it," commanded Tilly, with a pat on the yellow head, and a private resolve that Seth should have the largest piece of pie at dinner next day, as reward for his chivalry.

"Well, the men went off after turning the castle out of window, but they said they should come again; so faithful Matildy was full of trouble, and hardly dared to leave the room where the chair stood. All day she sat there, and at night her sleep was so full of fear about it, that she often got up and went to see that all was safe. The servants thought the fright had hurt her wits, and let her be, but Rupert, the boy, stood by her and never was afraid of her queer ways. She was 'a pious maid,' the book says, and often spent the long evenings reading the Bible, with her brother by her, all alone in the great room, with no one to help her bear her secret, and no good news of her father. At last, word came that the king was dead and his friends banished out of England. Then the poor children were in a sad plight, for they had no mother, and the servants all ran away, leaving only one faithful old man to help them."

"But the father did come?" cried Roxy, eagerly.

"You'll see," continued Eph, half telling, half reading.

"Matilda was sure he would, so she sat on in the big chair, guarding the papers, and no one could get her away, till one day a man came with her father's ring and told her to give up the secret. She knew the ring, but would not tell until she had asked many questions, so as to be very sure, and while the man answered all about her father and the king, she looked at him sharply. Then she stood up and said, in a tremble, for there was something strange about the man: 'Sir, I doubt you in spite of the ring, and I will not answer till you pull off the false beard you wear, that I may see your face and know if you are my father's friend or foe.' Off came the disguise, and Matilda found it was my lord himself, come to take them with him out of England. He was very proud of that faithful girl, I guess, for the old chair still stands in the castle, and the name keeps in the family,

Pa says, even over here, where some of the Bassetts came along with the Pilgrims."

"Our Tilly would have been as brave, I know, and she looks like the old picter down to Gran'ma's, don't she, Eph?" cried Prue, who admired her bold, bright sister very much.

"Well, I think you'd do the settin' part best, Prue, you are so patient. Till would fight like a wild cat, but she can't hold her tongue worth a cent," answered Eph; whereat Tilly pulled his hair, and the story ended with a general frolic.

When the moon-faced clock behind the door struck nine, Tilly tucked up the children under the "extry comfortables," and having kissed them all around, as Mother did, crept into her own nest, never minding the little drifts of snow that sifted in upon her coverlet between the shingles of the roof, nor the storm that raged without.

As if he felt the need of unusual vigilance, old Bose lay down on the mat before the door, and pussy had the warm hearth all to herself. If any late wanderer had looked in at midnight, he would have seen the fire blazing up again, and in the cheerful glow the old cat blinking her yellow eyes, as she sat bolt upright beside the spinning wheel, like some sort of household goblin, guarding the children while they slept.

When they woke, like early birds, it still snowed, but up the little Bassetts jumped, broke the ice in their jugs, and went down with cheeks glowing like winter apples, after a brisk scrub and scramble into their clothes. Eph was off to the barn, and Tilly soon had a great kettle of mush ready, which, with milk warm from the cows made a wholesome breakfast for the seven hearty children.

"Now about dinner," said the young housekeeper, as the pewter spoons stopped clattering, and the earthen bowls stood empty.

"Ma said, have what we liked, but she didn't expect us to have a real Thanksgiving dinner, because she won't be here to cook it, and we don't know how," began Prue, doubtfully.

"I can roast a turkey and make a pudding as well as anybody, I guess. The pies are all ready, and if we can't boil vegetables and so on, we don't deserve any dinner," cried Tilly, burning to distinguish herself, and bound to enjoy to the utmost her brief authority.

"Yes, yes!" cried all the boys, "let's have a dinner anyway; Ma won't care, and the good victuals will spoil if they ain't eaten right up."

"Pa is coming tonight, so we won't have dinner till late; that will be real genteel and give us plenty of time," added Tilly, suddenly realizing the novelty of the task she had undertaken.

"Did you ever roast a turkey?" asked Roxy, with an air of deep interest.

"Should you darst to try?" said Rhody, in an awe-stricken tone.

"You will see what I can do. Ma said I was to use my judgment about things, and I'm going to. All you children have got to do is to keep out of the way, and let Prue and me work. Eph, I wish you'd put a fire in the best room, so the little ones can play in there. We shall want the settin'-room for the table, and I won't have them pickin' 'round when we get things fixed," commanded Tilly, bound to make her short reign a brilliant one.

"I don't know about that. Ma didn't tell us to," began cautious Eph who felt that this invasion of the sacred best parlor was a daring step.

"Don't we always do it Sundays and Thanksgivings? Wouldn't Ma wish the children kept safe and warm anyhow? Can I get up a nice dinner with four rascals under my feet all the time? Come, now, if you want roast turkey and onions, plum-puddin' and mince-pie, you'll have to do as I tell you, and be lively about it."

Tilly spoke with such spirit, and her suggestion was so irresistible, that Eph gave in, and, laughing good-naturedly, tramped away to heat up the best room, devoutly hoping that nothing serious would happen to punish such audacity.

The young folks delightedly trooped away to destroy the order of that prim apartment with housekeeping under the black horsehair sofa, "horseback-riders" on the arms of the best rocking chair, and an Indian war dance all over the well-waxed furniture. Eph, finding the society of peaceful sheep and cows more to his mind than that of two excited sisters, lingered over his chores in the barn as long as possible, and left the girls in peace.

Now Tilly and Prue were in their glory, and as soon as the breakfast things were out of the way, they prepared for a grand cooking time. They were handy girls, though they had never heard of a cooking school, never touched a piano, and knew nothing of embroidery beyond the samplers which hung framed in the parlor; one ornamented with a pink mourner under a blue weeping willow, the other with this pleasing verse, each word being done in a different color, which gave the effect of a distracted rainbow:

> *This sampler neat was worked by me,*
> *In my twelfth year, Prudence B.*

Both rolled up their sleeves, put on their largest aprons, and got out all the spoons, dishes, pots, and pans they could find, "so as to have everything handy," Prue said.

"Now, sister, we'll have dinner at five; Pa will be here by that time, if he is coming tonight, and be so surprised to

find us all ready, for he won't have had any very nice victuals if Gran'ma is so sick," said Tilly, importantly. "I shall
give the children a piece at noon" (Tilly meant luncheon);
"doughnuts and cheese, with apple pie and cider, will
please 'em. There's beans for Eph; he likes cold pork, so we
won't stop to warm it up, for there's lots to do, and I don't
mind saying to you I'm dreadful dubersome about the
turkey."

"It's all ready but the stuffing, and roasting is as easy as
can be. I can baste first-rate. Ma always likes to have me,
I'm so patient and stiddy, she says," answered Prue, for the
responsibility of this great undertaking did not rest upon
her, so she took a cheerful view of things.

"I know, but it's the stuffin' that troubles me," said Tilly,
rubbing her round elbows as she eyed the immense fowl
laid out on a platter before her. "I don't know how much I
want, nor what sort of yarbs to put in, and he's so awful big,
I'm kind of afraid of him."

"I ain't! I fed him all summer, and he never gobbled at
me. I feel real mean to be thinking of gobbling him, poor
old chap," laughed Prue, patting her departed pet with an
air of mingled affection and appetite.

"Well, I'll get the puddin' off my mind fust, for it ought
to bile all day. Put the big kettle on, and see that the spit is
clean, while I get ready."

Prue obediently tugged away at the crane, with its black
hooks, from which hung the iron teakettle and three-legged
pot; then she settled the long spit in the grooves made for
it in the tall andirons, and put the dripping pan underneath,
for in those days meat was roasted as it should be, not
baked in ovens.

Meantime Tilly attacked the plum pudding. She felt
pretty sure of coming out right, here, for she had seen her

mother do it so many times, it looked very easy. So in went suet and fruit; all sorts of spice, to be sure she got the right ones, and brandy instead of wine. But she forgot both sugar and salt, and tied it in the cloth so tightly that it had no room to swell, so it would come out as heavy as lead and as hard as a cannonball, if the bag did not burst and spoil it all. Happily unconscious of these mistakes, Tilly popped it into the pot, and proudly watched it bobbing about before she put the cover on and left it to its fate.

"I can't remember what flavorin' Ma puts in," she said, when she had got her bread well soaked for stuffing. "Sage and onions and applesauce go with goose, but I can't feel sure of anything but pepper and salt for a turkey."

"Ma puts in some kind of mint, I know, but I forget whether it is spearmint, peppermint, or pennyroyal," answered Prue, in a tone of doubt, but trying to show her knowledge of "yarbs," or, at least, of their names.

"Seems to me it's sweet majoram or summer savory. I guess we'll put both in, and then we are sure to be right. The best is up garret; you run and get some, while I mash the bread," commanded Tilly, diving into the mess.

Away trotted Prue, but in her haste she got catnip and wormwood, for the garret was darkish, and Prue's little nose was so full of the smell of the onions she had been peeling, that everything smelt of them. Eager to be of use, she pounded up the herbs and scattered the mixture with a liberal hand into the bowl.

"It doesn't smell just right, but I suppose it will when it is cooked," said Tilly, as she filled the empty stomach, that seemed aching for food, and sewed it up with the blue yarn, which happened to be handy. She forgot to tie down his legs and wings, but she set him by till his hour came, well satisfied with her work.

"Shall we roast the little pig, too? I think he'd look nice with a necklace of sausages, as Ma fixed him at Christmas," asked Prue, elated with their success.

"I couldn't do it. I loved that little pig, and cried when he was killed. I should feel as if I was roasting the baby," answered Tilly, glancing toward the buttery where piggy hung, looking so pink and pretty it certainly did seem cruel to eat him.

It took a long time to get all the vegetables ready, for, as the cellar was full, the girls thought they would have every sort. Eph helped, and by noon all was ready for cooking, and the cranberry sauce, a good deal scorched, was cooking in the lean-to.

Luncheon was a lively meal, and doughnuts and cheese vanished in such quantities that Tilly feared no one would have an appetite for her sumptuous dinner. The boys assured her they would be starving by five o'clock, and Sol mourned bitterly over the little pig that was not to be served up.

"Now you all go and coast, while Prue and I set the table and get out the best chiny," said Tilly, bent on having her dinner look well, no matter what its other failings might be.

Out came the rough sleds, on went the round hoods, old hats, red cloaks, and moccasins, and away trudged the four younger Bassetts, to disport themselves in the snow, and try the ice down by the old mill, where the great wheel turned and splashed so merrily in the summertime.

Eph took his fiddle and scraped away to his heart's content in the parlor, while the girls, after a short rest, set the table and made all ready to dish up the dinner when that exciting moment came. It was not at all the sort of table we see now, but would look very plain and countrified to us, with its green-handled knives, and two-pronged steel forks, its red-and-white china, and pewter platters, scoured till they shone, with mugs and spoons to match, and a brown jug for the cider. The cloth was coarse, but white as snow, and the little maids had seen the blue-eyed flax grow, out of which their mother wove the linen; they had watched and watched while it bleached in the green meadow. They had no napkins and little silver; but the best tankard and Ma's few wedding spoons were set forth in state. Nuts and apples at the corners gave an air, and the place of honor was left in the middle for the oranges yet to come.

"Don't it look beautiful?" said Prue, when they paused to admire the general effect.

"Pretty nice, I think. I wish Ma could see how well we can do it," began Tilly, when a loud howling startled both girls, and sent them flying to the window. The short afternoon had passed so quickly that twilight had come before they knew it, and now, as they looked out through the gathering dusk, they saw four small black figures tearing up the road, to come bursting in, all screaming at once: "The bear, the bear! Eph, get the gun! He's coming, he's coming!"

Eph had dropped his fiddle, and got down his gun before the girls could calm the children enough to tell their story, which they did in a somewhat incoherent manner. "Down in the holler, coastin', we heard a growl," began Sol, with his eyes as big as saucers. "I see him fust lookin' over the wall," roared Seth, eager to get his share of honor.

"Awful big and shaggy," quavered Roxy, clinging to Tilly, while Rhody hid in Prue's skirts, and piped out: "His great paws kept clawing at us, and I was so scared my legs would hardly go."

"We ran away as fast as we could go, and he came growlin' after us. He's awful hungry, and he'll eat every one of us if he gets in," continued Sol, looking about him for a safe retreat.

"Oh, Eph, don't let him eat us," cried both little girls, flying upstairs to hide under their mother's bed, as their surest shelter.

"No danger of that, you little geese. I'll shoot him as soon as he comes. Get out of the way, boys," and Eph raised the window to get good aim.

"There he is! Fire away, and don't miss!" cried Seth, hastily following Sol, who had climbed to the top of the dresser as a good perch from which to view the approaching fray.

Prue retired to the hearth as if bent on dying at her post rather than desert the turkey, now "browning beautiful," as she expressed it. But Tilly boldly stood at the open window, ready to lend a hand if the enemy proved too much for Eph.

All had seen bears, but none had ever come so near before, and even brave Eph felt that the big brown beast slowly trotting up the dooryard was an unusually formidable specimen. He was growling horribly, and stopped now and then as if to rest and shake himself.

"Get the ax, Tilly, and if I should miss, stand ready to keep him off while I load again," said Eph, anxious to kill his first bear in style and alone; a girl's help didn't count.

Tilly flew for the ax, and was at her brother's side by the time the bear was near enough to be dangerous. He stood on his hind legs, and seemed to sniff with relish the savory odors that poured out of the window.

"Fire, Eph!" cried Tilly, firmly.

"Wait till he rears again. I'll get a better shot then," answered the boy, while Prue covered her ears to shut out the bang, and the small boys cheered from their dusty refuge among the pumpkins.

But a very singular thing happened next, and all who saw it stood amazed, for suddenly Tilly threw down the ax, flung open the door, and ran straight into the arms of the bear, who stood erect to receive her, while his growlings changed to a loud "Haw, haw!" that startled the children more than the report of a gun.

"It's Gad Hopkins, tryin' to fool us!" cried Eph, much disgusted at the loss of his prey, for these hardy boys loved to hunt and prided themselves on the number of wild animals and birds they could shoot in a year.

"Oh, Gad, how could you scare us so?" laughed Tilly, still held fast in one shaggy arm of the bear, while the other drew a dozen oranges from some deep pocket in the buffalo-skin coat, and fired them into the kitchen with such good aim that Eph ducked, Prue screamed, and Sol and Seth came down much quicker than they went up.

"Wal, you see I got upsot over yonder, and the old horse went home while I was floundering in a drift, so I tied on the buffalers to tote 'em easy, and come along till I see the children playin' in the holler. I jest meant to give 'em a little scare, but they run like partridges, and I kep' up the joke to see how Eph would like this sort of company," and Gad haw-hawed again.

"You'd have had a warm welcome if we hadn't found you out. I'd have put a bullet through you in a jiffy, old chap," said Eph, coming out to shake hands with the young giant, who was only a year or two older than himself.

"Come in and set up to dinner with us. Prue and I have done it all ourselves, and Pa will be along soon, I reckon," cried Tilly, trying to escape.

"Couldn't, no ways. My folks will think I'm dead ef I don't get along home, sence the horse and sleigh have gone ahead empty. I've done my arrant and had my joke; now I want my pay, Tilly," and Gad took a hearty kiss from the rosy cheeks of his "little sweetheart," as he called her. His own cheeks tingled with the smart slap she gave him as she ran away, calling out that she hated bears and would bring her ax next time.

"I ain't afeared—your sharp eyes found me out: and ef you run into a bear's arms you must expect a hug," answered Gad, as he pushed back the robe and settled his fur cap more becomingly.

"I should have known you in a minute if I hadn't been asleep when the girls squalled. You did it well, though, and I advise you not to try it again in a hurry, or you'll get shot," said Eph, as they parted, he rather crestfallen and Gad in high glee.

"My sakes alive—the turkey is all burnt one side, and the kettles have biled over so the pies I put to warm are all ashes!" scolded Tilly, as the flurry subsided and she remembered her dinner.

"Well, I can't help it. I couldn't think of victuals when I expected to be eaten alive myself, could I?" pleaded poor Prue, who had tumbled into the cradle when the rain of oranges began.

Tilly laughed, and all the rest joined in, so goodhumor was restored, and the spirits of the younger ones were revived by sucks from the one orange which passed from hand to hand with great rapidity while the older girls dished up the dinner. They were just struggling to get the pudding out of the cloth when Roxy called out: "Here's Pa!"

"There's folks with him," added Rhody.

"Lots of 'em! I see two big sleighs chock full," shouted Seth, peering through the dusk.

"It looks like a semintary. Guess Gran'ma's dead and come up to be buried here," said Sol, in a solemn tone. This startling suggestion made Tilly, Prue, and Eph hasten to look out, full of dismay at such an ending of their festival.

"If that is a funeral, the mourners are uncommonly jolly," said Eph, dryly, as merry voices and loud laughter broke the white silence without.

"I see Aunt Cinthy, and Cousin Hetty—and there's Mose and Amos. I do declare, Pa's bringin' 'em all home to have some fun here," cried Prue, as she recognized one familiar face after another.

"Oh, my patience! Ain't I glad I got dinner, and don't I hope it will turn out good!" exclaimed Tilly, while the twins pranced with delight, and the small boys roared:

"Hooray for Pa! Hooray for Thanksgivin'!"

The cheer was answered heartily, and in came Father, Mother, Baby, aunts, and cousins, all in great spirits, and all much surprised to find such a festive welcome awaiting them.

"Ain't Gran'ma dead at all?" asked Sol, in the midst of the kissing and handshaking.

"Bless your heart, no! It was all a mistake of old Mr. Chadwick's. He's as deaf as an adder, and when Mrs. Brooks told him Mother was mendin' fast, and she wanted me to come down today, certain sure, he got the message all wrong, and give it to the fast person passin' in such a way as to scare me 'most to death, and send us down in a hurry. Mother was sittin' up as chirk as you please, and dreadful sorry you didn't all come."

"So, to keep the house quiet for her, and give you a taste of the fun, your Pa fetched us all up to spend the evenin', and we are goin' to have a jolly time on't, to jedge by the looks of things," said Aunt Cinthy, briskly finishing the tale when Mrs. Bassett paused for want of breath.

"What in the world put it into your head we was comin', and set you to gittin' up such a supper?" asked Mr. Bassett, looking about him, well pleased and much surprised at the plentiful table.

Tilly modestly began to tell, but the others broke in and sang her praises in a sort of chorus, in which bears, pigs, pies, and oranges were oddly mixed. Great satisfaction was expressed by all, and Tilly and Prue were so elated by the commendation of Ma and the aunts, that they set forth their dinner, sure everything was perfect.

But when the eating began, which it did the moment wraps were off, then their pride got a fall; for the first person who tasted the stuffing (it was big Cousin Mose, and that made it harder to bear) nearly choked over the bitter morsel.

"Tilly Bassett, whatever made you put wormwood and catnip in your stuffin'?" demanded Ma, trying not to be severe, for all the rest were laughing, and Tilly looked ready to cry.

"I did it," said Prue, nobly taking all the blame, which caused Pa to kiss her on the spot, and declare that it didn't do a mite of harm, for the turkey was all right.

"I never see onions cooked better. All the vegetables is well done, and the dinner a credit to you, my dears," declared Aunt Cinthy, with her mouth full of the fragrant vegetable she praised.

The pudding was an utter failure in spite of the blazing brandy in which it lay—as hard and heavy as one of the stone balls on Squire Dunkin's great gate. It was speedily whisked out of sight, and all fell upon the pies, which were perfect. But Tilly and Prue were much depressed, and didn't recover their spirits till dinner was over and the evening fun well under way.

"Blind-man's bluff," "Hunt the slipper," "Come, Philander,"

and other lively games soon set everyone bubbling over with jollity, and when Eph struck up "Money Musk" on his fiddle, old and young fell into their places for a dance. All down the long kitchen they stood, Mr. and Mrs. Bassett at the top, the twins at the bottom, and then away they went, heeling and toeing, cutting pigeon-wings, and taking their steps in a way that would convulse modern children with their new-fangled romps called dancing. Mose and Tilly covered themselves with glory by the vigor with which they kept it up, till fat Aunt Cinthy fell into a chair, breathlessly declaring that a very little of such exercise was enough for a woman of her "heft."

Apples and cider, chat and singing, finished the evening, and after a grand kissing all round, the guests drove away in the clear moonlight which came out to cheer their long drive.

When the jingle of the last bell had died away, Mr. Bassett said soberly, as they stood together on the hearth: "Children, we have special cause to be thankful that the sorrow we expected was changed into joy, so we'll read a chapter 'fore we go to bed, and give thanks where thanks is due."

Then Tilly set out the light stand with the big Bible on it, and a candle on each side, and all sat quietly in the firelight, smiling as they listened with happy hearts to the sweet old words that fit all times and seasons so beautifully.

When the good-nights were over, and the children in bed, Prue put her arm round Tilly and whispered tenderly, for she felt her shake, and was sure she was crying:

"Don't mind about the old stuffin' and puddin', deary— nobody cared, and Ma said we really did do surprisin' well for such young girls."

The laughter Tilly was trying to smother broke out then,

and was so infectious, Prue could not help joining her, even before she knew the cause of the merriment.

"I was mad about the mistakes, but don't care enough to cry. I'm laughing to think how Gad fooled Eph and I found him out. I thought Mose and Amos would have died over it, when I told them, it was so funny," explained Tilly, when she got her breath.

"I was so scared that when the first orange hit me, I thought it was a bullet, and scrabbled into the cradle as fast as I could. It was real mean to frighten the little ones so," laughed Prue, as Tilly gave a growl.

Here a smart rap on the wall of the next room caused a sudden lull in the fun, and Mrs. Bassett's voice was heard, saying warningly, "Girls, go to sleep immediate, or you'll wake the baby."

"Yes'm," answered two meek voices, and after a few irrepressible giggles, silence reigned, broken only by an occasional snore from the boys, or the soft scurry of mice in the buttery, taking their part in this old-fashioned Thanksgiving.

2

The Silver Party

"SUCH A LONG morning! Seems as if dinnertime would *never* come!" sighed Tony, as he wandered into the dining room for a third pick at the nuts and raisins to beguile his weariness with a little mischief.

It was Thanksgiving Day. All the family were at church, all the servants busy preparing for the great dinner; and so poor Tony, who had a cold, had not only to stay at home, but to amuse himself while the rest said their prayers, made calls, or took a brisk walk to get an appetite. If he had been allowed in the kitchen, he would have been quite happy, but cook was busy and cross and rapped him on the head with a poker when he ventured near the door. Peeping through the slide that opened to the kitchen was also forbidden, and John, the man, bribed him with an orange to keep out of the way till the table was set.

That was now done. The dining room was empty and quiet, and poor Tony lay down on the sofa to eat his nuts and admire the fine sight before him. All the best damask, china, glass, and silver was set forth with great care. A basket of flowers hung from the chandelier, and the sideboard was beautiful to behold with piled-up fruit, dishes of cake, and many-colored finger bowls and glasses.

"That's all very nice, but the eating part is what *I* care for. Don't believe I'll get my share today, because Mamma found out about this horrid cold. A fellow can't help sneezing, though he *can* hide a sore throat. Oh, hum! Nearly two more hours to wait," and, with a long sigh, Tony closed his eyes for a luxurious yawn.

When he opened them, the strange sight he beheld kept him staring without a thought of sleep. The big soup ladle stood straight up at the head of the table with a face plainly to be seen in the bright bowl. It was a very heavy, handsome old ladle, so the face was old, but round and jolly, and the long handle stood very erect, like a tall, thin gentleman with a big head.

"Well, upon my word that's queer!" said Tony, sitting up also and wondering what would happen next.

To his great amazement the ladle began to address the assembled forks and spoons in a silvery tone very pleasant to hear.

"Ladies and gentlemen, at this festive season it is proper that we should enjoy ourselves. As we shall be tired after dinner, we will at once begin our sports by a grand promenade. Take partners and fall in!"

At these words a general uprising took place, and before Tony could get his breath a long procession of forks and spoons stood ready. The finger bowls struck up an airy tune as if invisible wet fingers were making music on their rims, and, led by the stately ladle like a drum major, the grand march began. The forks were the gentlemen, tall, slender, and with a fine curve to their backs; the spoons were the ladies, with full skirts, and the scallops on the handles stood up like silver combs; the large ones were the mamas, the teaspoons were the young ladies, and the little salts, the children. It was sweet to see the small things walk at the end of the procession, with the two silver rests for the carving knife and fork trotting behind like pet dogs. The mustard spoon and pickle fork went together, and quarreled all the way, both being hot-tempered and sharp-tongued. The steel knives looked on, for this was a very aristocratic party, and only the silver people could join in it.

"Here's fun!" thought Tony, staring with all his might, and so much interested in this remarkable state of things that he forgot hunger and time altogether.

Round and round went the glittering train, to the soft music of the many-toned finger bowls, till three turns about the long oval table had been made; then all fell into line for a country-dance, as in the good old times before everyone took to spinning like tops. Grandpa Ladle led off with his oldest daughter, Madam Gravy Ladle, and the little salts stood at the bottom prancing like real children impatient for their turn. When it came, they went down the middle in fine style, with a cling! clang! that made Tony's legs quiver with a longing to join in.

It was beautiful to see the older ones twirl round in a stately way, with bows and courtesies at the end, while the teaspoons and small forks romped a good deal, and Mr. Pickle and Miss Mustard kept everyone laughing at their smart speeches. The silver butter knife, who was an invalid, having broken her back and been mended, lay in the rack and smiled sweetly down upon her friends, while the little Cupid on the lid of the butter dish pirouetted on one toe in the most delightful manner.

When everyone had gone through the dance, the napkins were arranged as sofas, and the spoons rested, while the polite forks brought sprigs of celery to fan them with.

The little salts got into Grandpa's lap, and the silver dogs lay down panting, for they had frisked with the children. They all talked, and Tony could not help wondering if real ladies said such things when they put *their* heads together and nodded and whispered, for some of the remarks were so personal that he was much confused. Fortunately they took no notice of him, so he listened and learned something in this queer way.

"I have been in this family a hundred years," began the soup ladle, "and it seems to me that each generation is worse than the last. My first master was punctual to a minute, and madam was always down beforehand to see that all was ready. Now master comes at all hours, mistress lets the servants do as they like, and the manners of the children are very bad. Sad state of things, very sad!"

"Dear me, yes!" sighed one of the large spoons; "we don't see such nice housekeeping now as we did when we were young. Girls were taught all about it then, but now it is all books or parties, and few of them know a skimmer from a gridiron."

"Well, I'm sure the poor things are much happier than if they were messing about in kitchens as girls used to do in your day. It is much better for them to be dancing, skating, and studying than wasting their young lives darning and preserving and sitting by their mammas as prim as dishes. *I* prefer the present way of doing things, though the girls in this family *do* sit up too late, and wear too high heels to their boots."

The mustard spoon spoke in a pert tone, and the pickle fork answered sharply, "I agree with you, cousin. The boys also sit up too late. I'm tired of being waked to fish out olives or pickles for those fellows when they come in from the theatre or some dance; and as for that Tony, he is a real pig—eats everything he can lay hands on and is the torment of the maid's life."

"Yes," cried one little salt spoon, "we saw him steal cake out of the sideboard, and he never told when his mother scolded Norah."

"So mean!" added the other, and both the round faces were so full of disgust that Tony fell flat and shut his eyes as if asleep to hide his confusion. Someone laughed, but he dared not look and lay blushing and listening to remarks which plainly proved how careful we should be of our acts and words even when alone, for who knows what apparently dumb thing may be watching us.

"I have observed that Mr. Murry reads the paper at table instead of talking to his family, that Mrs. Murry worries about the servants, the girls gossip and giggle, the boys eat and plague one another, and that small child Nelly teases for all she sees and is never quiet till she gets the sugar bowl," said Grandpa Ladle, in a tone of regret. "Now, useful and pleasant chat at table would make meals delightful, instead of being scenes of confusion and discomfort."

"I bite their tongues when I get a chance, hoping to make them witty or to check unkind words, but they only sputter and get a lecture from Aunt Maria, who is a sour old spinster, always criticizing her neighbors."

As the mustard spoon spoke, the teaspoons laughed as if they thought *her* rather like Aunt Maria in that respect.

"I gave the baby a fit of colic to teach her to let pickles alone, but no one thanked me," said the pickle fork.

"Perhaps if we keep ourselves so bright that those who use us can see their faces in us, we shall be able to help them a little, for no one likes to see an ugly face or a dull spoon. The art of changing frowns to smiles is never old-fashioned, and lovely manners smooth away the little worries of life beautifully." A silvery voice spoke, and all looked respectfully at Madam Gravy Ladle, who was a very fine old spoon, with a coat of arms and a polish that all envied.

"People can't always be remembering how old and valuable and bright they are. Here in America we just go ahead and make manners and money for ourselves. *I* don't stop to ask what dish I'm going to help to; I just pitch in and take all I can hold and don't care a bit whether I shine or not. My grandfather was a kitchen spoon, but I'm smarter than he was, thanks to my plating, and look and feel as good as anyone, though I haven't got stags' heads and big letters on my handle."

No one answered these impertinent remarks of the sauce spoon, for all knew that she was not pure silver and was only used on occasions when many spoons were needed. Tony was ashamed to hear her talk in that rude way to the fine old silver he was so proud of and resolved he'd give the saucy spoon a good rap when he helped himself to the cranberry.

An impressive silence lasted till a lively fork exclaimed, as the clock struck, "Everyone is coasting out of doors. Why not have our share of the fun inside? It is very fashionable this winter, and ladies and gentlemen of the best families do it, I assure you."

"We will!" cried the other forks, and, as the dowagers did not object, all fell to work to arrange the table for this agreeable sport. Tony sat up to see how they would manage and was astonished at the ingenuity of the silver people. With a great clinking and rattling they ran to and fro, dragging the stiff white mats about; the largest they leaned up against the tall caster, and laid the rest in a long slope to the edge of the table, where a pile of napkins made a nice snowdrift to tumble into.

"What *will* they do for sleds?" thought Tony, and the next minute chuckled when he saw them take the slices of bread laid at each place, pile on, and spin away, with a great scattering of crumbs like snowflakes and much laughter as they landed in the white pile at the end of the coast.

"Won't John give it to 'em if he comes in and catches 'em turning his nice table topsy-turvy!" said the boy to himself, hoping nothing would happen to end this jolly frolic. So he kept very still and watched the gay forks and spoons climb up and whiz down till they were tired. The little salts got Baby Nell's own small slice and had lovely times on a short coast of their own made of one mat held up by Grandpa, who smiled benevolently at the fun, being too old and heavy to join in it.

They kept it up until the slices were worn thin, and one or two upsets alarmed the ladies; then they rested and conversed again. The mammas talked about their children, how sadly the silver basket needed a new lining, and what there was to be for dinner. The teaspoons whispered sweetly together, as young ladies do—one declaring that rouge powder was not as good as it used to be, another lamenting the sad effect upon her complexion, and all smiled amiably upon the forks, who stood about discussing wines and cigars, for both lived in the sideboard and were brought out after dinner, so the forks knew a great deal about such matters and found them very interesting, as all gentlemen seem to do.

Presently someone mentioned bicycles, and what fine rides the boys of the family told about. The other fellows proposed a race; and before Tony could grasp the possibility of such a thing, it was done. Nothing easier, for there stood a pile of plates, and just turning them on their edges, the forks got astride, and the big wheels spun away as if a whole bicycle club had suddenly arrived.

Old Pickle took the baby's plate, as better suited to his size. The little salts made a tricycle of napkin rings and rode gaily off, with the dogs barking after them. Even the carving fork, though not invited, could not resist the exciting sport, and tipping up the wooden bread platter, went whizzing off at a great pace, for his two prongs were better than four, and his wheel was lighter than the china ones. Grandpapa Ladle cheered them on, like a fine old gentleman as he was, for, though the new craze rather astonished him, he liked manly sports and would have taken a turn if his dignity and age had allowed. The ladies chimed their applause, for it really was immensely exciting to see fourteen plates with forks astride racing around the large table with cries of, "Go it, Pickle! Now, then, Prongs! Steady, Silver-top! Hurrah for the twins!"

The fun was at its height when young Prongs ran against Pickle, who did not steer well, and both went off the table with a crash. All stopped at once and crowded to the edge to see who was killed. The plates lay in pieces; old Pickle had a bend in his back that made him groan dismally; and Prongs had fallen down the register.

Wails of despair arose at that awful sight, for he was a favorite with everyone, and such a tragic death was too much for some of the tenderhearted spoons, who fainted at the idea of that gallant fork's destruction in what to them was a fiery volcano.

"Serves Pickle right! He ought to know he was too old for such wild games," scolded Miss Mustard, peering anxiously over at her friend, for they were fond of each another in spite of their tiffs.

"Now let us see what these fine folks will do when they get off the damask and come to grief. A helpless lot, I fancy, and those fellows deserve what they've got," said the sauce spoon, nearly upsetting the twins as she elbowed her way to the front to jeer over the fallen.

"I think you will see that gentle people are as brave as those who make a noise," answered Madam Gravy, and, leaning over the edge of the table, she added in her sweet voice, "Dear Mr. Pickle, we will let down a napkin and pull you up if you have strength to take hold."

"Pull away, ma'am," groaned Pickle, who well deserved his name just then, and, soon, thanks to Madam's presence of mind, he was safely laid on a pile of mats, while Miss Mustard put a plaster on his injured back.

Meanwhile brave Grandpapa Ladle had slipped from the table to a chair, and so to the floor without too great a jar to his aged frame; then, sliding along the carpet, he reached the register. Peering down that dark, hot abyss he cried, while all listened breathlessly for a reply, "Prongs, my boy, are you there?"

"Aye, aye, sir; I'm caught in the wire screen. Ask some of the fellows to lend a hand and get me out before I'm melted," answered the fork, with a gasp of agony.

Instantly the long handle of the patriarchal Ladle was put down to his rescue, and, after a moment of suspense, while Prongs caught firmly hold, up he came, hot and dusty, but otherwise unharmed by that dreadful fall. Cheers greeted them, and everyone lent a hand at the napkin as they were hoisted to the table to be embraced by their joyful relatives and friends.

"What did you think about down in that horrid place?" asked one of the twins.

"I thought of a story I once heard master tell, about a

child who was found one cold day sitting with his feet on a newspaper, and when asked what he was doing, answered, 'Warming my feet on the "Christian Register."' I hoped my register would be Christian enough not to melt me before help came. Ha! Ha! See the joke, my dears?" and Prongs laughed as gaily as if he never had taken a header into a volcano.

"What did you see down there?" asked the other twin, curious, as all small people are.

"Lots of dust and pins, a baby-doll's head put there, Norah's thimble, and the big red marble that boy Tony was raging about the other day. It's a regular catchall and shows how the work is shirked in this house," answered Prongs, stretching his legs, which were a little damaged by the fall.

"What shall we do about the plates?" asked Pickle, from his bed.

"Let them lie, for we can't mend them. John will think the boy broke them, and he'll get punished, as he deserves, for he broke a tumbler yesterday and put it slyly in the ash barrel," said Miss Mustard spitefully.

"Oh! I say, that's mean," began Tony, but no one listened.

In a minute Prongs answered bravely. "I'm a gentleman, and I don't let other people take the blame of my scrapes. Tony has enough of his own to answer for."

"I'll have that bent fork for mine and make John keep it as bright as a new dollar to pay for this. Prongs is a trump, and I wish I could tell him so," thought Tony, much gratified at this handsome behavior.

"Right, Grandson. I am pleased with you, but allow me to suggest that the Chinese mandarin on the chimney piece be politely requested to mend the plates. He can do that sort of thing nicely and will be charmed to oblige us, I am sure."

Grandpapa's suggestion was a good one, and Yam Ki Lo consented at once, skipped to the floor, tapped the bits of china with his fan, and in the twinkling of an eye was back on his perch, leaving two whole plates behind him, for he was a wizard and knew all about blue china.

Just as the silver people were rejoicing over this fine escape from discovery, the clock struck, a bell rang, voices were heard upstairs, and it was very evident that the family had arrived.

At these sounds a great flurry arose in the dining room as every spoon, fork, plate, and napkin flew back to its place. Pickle rushed to the jar, and plunged in head first, regardless of his back; Miss Mustard retired to the caster; the twins scrambled into the saltcellar; and the silver dogs lay down by the carving knife and fork as quietly as if they had never stirred a leg; Grandpapa slowly reposed in his usual place; Madam followed his example with dignity; the teaspoons climbed into the holder, uttering little cries of alarm; and Prongs stayed to help them till he had barely time to drop down at Tony's place and lie there with his bent leg in the air, the only sign of the great fall, about which he talked for a long time afterward. All was in order but the sauce spoon, who had stopped to laugh at the mandarin till it was too late to get to her corner, and before she could find any place of concealment, John came in and caught her lying in the middle of the table, looking very common and shabby among all the bright silver.

"What in the world is that old plated thing here for? Missis told Norah to put it in the kitchen, as she had a new one for a present today—real silver—so out you go," and as he spoke, John threw the spoon through the slide—an exile forevermore from the good society which she did not value as she should.

Tony saw the glimmer of a smile in Grandpapa Ladle's face, but it was gone like a flash, and by the time the boy reached the table nothing was to be seen in the silver bowl but his own round rosy countenance, full of wonder.

"I don't think anyone will believe what I've seen, but I mean to tell, it was so *very* curious," he said, as he surveyed the scene of the late frolic, now so neat and quiet that not a wrinkle or a crumb betrayed what larks had been going on.

Hastily fishing up his long-lost marble, the doll's head, and Norah's thimble, he went thoughtfully upstairs to welcome his cousins, still much absorbed by this very singular affair.

Dinner was soon announced, and while it lasted everyone was too busy eating the good things before them to observe how quiet the usually riotous Tony was. His appetite for turkey and cranberries seemed to have lost its sharp edge, and the mince pie must have felt itself sadly slighted by his lack of appreciation of its substance and flavor. He seemed in a brown study and kept staring about as if he saw more than other people did. He examined Nelly's plate as if looking for a crack, smiled at the little spoon when he took salt, refused pickles and mustard with a frown, kept a certain bent fork by him as long as possible, and tried to make music with a wet finger on the rim of his bowl at dessert.

But in the evening, when the young people sat around the fire, he amused them by telling the queer story of the silver party; but he very wisely left out the remarks made upon himself and family, remembering how disagreeable the sauce spoon had seemed, and he privately resolved to follow Madam Gravy Ladle's advice to keep his own face bright, manners polite, and speech kindly, that he might prove himself to be pure silver, and be stamped a gentleman.

3

Oh, the Beautiful Old Story

Oh, the beautiful old story!
   Of the little child that lay
In a manger on that morning,
   When the stars sang in the day;
When the happy shepherds kneeling,
   As before a holy shrine,
Blessed God and the tender mother
   For a life that was divine.

Oh, the pleasant, peaceful story!
   Of the youth who grew so fair,
In his father's humble dwelling,
   Poverty and toil to share,
Till around him, in the temple,
   Marvelling, the old men stood,
As through his wise innocency
   Shone the meek boy's angelhood.

Oh, the wonderful, true story!
   Of the messenger from God,
Who among the poor and lowly,

Bravely and devoutly trod,
Working miracles of mercy,
    Preaching peace, rebuking strife,
Blessing all the little children,
    Lifting up the dead to life.

Oh, the sad and solemn story!
    Of the cross, the crown, the spear,
Of the pardon, pain, and glory
    That have made this name so dear.
This example let us follow,
    Fearless, faithful to the end,
Walking in the sacred footsteps
    Of our brother, Master, friend.

4

Sophie's Secret

I.

A PARTY OF young girls, in their gay bathing-dresses, were sitting on the beach waiting for the tide to rise a little higher before they enjoyed the daily frolic which they called "mermaiding."

"I wish we could have a clam-bake; but we haven't any clams, and don't know how to cook them if we had. It's such a pity all the boys have gone off on that stupid fishing excursion," said one girl, in a yellow-and-black striped suit which made her look like a wasp.

"What is a clam-bake? I do not know that kind of fête," asked a pretty brown-eyed girl, with an accent that betrayed the foreigner.

The girls laughed at such sad ignorance, and Sophie colored, wishing she had not spoken.

"Poor thing! she has never tasted a clam. What *should* we do if we went to Switzerland?" said the wasp, who loved to tease.

"We should give you the best we had, and not laugh at your ignorance, if you did not know all our dishes. In *my*

country, we have politeness, though not the clam-bake,"
answered Sophie, with a flash of the brown eyes which
warned naughty Di to desist.

"We might row to the light-house, and have a picnic supper. Our mammas will let us do that alone," suggested Dora
from the roof of the bath-house, where she perched like a
flamingo.

"That's a good idea," cried Fanny, a slender brown girl
who sat dabbling her feet in the water, with her hair streaming in the wind. "Sophie should see that, and get some of
the shells she likes so much."

"You are kind to think of me. I shall be glad to have a
necklace of the pretty things, as a souvenir of this so
charming place and my good friend," answered Sophie,
with a grateful look at Fanny, whose many attentions had
won the stranger's heart.

"Those boys haven't left us a single boat, so we must dive
off the rocks, and that isn't half so nice," said Di, to change
the subject, being ashamed of her rudeness.

"A boat is just coming round the Point; perhaps we can
hire that, and have some fun," cried Dora, from her perch.
"There is only a girl in it; I'll hail her when she is near
enough."

Sophie looked about her to see where the *hail* was coming from; but the sky was clear, and she waited to see what
new meaning this word might have, not daring to ask for
fear of another laugh.

While the girls watched the boat float around the farther
horn of the crescent-shaped beach, we shall have time to
say a few words about our little heroine.

She was a sixteen-year-old Swiss girl, on a visit to some
American friends, and had come to the seaside for a month
with one of them who was an invalid. This left Sophie to

the tender mercies of the young people; and they gladly welcomed the pretty creature, with her fine manners, foreign ways, and many accomplishments. But she had a quick temper, a funny little accent, and dressed so very plainly that the girls could not resist criticising and teasing her in a way that seemed very ill-bred and unkind to the new-comer.

Their free and easy ways astonished her, their curious language bewildered her; and their ignorance of many things she had been taught made her wonder at the American education she had heard so much praised. All had studied French and German; yet few read or spoke either tongue correctly, or understood her easily when she tried to talk to them. Their music did not amount to much, and in the games they played, their want of useful information amazed Sophie. One did not know the signs of the zodiac; another could only say of cotton that "it was stuff that grew down South;" and a third was not sure whether a frog was an animal or a reptile, while the handwriting and spelling displayed on these occasions left much to be desired. Yet all were fifteen or sixteen, and would soon leave school "finished," as they expressed it, but not *furnished,* as they should have been, with a solid, sensible education. Dress was an all-absorbing topic, sweet-meats their delight; and in confidential moments sweethearts were discussed with great freedom. Fathers were conveniences, mothers comforters, brothers plagues, and sisters ornaments or playthings according to their ages. They were not hard-hearted girls, only frivolous, idle, and fond of fun; and poor little Sophie amused them immensely till they learned to admire, love, and respect her.

Coming straight from Paris, they expected to find that her trunks contained the latest fashions for demoiselles, and begged to see her dresses with girlish interest. But when Sophie obligingly showed a few simple, but pretty and appropriate gowns and hats, they exclaimed with one voice,—

"Why, you dress like a little girl! Don't you have ruffles and lace on your dresses; and silks and high-heeled boots and long gloves and bustles and corsets, and things like ours?"

"I *am* a little girl," laughed Sophie, hardly understanding their dismay. "What should I do with fine toilets at school? My sisters go to balls in silk and lace; but I—not yet."

"How queer! Is your father poor?" asked Di, with Yankee bluntness.

"We have enough," answered Sophie, slightly knitting her dark brows.

"How many servants do you keep?"

"But five, now that the little ones are grown up."

"Have you a piano?" continued undaunted Di, while the others affected to be looking at the books and pictures strewn about by the hasty unpacking.

"We have two pianos, four violins, three flutes, and an organ. We love music, and all play, from papa to little Franz."

"My gracious, how swell! You must live in a big house to hold all that and eight brothers and sisters."

"We are not peasants; we do not live in a hut. *Voilà*, this is my home." And Sophie laid before them a fine photograph of a large and elegant house on lovely Lake Geneva.

It was droll to see the change in the faces of the girls as they looked, admired, and slyly nudged one another, enjoying saucy Di's astonishment, for she had stoutly insisted that the Swiss girl was a poor relation.

Sophie meanwhile was folding up her plain pique and

muslin frocks, with a glimmer of mirthful satisfaction in her eyes, and a tender pride in the work of loving hands now far away.

Kind Fanny saw a little quiver of the lips as she smoothed the blue corn-flowers in the best hat, and put her arm around Sophie, whispering,—

"Never mind, dear, they don't mean to be rude; it's only our Yankee way of asking questions. I like *all* your things, and that hat is perfectly lovely."

"Indeed, yes! Dear mamma arranged it for me. I was thinking of her and longing for my morning kiss."

"Do you do that every day?" asked Fanny, forgetting herself in her sympathetic interest.

"Surely, yes. Papa and mamma sit always on the sofa, and we all have the hand-shake and the embrace each day before our morning coffee. I do not see that here," answered Sophie, who sorely missed the affectionate respect foreign children give their parents.

"Haven't time," said Fanny, smiling too, at the idea of American parents sitting still for five minutes in the busiest part of the busy day to kiss their sons and daughters.

"It is what you call old-fashioned, but a sweet fashion to me; and since I have not the dear warm cheeks to kiss, I embrace my pictures often. See, I have them all." And Sophie unfolded a Russia-leather case, displaying with pride a long row of handsome brothers and sisters with the parents in the midst.

More exclamations from the girls, and increased interest in "Wilhelmina Tell," as they christened the loyal Swiss maiden, who was now accepted as a companion, and soon became a favorite with old and young.

They could not resist teasing her, however,—her mistakes were so amusing, her little flashes of temper so dramatic, and her tongue so quick to give a sharp or witty answer when the new language did not perplex her. But Fanny always took her part, and helped her in many ways. Now they sat together on the rock, a pretty pair of mermaids with wind-tossed hair, wave-washed feet, and eyes fixed on the approaching boat.

The girl who sat in it was a great contrast to the gay creatures grouped so picturesquely on the shore, for the old straw hat shaded a very anxious face, the brown calico gown covered a heart full of hopes and fears, and the boat that drifted so slowly with the incoming tide carried Tilly Reed like a young Columbus toward the new world she longed for, believed in, and was resolved to discover.

It was a weather-beaten little boat, yet very pretty; for a pile of nets lay at one end, a creel of red lobsters at the other, and all between stood baskets of berries and water-lilies, purple marsh rosemary and orange butterfly-weed, shells and great smooth stones such as artists like to paint little sea-views on. A tame gull perched on the prow; and the morning sunshine glittered from the blue water to the bluer sky.

"Oh, how pretty! Come on, please, and sell us some lilies," cried Dora, and roused Tilly from her waking dream.

Pushing back her hat, she saw the girls beckoning, felt that the critical moment had come, and catching up her oars, rowed bravely on, though her cheeks reddened and her heart beat, for this venture was her last hope, and on its success depended the desire of her life. As the boat approached, the watchers forgot its cargo to look with surprise and pleasure at its rower, for she was not the rough country lass they expected to see, but a really splendid girl of fifteen, tall, broad-shouldered, bright-eyed, and blooming, with a certain shy dignity of her own and a very sweet smile, as she nodded and pulled in with strong, steady strokes. Before they could offer help, she had risen, planted an oar in the water, and leaping to the shore, pulled her boat high up on the beach, offering her wares with wistful eyes and a very expressive wave of both brown hands.

"Everything is for sale, if you'll buy," said she.

Charmed with the novelty of this little adventure, the girls, after scampering to the bathing-houses for purses and portemonnaies, crowded around the boat like butterflies about a thistle, all eager to buy, and to discover who this bonny fisher-maiden might be.

"Oh, see these beauties!" "A dozen lilies for me!" "All the yellow flowers for me, they'll be so becoming at the dance to-night!" "Ow! that lob bites awfully!" "Where do you come from?" "Why have we never seen you before?"

These were some of the exclamations and questions showered upon Tilly, as she filled little birch-bark panniers with berries, dealt out flowers, or dispensed handfuls of shells. Her eyes shone, her checks glowed, and her heart danced in her bosom; for this was a better beginning than she had dared to hope for, and as the dimes tinkled into the tin pail she used for her till, it was the sweetest music she had ever heard. This hearty welcome banished her shyness; and in these eager, girlish customers she found it easy to confide.

"I'm from the light-house. You have never seen me because I never came before, except with fish for the hotel. But I mean to come every day, if folks will buy my things, for I want to make some money, and this is the only way in which I can do it."

Sophie glanced at the old hat and worn shoes of the speaker, and dropping a bright half-dollar into the pail, said in her pretty way:

"For me all these lovely shells. I will make necklaces of

them for my people at home as souvenirs of this charming place. If you will bring me more, I shall be much grateful to you."

"Oh, thank you! I'll bring heaps; I know where to find beauties in places where other folks can't go. Please take these; you paid too much for the shells;" and quick to feel the kindness of the stranger, Tilly put into her hands a little bark canoe heaped with red raspberries.

Not to be outdone by the foreigner, the other girls emptied their purses and Tilly's boat also of all but the lobsters, which were ordered for the hotel.

"Is that jolly bird for sale?" asked Di, as the last berry vanished, pointing to the gull who was swimming near them while the chatter went on.

"If you can catch him," laughed Tilly, whose spirits were now the gayest of the party.

The girls dashed into the water, and with shrieks of merriment swam away to capture the gull, who paddled off as if he enjoyed the fun as much as they.

Leaving them to splash vainly to and fro, Tilly swung the creel to her shoulder and went off to leave her lobsters, longing to dance and sing to the music of the silver clinking in her pocket.

When she came back, the bird was far out of reach and the girls diving from her boat, which they had launched without leave. Too happy to care what happened now, Tilly threw herself down on the warm sand to plan a new and still finer cargo for next day.

Sophie came and sat beside her while she dried her curly hair, and in five minutes her sympathetic face and sweet ways had won Tilly to tell all her hopes and cares and dreams.

"I want schooling, and I mean to have it. I've got no folks

of my own; and uncle has married again, so he doesn't need me now. If I only had a little money, I could go to school somewhere, and take care of myself. Last summer I worked at the hotel, but I didn't make much, and had to have good clothes, and that took my wages pretty much. Sewing is slow work, and baby-tending leaves me no time to study; so I've kept on at home picking berries and doing what I could to pick up enough to buy books. Aunt thinks I'm a fool; but uncle, he says, 'Go ahead, girl, and see what you can do.' And I mean to show him!"

Tilly's brown hand came down on the sand with a resolute thump; and her clear young eyes looked bravely out across the wide sea, as if far away in the blue distance she saw her hope happily fulfilled.

Sophie's eyes shone approval, for she understood this love of independence, and had come to America because she longed for new scenes and greater freedom than her native land could give her. Education is a large word, and both girls felt that desire for self-improvement that comes to all energetic natures. Sophie had laid a good foundation, but still desired more; while Tilly was just climbing up the first steep slope which rises to the heights few attain, yet all may strive for.

"That is beautiful! You will do it! I am glad to help you if I may. See, I have many books; will you take some of them? Come to my room to-morrow and take what will best please you. We will say nothing of it, and it will make me a truly great pleasure."

As Sophie spoke, her little white hand touched the strong, sunburned one that turned to meet and grasp hers with grateful warmth, while Tilly's face betrayed the hunger that possessed her, for it looked as a starving girl's would look when offered a generous meal.

"I *will* come. Thank you so much! I don't know anything, but just blunder along and do the best I can. I got so discouraged I was real desperate, and thought I'd have one try, and see if I couldn't earn enough to get books to study this winter. Folks buy berries at the cottages; so I just added flowers and shells, and I'm going to bring my boxes of butterflies, birds' eggs, and seaweeds. I've got lots of such things; and people seem to like spending money down here. I often wish I had a little of what they throw away."

Tilly paused with a sigh, then laughed as an impatient movement caused a silver clink; and slapping her pocket, she added gayly,—

"I won't blame 'em if they'll only throw their money in here."

Sophie's hand went involuntarily toward her own pocket, where lay a plump purse, for papa was generous, and simple Sophie had few wants. But something in the intelligent face opposite made her hesitate to offer as a gift what she felt sure Tilly would refuse, preferring to earn her education if she could.

"Come often, then, and let me exchange these stupid bills for the lovely things you bring. We will come this afternoon to see you if we may, and I shall like the butterflies. I try to catch them; but people tell me I am too old to run, so I have not many."

Proposed in this way, Tilly fell into the little trap, and presently rowed away with all her might to set her possessions in order, and put her precious earnings in a safe place. The mermaids clung about the boat as long as they dared, making a pretty tableau for the artists on the rocks, then swam to shore, more than ever eager for the picnic on Light-house Island.

They went, and had a merry time; while Tilly did the

honors and showed them a room full of treasures gathered from earth, air, and water, for she led a lonely life, and found friends among the fishes, made playmates of the birds, and studied rocks and flowers, clouds and waves, when books were wanting.

The girls bought gulls' wings for their hats, queer and lovely shells, eggs and insects, seaweeds and carved wood, and for their small brothers, birch baskets and toy ships, made by Uncle Hiram, who had been a sailor.

When Tilly had sold nearly everything she possessed (for Fanny and Sophie bought whatever the others declined), she made a fire of drift-wood on the rocks, cooked fish for supper, and kept them till moonrise, telling sea stories or singing old songs, as if she could not do enough for these good fairies who had come to her when life looked hardest and the future very dark. Then she rowed them home, and promising to bring loads of fruit and flowers every day, went back along a shining road, to find a great bundle of books in her dismantled room, and to fall asleep with wet eye-lashes and a happy heart.

II.

FOR A MONTH Tilly went daily to the Point with a cargo of pretty merchandise, for her patrons increased; and soon the ladies engaged her berries, the boys ordered boats enough to supply a navy, the children clamored for shells, and the girls depended on her for bouquets and garlands for the dances that ended every summer day. Uncle Hiram's fish was in demand when such a comely saleswoman offered it; so he let Tilly have her way, glad to see the old tobacco-pouch in which she kept her cash fill fast with well-earned money.

She really began to feel that her dream was coming true, and she would be able to go to the town and study in some great school, eking out her little fund with light work. The other girls soon lost their interest in her, but Sophie never did; and many a book went to the island in the empty baskets, many a helpful word was said over the lilies or wild honeysuckle Sophie loved to wear, and many a lesson was given in the bare room in the light-house tower which no one knew about but the gulls and the sea-winds sweeping by the little window where the two heads leaned together over one page.

"You will do it, Tilly, I am very sure. Such a will and such a memory will make a way for you; and one day I shall see you teaching as you wish. Keep the brave heart, and all will be well with you," said Sophie, when the grand breaking-up came in September, and the girls were parting down behind the deserted bathhouses.

"Oh, Miss Sophie, what should I have done without you? Don't think I haven't seen and known all the kind things you have said and done for me. I'll never forget 'em; and I do hope I'll be able to thank you some day," cried grateful Tilly, with tears in her clear eyes that seldom wept over her own troubles.

"I am thanked if you do well. Adieu; write to me, and remember always that I am your friend."

Then they kissed with girlish warmth, and Tilly rowed away to the lonely island; while Sophie lingered on the shore, her handkerchief fluttering in the wind, till the boat vanished and the waves had washed away their footprints on the sand.

III.

December snow was falling fast, and the wintry wind whistled through the streets; but it was warm and cosy in the luxurious parlor where Di and Do were sitting making Christmas presents, and planning what they would wear at the party Fanny was to give on Christmas Eve.

"If I can get mamma to buy me a new dress, I shall have something yellow. It is always becoming to brunettes, and I'm so tired of red," said Di, giving a last touch to the lace that trimmed a blue satin sachet for Fanny.

"That will be lovely. I shall have pink, with roses of the same color. Under muslin it is perfectly sweet." And Dora eyed the sunflower she was embroidering as if she already saw the new toilet before her.

"Fan always wears blue, so we shall make a nice contrast. She is coming over to show me about finishing off my banner-screen; and I asked Sophie to come with her. I want to know what *she* is going to wear," said Di, taking a little sniff at the violet-scented bag.

"That old white cashmere. Just think! I asked her why she didn't get a new one, and she laughed and said she couldn't afford it. Fan told me Sophie's father sent her a hundred dollars not long ago, yet she hasn't got a thing that we know of. I do think she's mean."

"She bought a great bundle of books. I was there when the parcel came, and I peeped while she was out of the room, because she put it away in a great hurry. I'm afraid she *is* mean, for she never buys a bit of candy, and she wears shabby boots and gloves, and she has made over her old hat instead of having that lovely one with the pheasant's breast in it."

"She's very queer; but I can't help liking her, she's so

pretty and bright and obliging. I'd give anything if I could speak three languages and play as she does."

"So would I. It seems so elegant to be able to talk to foreigners. Papa had some Frenchmen to dinner the other day, and they were so pleased to find they needn't speak English to Sophie. I couldn't get on at all; and I was so mortified when papa said all the money he had spent on my languages was thrown away."

"I wouldn't mind. It's so much easier to learn those things abroad, she would be a goose if she didn't speak French better than we do. There's Fan! she looks as if something had happened. I hope no one is ill and the party spoiled."

As Dora spoke, both girls looked out to see Fanny shaking the snow from her seal-skin sack on the doorstep; then Do hastened to meet her, while Di hid the sachet, and was hard at work on an old-gold sofa cushion when the newcomer entered.

"What's the matter? Where's Sophie?" exclaimed the girls together, as Fan threw off her wraps and sat down with a tragic sigh.

"She will be along in a few minutes. I'm disappointed in her! I wouldn't have believed it if I hadn't seen them. Promise not to breathe a word to a living soul, and I'll tell you something dreadful," began Fanny, in a tone that caused her friends to drop their work and draw their chairs nearer, as they solemnly vowed eternal silence.

"I've seen Sophie's Christmas presents,—all but mine; and they are just nothing at all! She hasn't bought a thing, not even ribbons, lace, or silk, to make up prettily as we do. Only a painted shell for one, an acorn emery for another, her ivory fan with a new tassel for a third, and I suspect one of those nice handkerchiefs embroidered by the nuns for me, or her silver filigree necklace. I saw the box in the drawer with the other things. She's knit woollen cuffs and tippets for the children, and got some eight-cent calico gowns for the servants. I don't know how people do things in Switzerland, but I do know that if *I* had a hundred dollars in my pocket, I would be more generous than that!"

As Fanny paused, out of breath, Di and Do groaned in sympathy, for this was indeed a sad state of things; because the girls had a code that Christmas being the season for gifts, extravagance would be forgiven then as at no other time.

"I have a lovely smelling-bottle for her; but I've a great mind not to give it now," cried Di, feeling defrauded of the bracelet she had plainly hinted she would like.

"I shall heap coals of fire on her head by giving her *that;*" and Dora displayed a very useless but very pretty apron of muslin, lace, and carnation ribbon.

"It isn't the worth of the things. I don't care for that so much as I do for being disappointed in her; and I have been lately in more ways than one," said Fanny, listlessly taking up the screen she was to finish. "She used to tell me everything, and now she doesn't. I'm sure she has some sort of a secret; and I do think *I* ought to know it. I found her smiling over a letter one day; and she whisked it into her pocket and never said a word about it. I always stood by her, and I do feel hurt."

"I should think you might! It's real naughty of her, and I shall tell her so! Perhaps she'll confide in you then, and you can just give *me* a hint; I always liked Sophie, and never thought of not giving *my* present," said Dora, persuasively, for both girls were now dying with curiosity to know the secret.

"I'll have it out of her, without any dodging or bribing. I'm not afraid of any one, and I shall ask her straight out, no matter how much she scowls at me," said dauntless Di, with a threatening nod.

"There she is! Let us see you do it now!" cried Fanny, as the bell rang, and a clear voice was heard a moment later asking if Mademoiselle was in.

"You shall!" and Di looked ready for any audacity.

"I'll wager a box of candy that you don't find out a thing," whispered Do.

"Done!" answered Di, and then turned to meet Sophie, who came in looking as fresh as an Alpine rose with the wintry wind.

"You dear thing! we were just talking of you. Sit here and get warm, and let us show you our gifts. We are almost done, but it seems as if it got to be a harder job each Christmas. Don't you find it so?"

"But no; I think it the most charming work of all the year," answered Sophie, greeting her friend, and putting her well-worn boots toward the fire to dry.

"Perhaps you don't make as much of Christmas as we do, or give such expensive presents. That would make a great difference, you know," said Di, as she lifted a cloth from the table where her own generous store of gifts was set forth.

"I had a piano last year, a set of jewels, and many pretty trifles from all at home. Here is one;" and pulling the fine gold chain hidden under her frills, Sophie showed a locket set thick with pearls, containing a picture of her mother.

"It must be so nice to be rich, and able to make such fine presents. I've got something for you; but I shall be ashamed of it after I see your gift to me, I'm afraid."

Fan and Dora were working as if their bread depended on it, while Di, with a naughty twinkle in her eye, affected to be rearranging her pretty table as she talked.

"Do not fear that; my gifts this year are very simple ones. I did not know your custom, and now it is too late. My comfort is that you need nothing, and having so much, you will not care for my—what you call—coming short."

Was it the fire that made Sophie's face look so hot, and a cold that gave a husky sort of tone to her usually clear voice? A curious expression came into her face as her eyes roved from the table to the gay trifles in her friend's hands; and she opened her lips as if to add something impulsively. But nothing came, and for a moment she looked straight out at the storm as if she had forgotten where she was.

"'Shortcoming' is the proper way to speak it. But never mind that, and tell me why you say 'too late'?" asked Di, bent on winning her wager.

"Christmas comes in three days, and I have no time," began Sophie.

"But with money one can buy plenty of lovely things in one day," said Di.

"No, it is better to put a little love and hard work into what we give to friends. I have done that with my trifles, and another year I shall be more ready."

There was an uncomfortable pause, for Sophie did not speak with her usual frankness, but looked both proud and ashamed, and seemed anxious to change the subject, as she began to admire Dora's work, which had made very little progress during the last fifteen minutes.

Fanny glanced at Di with a smile that made the other toss her head and return to the charge with renewed vigor.

"Sophie, will you do me a favor?"

"With much pleasure."

"Do has promised me a whole box of French bonbons, and if you will answer three questions, you shall have it."

"*Allons*," said Sophie, smiling.

"Haven't you a secret?" asked Di, gravely.

"Yes."

"Will you tell us?"

"No."

Di paused before she asked her last question, and Fan and Dora waited breathlessly, while Sophie knit her brows and looked uneasy.

"Why not?"

"Because I do not wish to tell it."

"Will you tell if we guess?"

"Try."

"You are engaged."

At this absurd suggestion Sophie laughed gayly, and shook her curly head.

"Do you think we are betrothed at sixteen in my country?"

"I *know* that is an engagement ring,—you made such a time about it when you lost it in the water, and cried for joy when Tilly dived and found it."

"Ah, yes, I was truly glad. Dear Tilly, never do I forget that kindness!" and Sophie kissed the little pearl ring in her impulsive way, while her eyes sparkled and the frown vanished.

"I *know* a sweetheart gave it," insisted Di, sure now she had found a clue to the secret.

"He did," and Sophie hung her head in a sentimental way that made the three girls crowd nearer with faces full of interest.

"Do tell us all about it, dear. It's *so* interesting to hear love-stories. What is his name?" cried Dora.

"Hermann," simpered Sophie, drooping still more, while her lips trembled with suppressed emotion of some sort.

"How lovely!" sighed Fanny, who was very romantic.

"Tell on, do! Is he handsome?"

"To me the finest man in all the world," confessed Sophie, as she hid her face.

"And you love him?"

"I adore him!" and Sophie clasped her hands so dramatically that the girls were a little startled, yet charmed at this discovery.

"Have you his picture?" asked Di, feeling that she had won her wager now.

"Yes," and pulling out the locket again, Sophie showed in the other side the face of a fine old gentleman who looked very like herself.

"It's your father!" exclaimed Fanny, rolling her blue eyes excitedly. "You are a humbug!" cried Dora. "Then you fibbed about the ring," said Di, crossly.

"Never! It is mamma's betrothal ring; but her finger grew too plump, and when I left home she gave the ring to me as a charm to keep me safe. Ah, ha! I have my little joke as well as you, and the laugh is for me this time." And falling back among the sofa cushions, Sophie enjoyed it as only a gay girl could. Do and Fanny joined her; but Di was much disgusted, and vowed she *would* discover the secret and keep all the bonbons to herself.

"You are most welcome; but I will not tell until I like, and then to Fanny first. She will not have ridicule for what I do, but say it is well, and be glad with me. Come now and work. I will plait these ribbons, or paint a wild rose on this pretty fan. It is too plain now. Will you that I do it, dear Di?"

The kind tone and the prospect of such an ornament to her gift appeased Di somewhat; but the mirthful malice in Sophie's eyes made the other more than ever determined to be even with her by and by.

Christmas Eve came, and found Di still in the dark, which fact nettled her sadly, for Sophie tormented her and amused the other girls by pretended confidences and dark hints at the mystery which might never, never be disclosed.

Fan had determined to have an unusually jolly party; so she invited only her chosen friends, and opened the festivities with a Christmas tree, as the prettiest way of exchanging gifts and providing jokes for the evening in the shape of delusive bottles, animals full of candy, and every sort of musical instrument to be used in an impromptu concert afterward. The presents to one another were done up in secure parcels, so that they might burst upon the public eye in all their freshness. Di was very curious to know what Fan was going to give her,—for Fanny was a generous creature and loved to give. Di was a little jealous of her love for Sophie, and couldn't rest till she discovered which was to get the finer gift.

So she went early and slipped into the room where the tree stood, to peep and pick a bit, as well as to hang up a few trifles of her own. She guessed several things by feeling the parcels; but one excited her curiosity intensely, and she could not resist turning it about and pulling up one corner of the lid. It was a flat box, prettily ornamented with sea-weeds like red lace, and tied with scarlet ribbons. A tantalizing glimpse of jeweller's cotton, gold clasps, and something rose-colored conquered Di's last scruples; and she was just about to untie the ribbons when she heard Fanny's voice, and had only time to replace the box, pick up a paper that had fallen out of it, and fly up the back stairs to the dressing-room, where she found Sophie and Dora surveying each other as girls always do before they go down.

"You look like a daisy," cried Di, admiring Dora with great interest, because she felt ashamed of her prying, and the stolen note in her pocket.

"And you like a dandelion," returned Do, falling back a step to get a good view of Di's gold-colored dress and black velvet bows.

"Sophie is a lily of the valley, all in green and white," added Fanny, coming in with her own blue skirts waving in the breeze.

"It does me very well. Little girls do not need grand toilets, and I am fine enough for a 'peasant,'" laughed Sophie, as she settled the fresh ribbons on her simple white cashmere and the holly wreath in her brown hair, but secretly longing for the fine dress she might have had.

"Why didn't you wear your silver necklace? It would be lovely on your pretty neck," said Di, longing to know if she had given the trinket away.

But Sophie was not to be caught, and said with a contented smile, "I do not care for ornaments unless some one I love gives me them. I had red roses for my *bouquet de corsage*; but the poor Madame Page was so *triste*, I left them on her table to remember her of me. It seemed so heartless to go and dance while she had only pain; but she wished it."

"Dear little Sophie, how good you are!" and warm-hearted Fan kissed the blooming face that needed no roses to make it sweet and gay.

Half an hour later, twenty girls and boys were dancing round the brilliant tree. Then its boughs were stripped. Every one seemed contented; even Sophie's little gifts gave pleasure, because with each went a merry or affectionate verse, which made great fun on being read aloud. She was quite loaded with pretty things, and had no words to express her gratitude and pleasure.

"Ah, you are all so good to me! and I have nothing beautiful for you. I receive much and give little, but I cannot help it! Wait a little and I will redeem myself," she said to Fanny, with eyes full of tears, and a lap heaped with gay and useful things.

"Never mind that now; but look at this, for here's still another offering of friendship, and a very charming one, to judge by the outside," answered Fan, bringing the white box with the sea-weed ornaments.

Sophie opened it, and cries of admiration followed, for lying on the soft cotton was a lovely set of coral. Rosy pink branches, highly polished and fastened with gold clasps, formed necklace, bracelets, and a spray for the bosom. No note or card appeared, and the girls crowded round to admire and wonder who could have sent so valuable a gift.

"Can't you guess, Sophie?" cried Dora, longing to own the pretty things.

"I should believe I knew, but it is too costly. How came the parcel, Fan? I think you must know all," and Sophie turned the box about, searching vainly for a name.

"An expressman left it, and Jane took off the wet paper and put it on my table with the other things. Here's the wrapper; do you know that writing?" and Fan offered the brown paper which she had kept.

"No; and the label is all mud, so I cannot see the place. Ah, well, I shall discover some day, but I should like to thank this generous friend at once. See now, how fine I am! I do myself the honor to wear them at once."

Smiling with girlish delight at her pretty ornaments, Sophie clasped the bracelets on her round arms, the necklace about her white throat, and set the rosy spray in the lace on her bosom. Then she took a little dance down the room and found herself before Di, who was looking at her with an expression of naughty satisfaction on her face.

"Don't you wish you knew who sent them?"

"Indeed, yes;" and Sophie paused abruptly.

"Well, *I* know, and *I* won't tell till I like. It's my turn to have a secret; and I mean to keep it."

"But it is not right," began Sophie, with indignation.

"Tell me yours, and I'll tell mine," said Di, teasingly.

"I will not! You have no right to touch my gifts, and I am sure you have done it, else how know you who sends this fine *cadeau?*" cried Sophie, with the flash Di liked to see.

Here Fanny interposed, "If you have any note or card belonging to Sophie, give it up at once. She shall not be tormented. Out with it, Di. I see your hand in your pocket, and I'm sure you have been in mischief."

"Take your old letter, then. I know what's in it; and if I can't keep my secret for fun, Sophie shall not have hers. That Tilly sent the coral, and Sophie spent her hundred dollars in books and clothes for that queer girl, who'd better stay among her lobsters than try to be a lady," cried Di, bent on telling all she knew, while Sophie was reading her letter eagerly.

"Is it true?" asked Dora, for the four girls were in a corner together, and the rest of the company busy pulling crackers.

"Just like her! I thought it was that; but she wouldn't tell. Tell us now, Sophie, for *I* think it was truly sweet and beautiful to help that poor girl, and let us say hard things of you," cried Fanny, as her friend looked up with a face and a heart too full of happiness to help overflowing into words.

"Yes; I will tell you now. It was foolish, perhaps; but I did not want to be praised, and I loved to help that good Tilly. You know she worked all summer and made a little sum. So glad, so proud she was, and planned to study that she might go to school this winter. Well, in October the uncle fell very ill, and Tilly gave all her money for the doctors. The uncle had been kind to her, she did not forget; she was glad to help, and told no one but me. Then I said, 'What better can I do with my father's gift than give it to the dear creature, and let her lose no time?' I do it; she will not at first, but I write and say, 'It must be,' and she submits. She is made neat with some little dresses, and she goes at last, to be so happy and do so well that I am proud of her. Is not that better than fine toilets and rich gifts to those who need nothing? Truly, yes! yet I confess it cost me pain to give up my plans for Christmas, and to seem selfish or ungrateful. Forgive me that."

"Yes, indeed, you dear generous thing!" cried Fan and Dora, touched by the truth.

"But how came Tilly to send you such a splendid present?" asked Di. "Shouldn't think you'd like her to spend your money on such things."

"She did not. A sea-captain, a friend of the uncle, gave her these lovely ornaments, and she sends them to me with a letter that is more precious than all the coral in the sea. I cannot read it; but of all my gifts *this* is the dearest and the best!"

Sophie had spoken eagerly, and her face, her voice, her gestures, made the little story eloquent; but with the last words she clasped the letter to her bosom as if it well repaid her for all the sacrifices she had made. They might seem small to others, but she was sensitive and proud, anxious to be loved in the strange country, and fond of giving, so it cost her many tears to seem mean and thoughtless, to go poorly dressed, and be thought hardly of by those she wished to please. She did not like to tell of her own generosity, because it seemed like boasting; and she was not sure that it had been wise to give so much. Therefore, she waited to see if Tilly was worthy of the trust reposed in her and she now found a balm for many wounds in the loving letter that came with the beautiful and unexpected gift.

Di listened with hot cheeks, and when Sophie paused, she whispered regretfully,—

"Forgive me, I was wrong! I'll keep your gift all my life to remember you by, for you *are* the best and dearest girl I know."

Then with a hasty kiss she ran away, carrying with great care the white shell on which Sophie had painted a dainty little picture of the mermaids waiting for the pretty boat that brought good fortune to poor Tilly, and this lesson to those who were hereafter her faithful friends.

5
Rosa's Tale

"NOW, I BELIEVE everyone has had a Christmas present and a good time. Nobody has been forgotten, not even the cat," said Mrs. Ward to her daughter, as she looked at Pobbylinda, purring on the rug, with a new ribbon round her neck and the remains of a chicken bone between her paws.

It was very late, for the Christmas tree was decorated, the little folks in bed, the baskets and bundles left at poor neighbors' doors, and everything ready for the happy day which would begin as the clock struck twelve. They were resting after their mother's words reminded Belinda of one good friend who had received no gift that night.

"We've forgotten Rosa! Her mistress is away, but she shall have a present nevertheless. As late as it is, I know she would like some apples and cake and a Merry Christmas from the family."

Belinda jumped up as she spoke, and having collected such remnants of the feast as a horse would relish, she put on her hood, lighted a lantern, and trotted off to the barn to deliver her Christmas cheer.

As she opened the door of the loose box in which Rosa was kept, Belinda saw Rosa's eyes shining in the dark as she lifted her head with a startled air. Then, recognizing a friend, the horse rose and came rustling through the straw to greet her late visitor. She was evidently much pleased with the attention and gratefully rubbed her nose against Miss Belinda. At the same time, she poked her nose suspiciously into the contents of the basket.

Miss Belinda well knew that Rosa was an unusually social beast and would enjoy the little feast more if she had company, so she hung up the lantern, and sitting down on an inverted bucket, watched her as she munched contentedly.

"Now really," said Miss Belinda, when telling her story afterwards, "I am not sure whether I took a nap and dreamed what follows, or whether it actually happened, for strange things do occur at Christmastime, as everyone knows.

"As I sat there the town clock struck twelve, and the sound reminded me of the legend, which affirms that all animals are endowed with speech for one hour after midnight on Christmas eve, in memory of the animals who lingered near the manger when the blessed Christ Child was born.

"I wish this pretty legend were true and our Rosa could speak, if only for an hour. I'm sure she has an interesting history, and I long to know all about it.

"I said this aloud, and to my utter amazement the bay mare stopped eating, fixed her intelligent eyes upon my face, and answered in a language I understood perfectly well—'You shall indeed know my history, for whether the legend you mention is true or not, I do feel that I can confide in you and tell you all that I feel,' sweet Rosa told me.

"'I was lying awake listening to the fun in the house, thinking of my dear mistress so far away across the ocean and feeling very sad, for I heard you say that I was to be sold. That nearly broke my heart for no one has ever been so kind to me as Miss Merry, and nowhere shall I be taken care of, nursed, and loved as I have been since she bought me. I know I'm getting old and stiff in the knees. My fore-foot is lame, and sometimes I'm cross when my shoulder aches; but I do try to be a patient, grateful beast. I've gotten fat with good living, my work is not hard, and I dearly love to carry those who have done so much for me; I'll carry them about until I die in the harness if they will only keep me.'

"I was so astonished by Rosa's speech that I tumbled off the pail on which I was sitting and landed in the straw star-ing up at Rosa, as dumb as if I had lost the power she had gained. She seemed to enjoy my surprise, and added to it by letting me hear a genuine horse laugh, hearty, shrill, and clear, as she shook her pretty head and went on talking rapidly in the language which I now perceived to be a mix-ture of English and the peculiar dialect of the horse country.

"'Thank you for remembering me tonight, and in return for the goodies you bring I'll tell my story as quickly as I can, for I have often longed to recount the trials and tri-umphs of my life. Miss Merry came last Christmas eve to bring me sugar, and I wanted to speak, but it was too early and I could not say a word, though my heart was full.'

"Rosa paused an instant, and her fine eyes dimmed as if with tender tears at the recollection of the happy year, which followed the day she was bought from the drudgery of a livery stable to be a lady's special pet. I stroked her neck as she stooped to sniff affectionately at my hood, and eagerly said—

"'Tell away, dear, I'm full of interest, and understand every word you say.'

"Thus encouraged, Rosa threw up her head, and began

once again to speak with an air of pride, which plainly proved what we had always suspected, that she belonged to a good family.

"'My father was a famous racer, and I am very like him; the same color, spirit, and grace, and but for the cruelty of man, I might have been as renowned as he. I was a happy colt, petted by my master, tamed by love, and never struck a blow while he lived. I won one race for him, and my future seemed so promising that when he died, I brought a great price.

"'I mourned the death of my master, but I was glad to be sent to my new owner's racing stable, where I was made over by everyone. I heard many predictions that I would be another Goldsmith Maid or Flora Temple. Ah, how ambitious and proud I was in those days! I was truly vain in regard to my good blood, my speed, and my beauty; for indeed, I was handsome then, though you may find it difficult to believe now.' Rosa sighed regretfully as she stole a look at me, and turned her head in a way that accentuated the fine lines about her head and neck.

"'I do not find it hard to believe at all,' I answered. 'Miss Merry saw them, though you seemed to be nothing more than a skeleton when she bought you. The Cornish blacksmith who shod you noted the same. It is easy to see that you belong to a good family by the way you hold your head without a check-rein and carry your tail like a plume,' I said, with a look of admiration.

"'I must hurry over this part of my story because, though brilliant, it was very brief, and ended in a way that made it the bitterest portion of my life,' continued Rosa. 'I won several races and everyone predicted that I would earn great fame. You may guess how high my reputation was when

I tell you that before my last fatal trial thousands were bet on me, and my rival trembled at the thought of racing against me.

"'I was full of spirit, eager to show my speed and sure of success. Alas, how little I knew of the wickedness of human nature then, how dearly I bought the knowledge, and how completely it has changed my whole life! You do not know much about such matters, of course, and I won't digress to tell you all the tricks of the trade; only beware of jockeys and never bet.

"'I was kept carefully out of everyone's way for weeks and only taken out for exercise by my trainer. Poor Bill! I was fond of him, and he was so good to me that I never have forgotten him, though he broke his neck years ago. A few nights before the great race, as I was enjoying a good sleep carefully tucked away in my stall, someone stole in and gave me a dish of warm mash. It was dark, and I was but half awake. I ate it like a fool, even though I knew by instinct that it was not Bill who left it for me.

"'I was a trusting creature then, and used to all sorts of strange things being done to prepare me to race. For that reason, I never suspected that something could be wrong. Something was very wrong, however, and the deceit of it has caused me to be suspicious of any food ever since. You see, the mash was dosed in some way; it made me very ill and nearly allowed my enemies to triumph. What a shameful, cowardly trick.

"'Bill worked with me day and night, trying desperately to prepare me to run. I did my best to seem well, but there was not time for me to regain my lost strength and spirit. My pride was the only thing that kept me going. "I'll win for my master even if I die in doing it," I said to myself. When the hour came, I pranced to my place trying to look as well as ever, though my heart was heavy and I trembled with excitement. "Courage, my lass, and we'll beat them in spite of their dark tricks," Bill whispered, as he sprang into place.

"'I lost the first heat, but won the second, and the sound of the cheering gave me strength to walk away without staggering, though my legs shook under me. What a splendid minute that was when, encouraged and refreshed by my faithful Bill, I came on the track again! I knew my enemies began to fear. I carried myself so bravely that they fancied I was quite well, and now, excited by that first success, I was mad with impatience to be off and cover myself with glory.'

"Rosa looked as if her 'splendid moment' had come again, for she arched her neck, opened wide her red nostrils, and pawed the straw with one little foot. At the same time, her eyes shone with sudden fire, and her ears were pricked up as if to catch again the shouts of the spectators on that long ago day.

"'I wish I had been there to see you!' I exclaimed, quite carried away by her ardor.

"'I wish you had indeed,' she answered, 'for I won. I won! The big black horse did his best, but I had vowed to win or die, and I kept my word. For I beat him by a head, and as quickly as I had done so, I fell to the ground as if dead. I might as well have died then and there. I heard those around me whispering that the poison, the exercise, and the fall had ruined me as a racer.

"'My master no longer cared for me and would have had me shot if kind Bill had not saved my life. I was pronounced good for nothing and Bill was able to buy me cheaply. For quite a long time, I was lame and useless, but his patient care did wonders, and just as I was able to be of use to him, he was killed.

"'A gentleman in search of a saddle horse purchased me because my easy gait and quiet temper suited him; for I was meek enough now, and my size allowed me to carry his delicate daughter.

"'For more than a year, I served little Miss Alice, rejoicing to see how rosy her pale cheeks became, how upright her feeble figure grew, thanks to the hours she spent with me. My canter rocked her as gently as if she were in a cradle and fresh air was the medicine she needed. She often said she owed her life to me, and I liked to think so, for she made my life a very easy one.

"'But somehow my good times never lasted long, and when Miss Alice went west, I was sold. I had been so well treated that I looked as handsome and happy as ever. To be honest though, my shoulder never was strong again, and I often had despondent moods, longing for the excitement of the race track with the instinct of my kind; so I was glad when, attracted by my spirit and beauty, a young army officer bought me and I went to the war.

"'Ah! You never guessed that, did you? Yes, I did my part gallantly and saved my master's life more than once. You have observed how martial music delights me, but you don't know that it is because it reminds me of the proudest hour of my life. I've told you about the saddest—now listen as I tell you about the bravest and give me a pat for the courageous act that won my master his promotion though I got no praise for my part of the achievement.

"'In one of the hottest battles, my captain was ordered to lead his men on a most perilous mission. They hesitated, so did he, for it was certain to cost many lives, and, brave as they were, they paused an instant. But, I settled the point. Wild with the sound of drums, the smell of powder, and the excitement of the hour, I rebelled. Though I was sharply reined in, I took the bit between my teeth, and dashed straight ahead into the midst of the fight. Though he tried, my rider could do nothing to stop me. The men, thinking their captain was leading them on, followed cheering loudly and carrying all that was before them.

"'What happened just after that I never could remember, except that I got a wound here in my neck and a cut on my flank. The scar is there still, and I'm proud of it, though buyers always consider it a blemish. When the battle was won my master was promoted on the field, and I carried him up to the general as he sat among his officers under the torn flags.

"'Both of us were weary and wounded, both of us were full of pride at what we had done; but he received all the praise and honor. I received only a careless word and a better supper than usual.

"'It seemed so wrong that no one knew or appreciated my courageous action. Not a one seemed to care that it was the horse, not the man, who led that fearless charge. I did think I deserved at least a rosette—others received much more for far less dangerous deeds. My master alone knew the truth of the matter. He thanked me for my help by keeping me always with him until the sad day when he was killed in a skirmish and lay for hours with no one to watch and mourn over him but his faithful horse.

"'Then I knew how much he loved and thanked me. His hand stroked me while it had the strength, his eye turned to me until it grew too dim to see, and when help came at last, I heard him whisper to a comrade, "Be kind to Rosa and send her safely home. She has earned her rest."

"'I had earned it, but I did not get it. When I arrived

home, I was received by a mother whose heart was broken by the loss of her son. She did not live long to cherish me. The worst of my bad times were only beginning.

"'My next owner was a fast young man who treated me badly in many ways. At last the spirit of my father rose within me and I ran away with my master and caused him to take a brutal fall.

"'To tame me down, I was sold as a carriage horse. That almost killed me, for it was dreadful drudgery. Day after day, I pulled heavy loads behind me over the hard pavement. The horses that pulled alongside me were far from friendly and there was no affection to cheer my life.

"'I have often longed to ask why Mr. Bergh does not try to prevent such crowds from piling into those carriages. Now I beg you to do what you can to stop such an unmerciful abuse.

"'In snowstorms it was awful, and more than one of my mates dropped dead with overwork and discouragement. I used to wish I could do the same, for my poor feet, badly shod, became so lame I could hardly walk at times, and the constant strain on the up-grades brought back the old trouble in my shoulder worse than ever.

"'Why they did not kill me, I don't know. I was a miserable creature then, but there must be something attractive that lingers about me for people always seem to think I am worth saving. Whatever can it be, ma'am?'

"'Now, Rosa, don't talk so. You know you are an engaging little animal, and if you live to be forty, I'm sure you will still have certain pretty ways about you—ways that win the hearts of women, if not of men. Women sympathize with your afflictions, find themselves amused with your coquettish airs, and like your affectionate nature. Men, unfortunately, see your weak points and take a money view of the case. Now hurry up and finish. It's getting a bit cold out here.'

"I laughed as I spoke and Rosa eyed me with a sidelong glance and gently waved her docked tail, which was her delight. The sly thing liked to be flattered and was as fond of compliments as a girl.

"'Many thanks. I will come now to the most interesting portion of my narrative. As I was saying, instead of knocking me on the head, I was packed off to New Hampshire and had a fine rest among the green hills, with a dozen or so weary friends. It was during this holiday that I acquired the love of nature Miss Merry detected and liked in me when she found me ready to study sunsets with her, to admire new landscapes, and enjoy bright summer weather.

"'In the autumn, a livery stable keeper bought me, and through the winter, he fed me well. By spring, I was quite presentable. It was a small town, but a popular place to visit in the summertime. I was kept on the trot while the season lasted, mostly because ladies found me easy to drive. You, Miss Belinda, were one of the ladies, and I never shall forget, though I have long ago forgiven it, how you laughed at my odd gait the day you hired me.

"'My tender feet and stiff knees made me tread very gingerly and amble along with short mincing steps, which contrasted rather strangely with my proudly waving tail and high carried head. You liked me nevertheless because I didn't rattle you senseless as we traveled down the steep hills. You also seemed pleased that I didn't startle at the sight of locomotives and stood patiently while you gathered flowers and enjoyed the sights and sounds.

"'I have always felt a regard for you because you did not whip me and admired my eyes, which, I may say without vanity, have always been considered unusually fine. But no one ever won my whole heart like Miss Merry, and I never shall forget the happy day when she came to the stable to order a saddle horse. Her cheery voice caught my attention and when she said after looking at several showy beasts, "No, they don't suit me. This little one here has the right air," my heart danced within me and I looked 'round with a whinny of delight. "Can I ride her?" she asked, understanding my welcome. She came right up to me, patted me, peered into my face, rubbed my nose, and looked at my feet with an air of interest and sympathy that made me feel as if I'd like to carry her clear around the world.

"'Ah, what rides we had after that! What happy hours trotting merrily through the green woods, galloping over the breezy hills, and pacing slowly along quiet lanes, where I often lunched luxuriously on clover tops while Miss Merry took a sketch of some picturesque scene with me in the foreground.

"'I liked that very much. We had long chats at such times, and I was convinced that she understood me perfectly. She was never frightened when I danced for pleasure on the soft turf. She never chided me when I snatched a bite from the young trees as we passed through sylvan ways, never thought it any trouble to let me wet my tired feet in babbling brooks, and always kindly dismounted long enough to remove the stones that plagued me.

"'Then how well she rode! So firm yet light in the seat, so steady a hand on the reins, so agile a foot to spring on and off, and such infectious spirits. No matter how despondent or cross I might be, I felt happy and young again whenever dear Miss Merry was on my back.'

"Here Rosa gave a frisk that sent the straw flying and made me shrink into a corner. She pranced about the box, neighing so loudly that she woke the big brown colt in the next stall and set poor Buttercup to lowing for her lost calf, which she had managed to forget about for a few moments in sleep.

"'Ah, Miss Merry never ran away from me! She knew my heels were to be trusted, and she let me play as I would, glad to see me lively. Never mind, Miss Belinda, come out and I'll behave as befits my years,' laughed Rosa, composing herself, and adding in a way so like a woman that I could not help smiling in the dark—

"'When I say "years," I beg you to understand that I am not as old as that base man declared, but just in the prime of life for a horse. Hard usage has made me seem old before my time, but I am good for years of service yet.'

"'Few people have been through as much as you have, Rosa, and you certainly have earned the right to rest,' I said consolingly, for her little whims and vanities amused me.

"'You know what happened next,' she continued, 'but I must seize this opportunity to express my thanks for all the kindness I've received since Miss Merry bought me, in spite of the ridicule and dissuasion of all her friends.

"'I know I didn't look a good bargain. I was very thin and lame and shabby, but she saw and loved the willing spirit in me. She pitied my hard lot and felt that it would be a good deed to buy me even if she never got much work out of me.

"'I shall always remember that, and whatever happens to me hereafter, I never shall be as proud again as I was the day she put my new saddle and bridle on me. I was led out, sleek, plump, and handsome with blue rosettes at my ears, my tail cut in the English style, and on my back, Miss Merry sat in her London hat and habit, all ready to head a cavalcade of eighteen horsemen and horsewomen.

"'We were the most perfect pair of all, and when the troop pranced down the street six abreast, my head was the highest, my rider the straightest, and our two hearts the friendliest in all the goodly company.

"'Nor is it pride and love alone that bind me to her. It is gratitude as well. She often bathed my feet herself, rubbed me down, watered me, blanketed me, and came daily to see me when I was here alone for weeks in the winter. Didn't she write to the famous friend of my race for advice, and drive me seven miles to get a good smith to shoe me well? Didn't she give me weeks of rest without shoes in order to save my poor contracted feet? And am I not now fat and handsome, and barring the stiff knees, a very presentable horse? If I am, it is all owing to Miss Merry, and for that reason, I want to live and die in her service.

"'She doesn't want to sell me and only told you to do so because you didn't want to care for me while she is gone. Dear Miss Belinda, please keep me! I'll eat as little as I can. I won't ask for a new blanket, though this old army one is thin and shabby. I'll trot for you all winter and try not to show it if I am lame. I'll do anything a horse can, no matter how humble, in order to earn my living. Don't, I beg you, send me away among strangers who have neither interest nor pity for me!'

"Rosa had spoken rapidly, feeling that her plea must be made now or never. Before another Christmas, she might be far away and speech of no use to win her wish. I was greatly touched, even though she was only a horse. She was looking earnestly at me as she spoke and made the last words very eloquent by preparing to bend her stiff knees and lie down at my feet. I stopped her and answered with an arm about her neck and her soft nose in my hand—

"'You shall not be sold, Rosa! You shall go and board at Mr. Town's great stable, where you will have pleasant society among the eighty horses who usually pass the winter there. Your shoes shall be taken off so that you might rest until March at least. Your care will be only the best, my dear, and I will come and see you. In the spring, you shall return to us, even if Miss Merry is not here to welcome you.'

"'Thanks, many, many thanks! But I wish I could do something to earn my board. I hate to be idle, though rest is delicious. Is there nothing I can do to repay you, Miss Belinda? Please answer quickly. I know the hour is almost over,' cried Rosa, stamping with anxiety. Like all horses, she wanted the last word.

"'Yes, you can,' I cried, as a sudden idea popped into my head. 'I'll write down what you have told me and send the little story to a certain paper I know of. The money I get for it will pay your board. So rest in peace, my dear. You will have earned your living after all and you may rest knowing that your debt is paid.'

"Before she could reply, the clock struck one. A long sigh of satisfaction was all the response in her power. But, we understood each other now, and cutting a lock from her hair for Miss Merry, I gave Rosa a farewell caress and went on my way. I couldn't help wondering if I had made it all up or the charming beast had really broken a year's silence and freed her mind.

"However that may be, here is the tale. The sequel to it is that the bay mare has really gone to board at a first-class stable," concluded Miss Belinda. "I call occasionally and leave my card in the shape of an apple, finding Madam Rosa living like an independent lady, her large box and private yard on the sunny side of the barn, a kind ostler to wait upon her, and much genteel society from the city when she is inclined for company.

"What more could any reasonable horse desire?"

6

The Little Red Purse

AMONG THE PRESENTS which Lu found on her tenth birthday was a pretty red plush purse with a steel clasp and chain, just like mamma's, only much smaller. In it were ten bright new cents, that being the sum Lu received each week to spend as she liked. She enjoyed all her gifts very much; but this one seemed to please her even more than the French doll in blue silk, the pearl ring, or "Alice in Wonderland,"—three things which she had wanted for a long time.

"It is *so* cunning, and the snap makes such a loud noise, and the chain is so nice on my arm, and the plush so red and soft, I can't help loving my dear little purse. I shall spend all the money for candy, and eat it every bit myself, because it is my birthday, and I must celebrate it," said Lu, as she hovered like a bee round a honey-pot about the table where the gifts were spread.

Now she was in a great hurry to go out shopping, with the new purse proudly carried in her small fat hand. Aunty was soon ready, and away they went across the pleasant park, where the pretty babies were enjoying the last warm days of autumn as they played among the fallen leaves.

"You will be ill if you eat ten cents' worth of candy to-day," said aunty.

"I'll sprinkle it along through the day, and eat each kind seppyrut; then they won't intersturb me, I am sure," answered Lu, who still used funny words, and always got *interrupt* and *disturb* rather mixed.

Just then a poor man who had lost his legs came creeping along with a tray of little flower pots to sell.

"Only five cents, miss, help an unfortnit man, please, mum."

"Let me buy one for my baby-house. It would be sweet. Cora Pinky May would love to have that darling little rose in her best parlor," cried Lu, thinking of the fine new doll.

Aunty much preferred to help the poor man than to buy candy, so the flower-pot was soon bought, though the "red, red rose" was unlike any ever seen in a garden.

"Now I'll have five cents for my treat, and no danger of being ill," said Lu, as they went on again.

But in a few moments a new beggar appeared, and Lu's tender heart would not let her pass the old woman without dropping two of her bright cents in the tin cup.

"Do come to the candy-place at once, or I never shall get any," begged Lu, as the red purse grew lighter and lighter every minute.

Three sticks of candy were all she could buy, but she felt that she could celebrate the birthday on that, and was ready to go home and begin at once.

As they went on to get some flowers to dress the cake at tea-time, Lu suddenly stopped short, lifted both hands, and cried out in a tone of despair,—

"My purse! my purse! I've lost it. Oh, I've lost it!"

"Left it in the store probably. Come and look for it," said aunty; and back they turned, just in time to meet a shabby little girl running after them with the precious thing in her hand.

"Ain't this yours? I thought you dropped it, and would hate to lose it," she said, smiling pleasantly.

"Oh, I should. It's spandy new, and I love it dearly. I've got no more money to pay you, only this candy; do take a stick," and Lu presented the red barley sugar.

The little girl took it gladly, and ran off.

"Well, two sticks will do. I'd rather lose every bit of it than my darling purse," said Lu, putting it carefully in her pocket.

"I love to give things away and make people happy," began Lu, but stopped to watch a dog who came up to her, wagging his tail as if he knew what a kind little girl she was, and wanted to be made happy. She put out her hand to pat him, quite forgetting the small parcel in it; but the dog snapped it up before she could save it.

"Oh, my last stick! I didn't mean to give it to him. You naughty dog, drop it this minute!" cried poor Lu.

But the beautiful pink cream candy was forever lost, and the ungrateful thief ran off, after a vain attempt to eat the flower-pot also. It was so funny that aunty laughed, and Lu joined her, after shaking her finger at the dog, who barked and frisked as if he felt that he had done a clever thing.

"Now I am quite satisfied, and you will have a pleasanter birthday for having made four people and a dog happy, instead of yourself sick with too many goodies. Charity is a nice sort of sweetie; and I hope you will buy that kind with your pocket-money now and then, my dear," said aunty, as they walked on again.

"Could I do much with ten cents a week?" asked Lu.

"Yes, indeed; you could buy a little book for lame Sammy, who loves to read, or a few flowers for my sick girl at the hospital, or a loaf of bread for some hungry person, or milk for a poor baby, or you could save up your money till Christmas, and get presents for children who otherwise would have none."

"Could I do all those things? I'd like to get presents best, and I will—I will!" cried Lu, charmed with the idea of playing Santa Claus. "I didn't think ten cents would be so useful. How long to Christmas, aunty?"

"About ten weeks. If you save all your pocket-money till then, you will have a dollar to spend."

"A truly dollar! How fine! But all that time I shouldn't have any candy. I don't think I could get along without *some*. Perhaps if I was *very* good someone would give me a bit now and then;" and Lu looked up with her most engaging smile and a twinkle in her eye.

"We will see about that. Perhaps 'someone' will give extra cents for work you may do, and leave you to decide which kind of sweeties you would buy."

"What can I do to earn money?" asked Lu.

"Well, you can dry and fold the paper every morning for grandpa. I will pay you a cent for that, because nurse is apt to forget it, and he likes to have it nicely ready for him after breakfast. Then you might run up and down for mamma, and hem some towels for me, and take care of Jip and the parrot. You will earn a good deal if you do your work regularly and well."

"I shall have dreadful trials going by the candy-shops and never buying any. I do long so to go in that I have to look away when you say No. I want to be good and help poor people, but I'm afraid it will be too hard for me," sighed Lu, foreseeing the temptations before her.

"We might begin to-day, and try the new plan for a while. If it is too hard, you can give it up; but I think you will soon like my way best, and have the merriest Christmas you ever knew with the money you save."

Lu walked thoughtfully home, and put the empty purse away, resolved to see how long she could hold out, and how much she could earn. Mamma smiled when she heard the plan, but at once engaged the little girl to do errands about the house at a cent a job, privately quite sure that her pretty express would soon stop running. Grandpapa was pleased to find his paper ready, and nodded and patted Lu's curly head when she told him about her Christmas plans. Mary, the maid, was glad to get rid of combing Jip and feeding Polly, and aunty made towel hemming pleasant by telling stories as the little needle-woman did two hems a day.

Every cent went into the red purse, which Lu hung on one of the gilt pegs of the easel in the parlor, for she thought it very ornamental, and hoped contributions might drop in occasionally. None did; but as every one paid her in bright cents, there was soon a fine display, and the little bag grew heavy with delightful rapidity.

Only once did Lu yield to temptation, and that was when two weeks of self-denial made her trials so great that she felt as if she really must reward herself, as no one else seemed to remember how much little girls loved candy.

One day she looked pale, and did not want any dinner, saying she felt sick. Mamma was away, so aunty put her on the bed and sat by her, feeling very anxious, as scarlet-fever was about. By and by Lu took her handkerchief out, and there, sticking to it, was a large brown cough-drop. Lu turned red, and hid her face, saying with a penitent sob, "I don't deserve to be cuddled. I've been selfish and silly, and spent some of my money for candy. I had a little cold, and I thought cough-drops would do me good. I ate a good many, and they were bitter and made me sick, and I'm glad of it."

Aunty wanted to laugh at the dear little sinner and her funny idea of choosing bitter candy as a sort of self-denial; but she comforted her kindly, and soon the invalid was skipping about again, declaring that she never would do so any more.

Next day something happened which helped her very much, and made it easier to like the new kind of sweeties better than the old. She was in the dining-room getting an apple for her lunch, when she saw a little girl come to the lower door to ask for cold food. The cook was busy, and sent her away, telling her begging was forbidden. Lu, peeping out, saw the little girl sit down on the steps to eat a cold potato as if she was very hungry, and while she ate she was trying to tie on a pair of very old boots some one had given her. It was a rainy day, and she had only a shawl over her head; her hands were red with cold; her gown was a faded cotton one; and her big basket seemed to have very few scraps in it. So poor, so sad, and tired did she look, that Lu could not bear to see it, and she called out in her pitiful child's voice,—

"Come in and get warm, little girl. Don't mind old Sarah. I'll give you something to eat, and lend you my rubber boots and water-proof to go home in."

The poor child gladly went to sit by the comfortable fire, while Lu with hospitable haste got crackers and cheese and cake and apples, and her own silver mug of milk, for her guest, forgetting, in her zeal, to ask leave. Fortunately aunty came down for her own lunch in time to see what was going on, and found Lu busily buttoning the waterproof, while the little girl surveyed her rubber boots and small umbrella with pride.

"I'm only *lending* my things, and she will return them to-morrow, aunty. They are too small for me, and the umbrella is broken; and I'd love to *give* them all to Lucy if I could. *She* has to go out in the rain to get food for her family, like a bird, and I don't."

"Birds don't need waterproofs and umbrellas," began aunty; and both children laughed at the idea of sparrows with such things, but looked a little anxious till aunty went on to say that Lucy could have these comforts, and to fill the basket with something better than cold potatoes, while she asked questions and heard the sad little story: how father was dead, and the baby sick, so mother could not work, and the boys had to pick up chips and cinders to burn, and Lucy begged food to eat. Lu listened with tears in her blue eyes, and a great deal of pity as well as admiration for poor little Lucy, who was only nine, yet had so many cares and troubles in her life. While aunty went to get some flannel for baby, Lu flew to her red purse and counted out ten cents from her store, feeling so rich, so glad to have it instead of an empty bonbon box, and a headache after a candy feast.

"Buy some nice fresh milk for little Totty, and tell her I sent it—all myself—with my love. Come again to-morrow, and I will tell mamma all about you, and you shall be my poor people, and I'll help you if I can," she said, full of interest and good-will, for the sight of this child made her feel what poverty really was, and long to lighten it if she could.

Lucy was smiling when she went away, sung and dry in her comfortable clothes, with the full basket on her arm; and all that day Lu talked and thought about her "own poor people," and what she hoped to do for them. Mamma inquired, and finding them worthy of help, let her little girl send many comforts to the children, and learn how to be wisely charitable.

"I shall give *all* my money to my 'Lucy children' on Christmas," announced Lu, as that pleasant time drew near. "I know what they want, and though I can't save money enough to give them half the things they need, maybe I can help a good deal, and really have a nice bundle to s'prise them with."

This idea took possession of little Lu, and she worked like a beaver in all sorts of funny ways to fill her purse by Christmas-time. One thing she did which amused her family very much, though they were obliged to stop it. Lu danced very prettily, and often had what she called ballets before she went to bed, when she tripped about the parlor like a fairy in the gay costumes aunty made for her. As the purse did not fill as fast as she hoped, Lu took it into her head one fine day to go round the square where she lived, with her tambourine, and dance as some of the girls with the hand-organ men did. So she dressed herself in her red skirt and black velvet jacket, and with a fur cap on her head and a blue cloak over her shoulders, slipped out into the quiet square, and going to the farther corner, began to dance and beat her tambourine on the sidewalk before a house where some little children lived.

As she expected, they soon came running to the window, and were charmed to see the pretty dancer whirling to and fro, with her ribbons flying and her tambourine bells ringing, till her breath was gone. Then she held up the instrument and nodded smilingly at them; and they threw down cents wrapped in paper, thinking her music much better than any the organ men made. Much encouraged, Lu went on from house to house, and was doing finely, when one of the ladies who looked out recognized the child, and asked her if her mother knew where she was. Lu had to say "No;" and the lady sent a maid to take her home at once.

That spoiled all the fun; and poor Lu did not hear the last of her prank for a long time. But she had made forty-two cents, and felt comforted when she added that handsome sum to her store. As if to console her for this disappointment, after that day several bright ten-cent pieces got into the red purse in a most mysterious manner. Lu asked every one in the house, and all declared that they did not do it. Grandpa could not get out of his chair without help, and nurse said she never took the purse to him; so of course it could not be he who slipped in those welcome bits of silver. Lu asked him; but he was very deaf that day, and did not seem to understand her at all.

"It must be fairies," she said, pondering over the puzzle, as she counted her treasure and packed it away, for now the little red purse was full. "Aunty says there are no fairies; but I like to think so. Perhaps angels fly around at Christmastime as they did long ago, and love to help poor people, and put those beautiful bright things here to show that they are pleased with me." She liked that fancy, and aunty agreed that some good spirit must have done it, and was sure they would find out the secret some time.

Lucy came regularly; and Lu always tried to see her, and so learned what she and Totty and Joe and Jimmy wanted, but never dreamed of receiving Christmas morning. It did both little girls much good, for poor Lucy was comforted by the kindness of these friends, and Lu learned about far harder trials than the want of sugarplums. The day before Christmas she went on a grand shopping expedition with aunty, for the purse now held three dollars and seven cents. She had spent some of it for trifles for her "Lucy children," and had not earned as much as she once hoped, various fits of idleness and other more amusing but less profitable work having lessened her wages. But she had enough, thanks to the good spirit, to get toys and books and candy for her family, and went joyfully away Christmas Eve to carry her little basket of gifts, accompanied by aunty with a larger store of comforts for the grateful mother.

When they got back, Lu entertained her mother with an account of the delight of the children, who never had such a Christmas before.

"They couldn't wait till morning, and I couldn't either, and we opened the bundles right away; and they *screamed*, mamma, and jumped for joy and ate everything and hugged me. And the mother cried, she was so pleased; and the boys can go to school all neat now, and so could Lucy, only she has to take care of Totty while her mother goes to work. Oh, it was lovely! I felt just like Santa Claus, only he doesn't stay to see people enjoy their things, and I did."

Here Lu stopped for breath, and when she got it, had a fine ballet as the only way to work off her excitement at the success of her "s'prise." It was a trial to go to bed, but she went at last, and dreamed that her "Lucy children" all had wings, and were flying round her bed with tambourines full of heavenly bonbons, which they showered down upon her; while aunty in an immense nightcap stood by clapping her hands and saying, "Eat all you like, dear; this sort won't hurt you."

Morning came very soon; and she popped up her head to see a long knobby stocking hanging from the mantel-piece. Out of bed skipped the little white figure, and back again, while cries of joy were heard as the treasures appeared one by one. There was a tableful beside the stocking, and Lu was so busy looking at them that she was late to breakfast. But aunty waited for her, and they went down together some time after the bell rang.

"Let me peep and see if grandpa has found the silk

handkerchief and spectacle-case I made for him," whispered Lu, as they passed the parlor door, which stood half open, leaving a wide crack for the blue eyes to spy through.

The old gentleman sat in his easy-chair as usual, waiting while nurse got his breakfast; but what was he doing with his long staff? Lu watched eagerly, and to her great surprise saw him lean forward, and with the hook at the end take the little red purse off the easel, open it, and slip in a small white parcel, then hang it on the gilt peg again, put away the cane, and sit rubbing his hands and laughing to himself at the success of his little trick, quite sure that this was a safe time to play it. Lu was about to cry out and rush in, but aunty whispered, "Don't spoil his fun yet. Go and see what is in the purse, then thank him in the way he likes best."

So Lu skipped into the parlor, trying to look very innocent, and ran to open the dear red purse, as she often did, eager to see if the good fairy had added to the charity fund.

"Why, here's a great gold medal, and some queer, shaky writing on the paper. Please see what it is," said Lu, very loud, hoping grandpa would hear her this time, for his face was hidden behind the newspaper he pretended to read.

"For Lu's poor's purse, from Santa Claus," read aunty, glad that at last the kind old fairy was discovered and ready for his reward.

Lu had never seen a twenty-dollar gold-piece before; but she could not stop to find out whether the shining medal was money or a locket, and ran to grandpa, crying as she pulled away the paper and threw her arms about his neck,—

"I've found you out, I've found you out, my dear old Santa Claus! Merry Christmas, grandpa, and lots of thanks and kisses!"

It was pretty to see the rosy cheek against the wrinkled

one, the golden and the silver heads close together, as the old man and the little girl kissed and laughed, and both talked at once for a few minutes.

"Tell me all about it, you sly grandpa. What made you think of doing it that way, and not let any one know?" cried Lu, as the old gentleman stopped to rest after a kindly "cuddle," as Lu called these caresses.

"Well, dear, I liked to see you trying to do good with your little pennies, and I wanted to help. I'm a feeble old man, tied to my chair and of no use now; but I like a bit of fun, and love to feel that it is not quite too late to make some one happy."

"Why, grandpa, you do heaps of good, and make many, many people happy," said Lu, with another hug. "Mamma told me all about the hospital for little children you built, and the money you gave to the poor soldiers in the war, and ever so many more good things you've done. I won't have you say you are of no use now. We want you to love and take care of; and we couldn't do without you, could we, aunty?"

Aunty sat on the arm of the chair with her arm round the old man's shoulder, and her only answer was a kiss. But it was enough, and grandpa went on quite cheerfully, as he held two plump hands in his own, and watched the blooming face that looked up at him so eagerly:

"When I was younger, I loved money, and wanted a great deal. I cared for nothing else, and worked hard to get it, and did get it after years of worry. But it cost me my health, and then I saw how foolish I had been, for all my money could not buy me any strength or pleasure and very little comfort. I could not take it with me when I died, and did not know what to do with it, because there was so much. So I tried to see if giving it away would not amuse me, and make me feel better about having wasted my life instead of using it wisely. The more I gave away the better I felt; and now I'm quite jolly, though I'm only a helpless old baby just fit to play jokes and love little girls. You have begun early at this pretty game of give-away, my dear, and aunty will see that you keep it up; so that when you are old you will have much treasure in the other world where the blessings of the poor are more precious than gold and silver."

Nobody spoke for a minute as the feeble old voice stopped; and the sunshine fell on the white head like a blessing. Then Lu said very soberly, as she turned the great coin in her hand, and saw the letters that told its worth,—

"What shall I do with all this money? I never had so much, and I'd like to spend it in some very good and pleasant way. Can you think of something, aunty, so I can begin at once to be like grandpa?"

"How would you like to pay two dollars a month, so that Totty can go to the Sunnyside Nursery, and be taken care of every day while Lucy goes to school? Then she will be safe and happy, and Lucy be learning, as she longs to do, and the mother free to work," said aunty, glad to have this dear child early learn to help those less blessed than herself.

"Could I? How splendid it would be to pay for a real live baby all myself! How long would my money do it?" said Lu, charmed with the idea of a living dolly to care for.

"All winter, and provide clothes besides. You can make them yourself, and go and see Totty, and call her your baby. This will be a sweet charity for you; and to-day is a good day to begin it, for this is the birthday of the Divine Child, who was born in a poorer place even than Lucy's sister. In His name pity and help this baby, and be sure He will bless you for it."

Lu looked up at the fine picture of the Good Shepherd

hanging over the sofa with holly-leaves glistening round it, and felt as if she too in her humble way was about to take a helpless little lamb in her arms and comfort it. Her childish face was very sweet and sober as she said softly,—

"Yes, I will spend my Christmas money so; for, aunty, I do think your sort of sweetie is better than mine, and making people happy a much wiser way to spend my pennies than in buying the nicest candy in the world."

Little Lu remembered that morning long after the dear old grandfather was gone, and kept her Christmas promise so well that very soon a larger purse was needed for charity money, which she used so wisely and so happily. But all her life in one corner of her desk lay carefully folded up, with the bit of paper inside, the little red purse.

7
Tessa's Surprises

I

LITTLE TESSA SAT alone by the fire, waiting for her father to come home from work. The children were fast asleep, all four in the big bed behind the curtain; the wind blew hard outside, and the snow beat on the windowpanes; the room was large and the fire so small and feeble that it didn't half warm the little bare toes peeping out of the old shoes on the hearth.

Tessa's father was an Italian plaster-worker, very poor, but kind and honest. The mother had died not long ago, and left twelve-year-old Tessa to take care of the little children. She tried to be very wise and motherly, and worked for them like any little woman; but it was so hard to keep the small bodies warm and fed, and the small souls good and happy, that poor Tessa was often at her wits' end. She always waited for her father, no matter how tired she was, so that he might find his supper warm, a bit of fire, and a loving little face to welcome him. Tessa thought over her troubles at these quiet times, and made her plans; for her father left things to her a good deal, and she had no friends but Tommo, the harp-boy upstairs, and the lively cricket who lived in the chimney. Tonight her face was very sober, and her pretty brown eyes very thoughtful as she stared at the fire and knit her brows, as if perplexed. She was not thinking of her old shoes, nor the empty closet, nor the boys' ragged clothes just then. No; she had a fine plan in her good little head, and was trying to discover how she could carry it out.

You see, Christmas was coming in a week; and she had set her heart on putting something in the children's stockings, as the mother used to do, for while she lived things were comfortable. Now Tessa had not a penny in the world, and didn't know how to get one, for all the father's earnings had to go for food, fire, and rent.

"If there were only fairies, ah! How heavenly that would be; for then I should tell them all I wish, and, pop! Behold the fine things in my lap!" said Tessa to herself. "I must earn the money; there is no one to give it to me, and I cannot beg. But what can I do, so small and stupid and shy as I am? I *must* find some way to give the little ones a nice Christmas. I *must*! I *must*!" and Tessa pulled her long hair, as if that would help her think.

But it didn't, and her heart got heavier and heavier; for it did seem hard that in a great city full of fine things, there should be none for poor Nono, Sep, and little Speranza. Just as Tessa's tears began to tumble off her eyelashes on to her brown cheeks, the cricket began to chirp. Of course, he didn't say a word; but it really did seem as if he had answered her question almost as well as a fairy; for, before he had piped a dozen shrill notes, an idea popped into Tessa's head—such a truly splendid idea that she clapped her hands and burst out laughing. "I'll do it! I'll do it! If father will let me," she said to herself, smiling and nodding at the fire. "Tommo will like to have me go with him and sing, while he plays his harp in the streets. I know many songs, and may get money if I am not frightened; for people throw pennies to other little girls who only play the tambourine. Yes, I will try; and then, if I do well, the little ones shall have a Merry Christmas."

So full of her plan was Tessa that she ran upstairs at once, and asked Tommo if he would take her with him on the morrow. Her friend was delighted, for he thought Tessa's songs very sweet, and was sure she would get money if she tried.

"But see, then, it is cold in the streets; the wind bites, and the snow freezes one's fingers. The day is very long, people are cross, and at night one is ready to die with weariness. Thou art so small, Tessa, I am afraid it will go badly with thee," said Tommo, who was a merry, black-eyed boy of fourteen, with the kindest heart in the world under his old jacket.

"I do not mind cold and wet, and cross people, if I can get the pennies," answered Tessa, feeling very brave with such a friend to help her. She thanked Tommo, and ran away to get ready, for she felt sure her father would not refuse her anything. She sewed up the holes in her shoes as well as she could, for she had much of that sort of cobbling to do; she mended her only gown, and laid ready the old hood and shawl which had been her mother's. Then she washed out little Ranza's frock and put it to dry, because she would not be able to do it the next day. She set the table and got things ready for breakfast, for Tommo went out early, and must not be kept waiting for her. She longed to make the beds and dress the children overnight, she was in such a hurry to have all in order; but, as that could not be, she sat down again, and tried over all the songs she knew. Six pretty ones were chosen; and she sang away with all her heart in a fresh little voice so sweetly that the children smiled in their sleep, and her father's tired face brightened as he entered, for Tessa was his cheery cricket on the hearth. When she had told her plan, Peter Benari shook his head, and thought it would never do; but Tessa begged so hard, he consented at last that she should try it for one week, and sent her to bed the happiest little girl in New York.

Next morning the sun shone, but the cold wind blew, and the snow lay thick in the streets. As soon as her father was gone, Tessa flew about and put everything in nice order, telling the children she was going out for the day, and they were to mind Tommo's mother, who would see about the fire and the dinner; for the good woman loved Tessa, and entered into her little plans with all her heart. Nono and Guiseppe, or Sep, as they called him, wondered what she was going away for, and little Ranza cried at being left; but Tessa told them they would know all about it in a week, and have a fine time if they were good; so they kissed her all round and let her go.

Poor Tessa's heart beat fast as she trudged away with Tommo, who slung his harp over his shoulder, and gave her his hand. It was rather a dirty hand, but so kind that Tessa clung to it, and kept looking up at the friendly brown face for encouragement.

"We go first to the *café*, where many French and Italians eat the breakfast. They like my music, and often give me sips of hot coffee, which I like much. You too shall have the sips, and perhaps the pennies, for these people are greatly kind," said Tommo, leading her into a large smoky place, where many people sat at little tables, eating and drinking. "See, now, have no fear; give them 'Bella Monica'; that is merry and will make the laugh," whispered Tommo, tuning his harp.

For a moment Tessa felt so frightened that she wanted to run away; but she remembered the empty stockings at home, and the fine plan, and she resolved *not* to give it up. One fat old Frenchman nodded to her, and it seemed to help her very much; for she began to sing before she thought, and that was the hardest part of it. Her voice trembled, and her cheeks grew redder and redder as she went on; but she kept her eyes fixed on her old shoes, and so got through without breaking down, which was very nice. The people laughed, for the song *was* merry; and the fat man smiled and nodded again. This gave her courage to try another, and she sang better and better each time; for Tommo played his best, and kept whispering to her, "Yes; we go well; this is fine. They will give the money and the blessed coffee."

So they did; for, when the little concert was over, several men put pennies in the cap Tessa offered, and the fat man took her on his knee, and ordered a mug of coffee, and some bread and butter for them both. This quite won her heart; and when they left the *café*, she kissed her hand to the old Frenchman, and said to her friend, "How kind they are! I like this very much; and now it is not hard."

But Tommo shook his curly head, and answered, soberly, "Yes, I took you there first, for they love music, and are of our country; but up among the great houses we shall not always do well. The people there are busy or hard or idle, and care nothing for harps and songs. Do not skip and laugh too soon, for the day is long, and we have but twelve pennies yet."

Tessa walked more quietly, and rubbed her cold hands, feeling that the world was a very big place, and wondering how the children got on at home without the little mother. Till noon they did not earn much, for everyone seemed in a hurry, and the noise of many sleigh-bells drowned the music. Slowly they made their way up to the great squares where the big houses were, with fine ladies and pretty children at the windows. Here Tessa sang all her best songs, and Tommo played as fast as his fingers could fly; but it was too cold to have the windows open, so the pretty children could not listen long, and the ladies tossed out a little money, and soon went back to their own affairs.

All the afternoon the two friends wandered about, singing and playing, and gathering up their small harvest. At dusk they went home—Tessa so hoarse she could hardly speak, and so tired she fell asleep over her supper. But she had made half a dollar, for Tommo divided the money fairly, and she felt rich with her share. The other days were very much like this; sometimes they made more, sometimes less, but Tommo always "went halves"; and Tessa kept on, in spite of cold and weariness, for her plans grew as her earnings increased, and now she hoped to get useful things, instead of candy and toys alone.

On the day before Christmas she made herself as tidy as she could, for she hoped to earn a good deal. She tied a bright scarlet handkerchief over the old hood, and the brilliant color set off her brown cheeks and bright eyes, as well as the pretty black braids of her hair. Tommo's mother lent her a pair of boots so big that they turned up at the toes, but there were no holes in them, and Tessa felt quite elegant in whole boots. Her hands were covered with chilblains, for she had no mittens; but she put them under her shawl, and scuffled merrily away in her big boots, feeling so glad that the week was over, and nearly three dollars safe in her pocket. How gay the streets were that day! How brisk everyone was, and how bright the faces looked, as people trotted about with big baskets, holly wreaths, and young evergreens going to blossom into splendid Christmas trees!

"If I could have a tree for the children, I'd never want anything again. But I can't; so I'll fill the socks all full, and be happy," said Tessa, as she looked wistfully into the gay stores, and saw the heavy baskets go by.

"Who knows what may happen if we do well?" returned Tommo, nodding wisely, for he had a plan as well as Tessa, and kept chuckling over it as he trudged through the mud. They did *not* do well, somehow, for people seemed so full of their own affairs they could not stop to listen, even to "Bella Monica," but bustled away to spend their money on turkeys, toys, and trees. In the afternoon it began to rain, and poor Tessa's heart to fail her; for the big boots tired her feet, the cold wind made her hands ache, and the rain spoiled the fine red handkerchief. Even Tommo looked sober, and didn't whistle as he walked, for he also was disappointed, and his plan looked rather doubtful, the pennies came in so slowly.

"We'll try one more street, and then go home, thou art so tired, little one. Come; let me wipe thy face, and give me thy hand here in my jacket pocket; there it will be as warm as any kitten"; and kind Tommo brushed away the drops which were not *all* rain from Tessa's cheeks, tucked the poor hand into his ragged pocket, and led her carefully along the slippery streets, for the boots nearly tripped her up.

II

At the first house, a cross old gentleman flapped his newspaper at them; at the second, a young gentleman and lady were so busy talking that they never turned their heads; and at the third, a servant came out and told them to go away, because someone was sick. At the fourth, some people let them sing all their songs, and gave nothing. The next three houses were empty; and the last of all showed not a single face, as they looked up anxiously. It was so cold, so dark and discouraging, that Tessa couldn't help one sob; and, as he glanced down at the little red nose and wet figure beside him, Tommo gave his harp an angry thump, and said something very fierce in Italian. They were just going to turn away; but they didn't, for that angry thump happened to be the best thing they could have done. All of a sudden a little head appeared at the window, as if the sound had brought it; then another and another, till there were five, of all heights and colors, and five eager faces peeped out, smiling and nodding to the two below.

"Sing, Tessa; sing! Quick! Quick!" cried Tommo, twanging away with all his might, and showing his white teeth, as he smiled back at the little gentlefolk.

Bless us! How Tessa did tune up at that! She chirped away like a real bird, forgetting all about the tears on her cheeks, the ache in her hands, and the heaviness at her heart. The children laughed and clapped their hands, and cried "More! More! Sing another, little girl! Please, do!" And away they went again, piping and playing, till Tessa's breath was gone, and Tommo's stout fingers tingled well.

"Mamma says, come to the door; it's too muddy to throw the money in the street!" cried out a kindly child's voice, as Tessa held up the old cap, with beseeching eyes.

Up the wide stone steps went the street musicians, and the whole flock came running down to give a handful of silver, and ask all sorts of questions. Tessa felt so grateful, that, without waiting for Tommo, she sang her sweetest little song all alone. It was about a lost lamb, and her heart was in the song; therefore, she sang it well, so well, that a pretty young lady came down to listen, and stood watching the bright-eyed child, who looked about her as she sang, evidently enjoying the light and warmth of the fine hall, and the sight of the lovely children with their gay dresses, shining hair, and dainty little shoes.

"You have a charming voice, child. Who taught you to sing?" asked the young lady, kindly.

"My mother. She is dead now; but I do not forget," answered Tessa, in her pretty broken English.

"I wish she could sing at our tree, since Bella is ill," cried one of the children, peeping through the banisters.

"She is not fair enough for the angel, and too large to go up in the tree. But she sings sweetly, and looks as if she would like to see a tree," said the young lady.

"Oh, so much!" exclaimed Tessa; adding eagerly, "my sister Ranza is small and pretty as a baby-angel. She could sit up in the fine tree, and I could sing for her from under the table."

"Sit down and warm yourself, and tell me about Ranza," said the kind elder sister, who liked the confiding little girl, in spite of her shabby clothes.

So Tessa sat down and dried the big boots over the furnace, and told her story, while Tommo stood modestly in the background, and the children listened with faces full of interest.

"Oh, Rose! Let us see the little girl; and if she will do, let us have her, and Tessa can learn our song, and it will be splendid!" cried the biggest boy, who sat astride of a chair, and stared at the harp with round eyes.

"I'll ask Mamma," said Rose; and away she went into the dining room close by. As the door opened, Tessa saw what looked to her like a fairy feast—all silver mugs and flowery plates and oranges and nuts and rosy wine in tall glass pitchers, and smoking dishes that smelt so deliciously she could not restrain a little sniff of satisfaction.

"Are you hungry?" asked the boy, in a grand tone.

"Yes, sir," meekly answered Tessa.

"I say, Mamma; she wants something to eat. Can I give her an orange?" called the boy, prancing away into the splendid room; quite like a fairy prince, Tessa thought.

A plump, motherly lady came out and looked at Tessa, asked a few questions, and then told her to come tomorrow with Ranza, and they would see what could be done. Tessa clapped her hands for joy—she didn't mind the chilblains now—and Tommo played a lively march, he was so pleased.

"Will you come, too, and bring your harp? You shall be paid, and shall have something from the tree, likewise," said the motherly lady, who liked what Tessa gratefully told about his kindness to her.

"Ah, yes; I shall come with much gladness, and play as never in my life before," cried Tommo, with a flourish of the old cap that made the children laugh.

"Give these to your brothers," said the fairy prince, stuffing nuts and oranges into Tessa's hands.

"And these to the little girl," added one of the young princesses, flying out of the dining room with cakes and rosy apples for Ranza.

Tessa didn't know what to say; but her eyes were full, and she just took the mother's white hand in both her little grimy ones, and kissed it many times in her pretty Italian fashion. The lady understood her, and stroked her cheek softly, saying to her elder daughter, "We must take care of this good little creature. Freddy, bring me your mittens; these poor hands must be covered. Alice, get your play-hood; this handkerchief is all wet; and, Maud, bring the old chinchilla tippet."

The children ran, and in a minute there were lovely blue mittens on the red hands, a warm hood over the black braids, and a soft "pussy" round the sore throat.

"Ah! so kind, so very kind! I have no way to say 'thank you'; but Ranza shall be for you a heavenly angel, and I will sing my heart out for your tree!" cried Tessa, folding the mittens as if she would say a prayer of thankfulness if she knew how.

Then they went away, and the pretty children called after them, "Come again, Tessa! Come again, Tommo!" Now the rain didn't seem dismal, the wind cold, nor the way long, as they bought their gifts and hurried home, for kind words and the sweet magic of charity had changed all the world to them.

I think the good spirits who fly about on Christmas Eve, to help the loving fillers of little stockings, smiled very kindly on Tessa as she brooded joyfully over the small store of presents that seemed so magnificent to her. All the goodies were divided evenly into three parts and stowed away in father's three big socks, which hung against the curtain. With her three dollars, she had got a pair of shoes for Nono, a knit cap for Sep, and a pair of white stockings for Ranza; to her she also gave the new hood; to Nono the mittens; and to Sep the tippet.

"Now the dear boys can go out, and my Ranza will be ready for the lady to see, in her nice new things," said Tessa, quite sighing with pleasure to see how well the gifts looked pinned up beside the bulging socks, which wouldn't hold them all. The little mother kept nothing for herself but the pleasure of giving everything away; yet I think she was both richer and happier than if she had kept them all. Her father laughed as he had not done since the mother died, when he saw how comically the old curtain had broken out into boots and hoods, stockings and tippets.

"I wish I had a gold gown and a silver hat for thee, my Tessa, thou art so good. May the saints bless and keep thee always!" said Peter Benari tenderly, as he held his little daughter close, and gave her the good-night kiss.

Tessa felt very rich as she crept under the faded counterpane, feeling as if she had received a lovely gift, and fell happily asleep with chubby Ranza in her arms, and the two rough black heads peeping out at the foot of the bed. She dreamed wonderful dreams that night, and woke in the morning to find real wonders before her eyes. She got up early, to see if the socks were all right, and there she found the most astonishing sight. Four socks, instead of three; and by the fourth, pinned out quite elegantly, was a little dress, evidently meant for her—a warm, woollen dress, all made, and actually with bright buttons on it. It nearly took her breath away; so did the new boots on the floor, and the funny long stocking like a gray sausage, with a wooden doll staring out at the top, as if she said, politely, "A Merry Christmas, ma'am!" Tessa screamed and danced in her delight, and up tumbled all the children to scream and dance with her, making a regular carnival on a small scale. Everybody hugged and kissed everybody else, offered sucks of orange, bites of cake, and exchanges of candy; everyone tried on the new things, and pranced about in them like a flock of peacocks. Ranza skipped to and fro airily, dressed in her white socks and the red hood; the boys promenaded in their little shirts, one with his creaking new shoes and mittens, the other in his gay cap and fine tippet; and Tessa put her dress straight on, feeling that her father's "gold gown" was not all a joke. In her long stocking she found all sorts of treasures; for Tommo had stuffed it full of queer things, and his mother had made gingerbread into every imaginable shape, from fat pigs to full omnibuses.

Dear me! What happy little souls they were that morning; and when they were quiet again, how like a fairy tale did Tessa's story sound to them. Ranza was quite ready to be an angel; and the boys promised to be marvelously good, if they were only allowed to see the tree at the "palace," as they called the great house.

Little Ranza was accepted with delight by the kind lady and her children, and Tessa learned the song quite easily. The boys *were* asked; and, after a happy day, the young Italians all returned, to play their parts at the fine Christmas party. Mamma and Miss Rose drilled them all; and, when the folding doors flew open, one rapturous "Oh!" arose from the crowd of children gathered to the festival. I assure you, it was splendid; the great tree glittering with lights and gifts; and on her invisible perch up among the green boughs sat the little golden-haired angel, all in white, with downy wings, a shining crown on her head, and the most serene satisfaction in her blue eyes, as she stretched her chubby arms to those below, and smiled her baby smile at them. Before anyone could speak, a voice, as fresh and sweet as a lark's, sang the Christmas Carol so blithely that everyone stood still to hear, and then clapped till the little angel shook on her perch, and cried out, "Be 'till, or me'll fall!" How they laughed at that; and what fun they had talking to Ranza, while Miss Rose stripped the tree, for the angel could not resist temptation, and amused herself by eating all the bonbons she could reach, till she was taken down, to dance about like a fairy in a white frock and red shoes. Tessa and her friends had many presents; the boys were perfect lambs, Tommo played for the little folks to dance, and everyone said something friendly to the strangers, so that they did not feel shy, in spite of shabby clothes. It was a happy night; and all their lives they remembered it as something too beautiful and bright to be quite true. Before they went home, the kind mamma told Tessa she should be her friend, and gave her a motherly kiss, which warmed the child's heart and seemed to set a seal upon that promise. It was faithfully kept, for the rich lady had been touched by Tessa's patient struggles and sacrifices; and for many years, thanks to her benevolence, there was no end to Tessa's Surprises.

8

A Song for a Christmas Tree

Cold and wintry is the sky,
Bitter winds go whistling by,
Orchard boughs are bare and dry,
Yet here stands a fruitful tree;
Household fairies kind and dear,
With loving magic none need fear,
Bade it rise and blossom here,
Little friends, for you and me.

Come and gather as they fall,
Shining gifts for great and small;
Santa Claus remembers all
When he comes with goodies piled;
Corn and candy, apples red,
Sugar horses, gingerbread,
Babies who are never fed,
Are hanging here for every child.

Shake the boughs and down they come,
Better fruit than peach or plum,
'Tis our little harvest home;
For though frosts the flowers kill,

Though birds depart, and squirrels sleep;
Though snows may gather cold and deep,
Little folk their sunshine keep,
And mother-love makes summer still.

Gathered in a smiling ring,
Lightly dance and gayly sing,
Still at heart remembering
The sweet story all should know,
Of the little Child whose birth
Has made this day, throughout the earth,
A festival for childish mirth,
Since that first Christmas long ago.

9

A Christmas Turkey, and How It Came

"I KNOW WE couldn't do it."

"I say we could, if we all helped."

"How can we?"

"I've planned lots of ways; only you mustn't laugh at them, and you mustn't say a word to mother. I want it to be all a surprise."

"She'll find us out."

"No, she won't, if we tell her we won't get into mischief."

"Fire away, then, and let's hear your fine plans."

"We must talk softly, or we shall wake father. He's got a headache."

A curious change came over the faces of the two boys as their sister lowered her voice, with a nod toward a half-opened door. They looked sad and ashamed, and Kitty sighed as she spoke, for all knew that father's headaches always began by his coming home stupid or cross, with only a part of his wages; and mother always cried when she thought they did not see her, and after the long sleep father looked as if he didn't like to meet their eyes, but went off early.

They knew what it meant, but never spoke of it,—only

pondered over it, and mourned with mother at the change which was slowly altering their kind industrious father into a moody man, and mother into an anxious over-worked woman.

Kitty was thirteen, and a very capable girl, who helped with the housekeeping, took care of the two little ones, and went to school. Tommy and Sammy looked up to her and thought her a remarkably good sister. Now, as they sat round the stove having "a go-to-bed warm," the three heads were close together; and the boys listened eagerly to Kitty's plans, while the rattle of the sewing-machine in another room went on as tirelessly as it had done all day, for mother's work was more and more needed every month.

"Well!" began Kitty, in an impressive tone, "we all know that there won't be a bit of Christmas in this family if we don't make it. Mother's too busy, and father don't care, so we must see what *we* can do; for I should be mortified to death to go to school and say I hadn't had any turkey or plum-pudding. Don't expect presents; but we *must* have some kind of a decent dinner."

"So I say; I'm tired of fish and potatoes," said Sammy, the younger.

"But where's the dinner coming from?" asked Tommy, who had already taken some of the cares of life on his young shoulders, and knew that Christmas dinners did not walk into people's houses without money.

"We'll earn it;" and Kitty looked like a small Napoleon planning the passage of the Alps. "You, Tom, must go early to-morrow to Mr. Brisket and offer to carry baskets. He will be dreadfully busy, and want you, I know; and you are so strong you can lug as much as some of the big fellows. He pays well, and if he won't give much money, you can take your wages in things to eat. We want everything."

"What shall I do?" cried Sammy, while Tom sat turning this plan over in his mind.

"Take the old shovel and clear sidewalks. The snow came on purpose to help you."

"It's awful hard work, and the shovel's half gone," began Sammy, who preferred to spend his holiday coasting on an old tea-tray.

"Don't growl, or you won't get any dinner," said Tom, making up his mind to lug baskets for the good of the family, like a manly lad as he was.

"I," continued Kitty, "have taken the hardest part of all; for after my work is done, and the babies safely settled, I'm going to beg for the leavings of the holly and pine swept out of the church down below, and make some wreaths and sell them."

"If you can," put in Tommy, who had tried pencils, and failed to make a fortune.

"Not in the street?" cried Sam, looking alarmed.

"Yes, at the corner of the Park. I'm bound to make some money, and don't see any other way. I shall put on an old hood and shawl, and no one will know me. Don't care if they do." And Kitty tried to mean what she said, but in her heart she felt that it would be a trial to her pride if any of her schoolmates should happen to recognize her.

"Don't believe you'll do it."

"See if I don't; for I *will* have a good dinner one day in the year."

"Well, it doesn't seem right for us to do it. Father ought to take care of us, and we only buy some presents with the little bit we earn. He never gives us anything now." And Tommy scowled at the bedroom door, with a strong sense of injury struggling with affection in his boyish heart.

"Hush!" cried Kitty. "Don't blame him. Mother says we never must forget he's our father. I try not to; but when she cries, it's hard to feel as I ought." And a sob made the little girl stop short as she poked the fire to hide the trouble in the face that should have been all smiles.

For a moment the room was very still, as the snow beat on the window, and the fire-light flickered over the six shabby little boots put up on the stove hearth to dry.

Tommy's cheerful voice broke the silence, saying stoutly, "Well, if I've got to work all day, I guess I'll go to bed early. Don't fret, Kit. We'll help all we can, and have a good time; see if we don't."

"I'll go out real early, and shovel like fury. Maybe I'll get a dollar. Would that buy a turkey?" asked Sammy, with the air of a millionnaire.

"No, dear; one big enough for us would cost two, I'm afraid. Perhaps we'll have one sent us. We belong to the church, though folks don't know how poor we are now, and we can't beg." And Kitty bustled about, clearing up, rather exercised in her mind about going and asking for the much-desired fowl.

Soon all three were fast asleep, and nothing but the whir of the machine broke the quiet that fell upon the house. Then from the inner room a man came and sat over the fire with his head in his hands and his eyes fixed on the ragged little boots left to dry. He had heard the children's talk; and his heart was very heavy as he looked about the shabby room that used to be so neat and pleasant. What he thought no one knows, what he did we shall see by-and-by; but the sorrow and shame and tender silence of his children worked a miracle that night more lasting and lovely than the white beauty which the snow wrought upon the sleeping city.

Bright and early the boys were away to their work; while Kitty sang as she dressed the little sisters, put the house in order, and made her mother smile at the mysterious hints she gave of something splendid which was going to happen. Father was gone, and though all rather dreaded evening, nothing was said; but each worked with a will, feeling that Christmas should be merry in spite of poverty and care.

All day Tommy lugged fat turkeys, roasts of beef, and every sort of vegetable for other people's good dinners on the morrow, wondering meanwhile where his own was coming from. Mr. Brisket had an army of boys trudging here and there, and was too busy to notice any particular lad till the hurry was over, and only a few belated buyers remained to be served. It was late; but the stores kept open, and though so tired he could hardly stand, brave Tommy held on when the other boys left, hoping to earn a trifle more by extra work. He sat down on a barrel to rest during a leisure moment, and presently his weary head nodded sideways into a basket of cranberries, where he slept quietly till the sound of gruff voices roused him.

It was Mr. Brisket scolding because one dinner had been forgotten.

"I told that rascal Beals to be sure and carry it, for the old gentleman will be in a rage if it doesn't come, and take away his custom. Every boy gone, and I can't leave the store, nor you either, Pat, with all the clearing up to do."

"Here's a boy, sir; a sleeping beauty in the cranberries, bad luck to him!" answered Pat, with a shake that set poor Tom on his legs, wide awake at once.

"*Good* luck to him, you mean. Here, What's-your-name, you take this basket to that number, and I'll make it worth your while," said Mr. Brisket, much relieved by this unexpected help.

"All right, sir;" and Tommy trudged off as briskly as his tired legs would let him, cheering the long cold walk with visions of the turkey with which his employer might reward him, for there were piles of them, and Pat was to have one for his family.

His brilliant dreams were disappointed, however, for Mr. Brisket naturally supposed Tom's father would attend to that part of the dinner, and generously heaped a basket with vegetables, rosy apples, and a quart of cranberries.

"There, if you ain't too tired, you can take one more load to that number, and a merry Christmas to you!" said the stout man, handing over his gift with the promised dollar.

"Thank you, sir; good-night," answered Tom, shouldering his last load with a grateful smile, and trying not to look longingly at the poultry; for he had set his heart on at least a skinny bird as a surprise to Kit.

Sammy's adventures that day had been more varied and his efforts more successful, as we shall see, in the end, for Sammy was a most engaging little fellow, and no one could look into his blue eyes without wanting to pat his curly yellow head with one hand while the other gave him something. The cares of life had not lessened his confidence in people; and only the most abandoned ruffians had the heart to deceive or disappoint him. His very tribulations usually led to something pleasant, and whatever happened, sunshiny Sam came right side up, lucky and laughing.

Undaunted by the drifts or the cold wind, he marched off with the remains of the old shovel to seek his fortune, and found it at the third house where he called. The first two sidewalks were easy jobs; and he pocketed his ninepences with a growing conviction that this was his chosen work. The third sidewalk was a fine long one, for the house stood on the corner, and two pavements must be cleared.

"It ought to be fifty cents; but perhaps they won't give me

so much, I'm such a young one. I'll show 'em I can work, though, like a man;" and Sammy rang the bell with the energy of a telegraph boy.

Before the bell could be answered, a big boy rushed up, exclaiming roughly, "Get out of this! I'm going to have the job. You can't do it. Start, now, or I'll chuck you into a snow-bank."

"I won't! answered Sammy, indignant at the brutal tone and unjust claim. "I got here first, and it's my job. You let me alone. I ain't afraid of you or your snow-banks either."

The big boy wasted no time in words, for steps were heard inside, but after a brief scuffle hauled Sammy, fighting bravely all the way, down the steps, and tumbled him into a deep drift. Then he ran up the steps, and respectfully asked for the job when a neat maid opened the door. He would have got it if Sam had not roared out, as he floundered in the drift, "I came first. He knocked me down 'cause I'm the smallest. Please let me do it; please!"

Before another word could be said, a little old lady appeared in the hall, trying to look stern, and failing entirely, because she was the picture of a dear fat, cosy grandma.

"Send that *bad* big boy away, Maria, and call in the poor little fellow. I saw the whole thing, and *he* shall have the job if he can do it."

The bully slunk away, and Sammy came panting up the steps, white with snow, a great bruise on his forehead, and a beaming smile on his face, looking so like a jolly little Santa Claus who had taken a "header" out of his sleigh that the maid laughed, and the old lady exclaimed, "Bless the boy! he's dreadfully hurt, and doesn't know it. Come in and be brushed and get your breath, child, and tell me how that scamp came to treat you so."

Nothing loath to be comforted, Sammy told his little tale while Maria dusted him off on the mat, and the old lady hovered in the doorway of the dining-room, where a nice breakfast smoked and smelled so deliciously that the boy sniffed the odor of coffee and buckwheats like a hungry hound.

"He'll get his death if he goes to work before he's dried a bit. Put him over the register, Maria, and I'll give him a hot drink, for it's bitter cold, poor dear!"

Away trotted the kind old lady, and in a minute came back with coffee and cakes, on which Sammy feasted as he warmed his toes and told Kitty's plans for Christmas, led on by the old lady's questions, and quite unconscious that he was letting all sorts of cats out of the bag.

Mrs. Bryant understood the little story, and made her plans also, for the rosy-faced boy was very like a little grandson who died last year, and her sad old heart was very tender to all other small boys. So she found out where Sammy lived, and nodded and smiled at him most cheerily as he tugged stoutly away at the snow on the long pavements till all was done, and the little workman came for his wages.

A bright silver dollar and a pocketful of gingerbread sent him off a rich and happy boy to shovel and sweep till noon, when he proudly showed his earnings at home, and feasted the babies on the carefully hoarded cake, for Dilly and Dot were the idols of the household.

"Now, Sammy dear, I want you to take my place here this afternoon, for mother will have to take her work home by-and-by, and I must sell my wreaths. I only got enough green for six, and two bunches of holly; but if I can sell them for ten or twelve cents apiece, I shall be glad. Girls never *can* earn as much money as boys somehow," sighed Kitty, surveying the thin wreaths tied up with carpet ravellings, and vainly puzzling her young wits over a sad problem.

"I'll give you some of my money if you don't get a dollar; then we'll be even. Men always take care of women, you know, and ought to," cried Sammy, setting a fine example to his father, if he had only been there to profit by it.

With thanks Kitty left him to rest on the old sofa, while the happy babies swarmed over him; and putting on the shabby hood and shawl, she slipped away to stand at the Park gate, modestly offering her little wares to the passers-by. A nice old gentleman bought two, and his wife scolded him for getting such bad ones; but the money gave more happiness than any other he spent that day. A child took a ten-cent bunch of holly with its red berries, and there Kitty's market ended. It was very cold, people were in a hurry, bolder hucksters pressed before the timid little girl, and the balloon man told her to "clear out."

Hoping for better luck, she tried several other places; but the short afternoon was soon over, the streets began to thin, the keen wind chilled her to the bone, and her heart was very heavy to think that in all the rich, merry city, where Christmas gifts passed her in every hand, there were none for the dear babies and boys at home, and the Christmas dinner was a failure.

"I must go and get supper anyway; and I'll hang these up in our own rooms, as I can't sell them," said Kitty, wiping a very big tear from her cold cheek, and turning to go away.

A smaller, shabbier girl than herself stood near, looking at the bunch of holly with wistful eyes; and glad to do to others as she wished some one would do to her, Kitty offered the only thing she had to give, saying kindly, "You may have it; merry Christmas!" and ran away before the delighted child could thank her.

I am very sure that one of the spirits who fly about at this season of the year saw the little act, made a note of it, and in about fifteen minutes rewarded Kitty for her sweet remembrance of the golden rule.

As she went sadly homeward she looked up at some of the big houses where every window shone with the festivities of Christmas Eve, and more than one tear fell, for the little girl found life pretty hard just then.

"There don't seem to be any wreaths at these windows; perhaps they'd buy mine. I can't bear to go home with so little for my share," she said, stopping before one of the biggest and brightest of these fairy palaces, where the sound of music was heard, and many little heads peeped from behind the curtains as if watching for some one.

Kitty was just going up the steps to make another trial, when two small boys came racing round the corner, slipped on the icy pavement, and both went down with a crash that would have broken older bones. One was up in a minute, laughing; the other lay squirming and howling, "Oh, my knee! my knee!" till Kitty ran and picked him up with the motherly consolations she had learned to give.

"It's broken; I know it is," wailed the small sufferer as Kitty carried him up the steps, while his friend wildly rang the doorbell.

It was like going into fairy-land, for the house was all astir with a children's Christmas party. Servants flew about with smiling faces; open doors gave ravishing glimpses of a feast in one room and a splendid tree in another; while a crowd of little faces peered over the balusters in the hall above, eager to come down and enjoy the glories prepared for them.

A pretty young girl came to meet Kitty, and listened to her story of the accident, which proved to be less severe than it at first appeared; for Bertie, the injured party, forgot his anguish at sight of the tree, and hopped upstairs so nimbly that every one laughed.

"He said his leg was broken, but I guess he's all right," said Kitty, reluctantly turning from this happy scene to go out into the night again.

"Would you like to see our tree before the children come down?" asked the pretty girl, seeing the wistful look in the child's eyes, and the shine of half-dried tears on her cheek.

"Oh, yes; I never saw anything so lovely. I'd like to tell the babies all about it;" and Kitty's face beamed at the prospect, as if the kind words had melted all the frost away.

"How many babies are there?" asked the pretty girl, as she led the way into the brilliant room. Kitty told her, adding several other facts, for the friendly atmosphere seemed to make them friends at once.

"I will buy the wreaths, for we haven't any," said the girl in silk, as Kitty told how she was just coming to offer them when the boys fell.

It was pretty to see how carefully the little hostess laid away the shabby garlands and slipped a half-dollar into Kitty's hand; prettier still, to watch the sly way in which she tucked some bonbons, a red ball, a blue whip, two china dolls, two pairs of little mittens, and some gilded nuts into an empty box for "the babies;" and prettiest of all, to see the smiles and tears make April in Kitty's face as she tried to tell her thanks for this beautiful surprise.

The world was all right when she got into the street again and ran home with the precious box hugged close, feeling that at last she had something to make a merry Christmas of.

Shrieks of joy greeted her, for Sammy's nice old lady had sent a basket full of pies, nuts and raisins, oranges and cake, and—oh, happy Sammy!—a sled, all for love of the blue eyes that twinkled so merrily when he told her about the tea-tray. Piled upon his red car of triumph, Dilly and Dot were being dragged about, while the other treasures were set forth on the table.

"I must show mine," cried Kitty; "we'll look at them to-night, and have them to-morrow;" and amid more cries of rapture *her* box was unpacked, *her* money added to the pile in the middle of the table, where Sammy had laid his handsome contribution toward the turkey.

Before the story of the splendid tree was over, in came Tommy with his substantial offering and his hard-earned dollar.

"I'm afraid I ought to keep my money for shoes. I've walked the soles off these to-day, and can't go to school barefooted," he said, bravely trying to put the temptation of skates behind him.

"We've got a good dinner without a turkey, and perhaps we'd better not get it," added Kitty, with a sigh, as she surveyed the table, and remembered the blue knit hood marked seventy-five cents that she saw in a shop-window.

"Oh, we *must* have a turkey! We worked so hard for it, and it's so Christmasy," cried Sam, who always felt that pleasant things ought to happen.

"Must have turty," echoed the babies, as they eyed the dolls tenderly.

"You *shall* have a turkey, and there he is," said an unexpected voice, as a noble bird fell upon the table, and lay there kicking up his legs as if enjoying the surprise immensely.

It was father's voice, and there stood father, neither cross nor stupid, but looking as he used to look, kind and happy, and beside him was mother, smiling as they had not seen her smile for months. It was not because the work was well paid for, and more promised, but because she had received

a gift that made the world bright, a home happy again,—
father's promise to drink no more.

"I've been working to-day as well as you, and you may
keep your money for yourselves. There are shoes for all; and
never again, please God, shall my children be ashamed of
me, or want a dinner Christmas Day."

As father said this with a choke in his voice, and
mother's head went down on his shoulder to hide the happy
tears that wet her cheeks, the children didn't know whether
to laugh or cry, till Kitty, with the instinct of a loving heart,
settled the question by saying, as she held out her hands,
"We haven't any tree, so let's dance around our goodies and
be merry."

Then the tired feet in the old shoes forgot their weariness, and five happy little souls skipped gayly round the
table, where, in the midst of all the treasures earned and
given, father's Christmas turkey proudly lay in state.

10

What the Bells Saw and Said

"Bells ring others to church, but go not in themselves."

NO ONE SAW the spirits of the bells up there in the old steeple at midnight on Christmas Eve. Six quaint figures, each wrapped in a shadowy cloak and wearing a bell-shaped cap. All were gray-headed, for they were among the oldest bell-spirits of the city, and "the light of other days" shone in their thoughtful eyes. Silently they sat, looking down on the snow-covered roofs glittering in the moonlight, and the quiet streets deserted by all but the watchmen on their chilly rounds, and such poor souls as wandered shelterless in the winter night. Presently one of the spirits said, in a tone, which, low as it was, filled the belfry with reverberating echoes,—

"Well, brothers, are your reports ready of the year that now lies dying?"

All bowed their heads, and one of the oldest answered in a sonorous voice:—

"My report isn't all I could wish. You know I look down on the commercial part of our city and have fine opportunities for seeing what goes on there. It's my business to watch the business men, and upon my word I'm heartily ashamed of them sometimes. During the war they did nobly, giving their time and money, their sons and selves to the good cause, and I was proud of them. But now too many of them have fallen back into the old ways, and their motto seems to be, 'Every one for himself, and the devil take the hindmost.' Cheating, lying and stealing are hard words, and I don't mean to apply them to *all* who swarm about below there like ants on an ant-hill—*they* have other names for these things, but I'm old-fashioned and use plain words. There's a deal too much dishonesty in the world, and business seems to have become a game of hazard in which luck, not labor, wins the prize. When I was young, men were years making moderate fortunes, and were satisfied with them. They built them on sure foundations, knew how to enjoy them while they lived, and to leave a good name behind them when they died.

"Now it's anything for money; health, happiness, honor, life itself, are flung down on that great gaming-table, and they forget everything else in the excitement of success or the desperation of defeat. Nobody seems satisfied either, for those who win have little time or taste to enjoy their prosperity, and those who lose have little courage or patience to support them in adversity. They don't even fail as they used to. In my day when a merchant found himself embarrassed he didn't ruin others in order to save himself, but honestly confessed the truth, gave up everything, and began again. But now-a-days after all manner of dishonorable shifts there comes a grand crash; many suffer, but by some hocus-pocus the merchant saves enough to retire upon and live comfortably here or abroad. It's very evident that honor and honesty don't mean now what they used to mean in the days of old May, Higginson and Lawrence.

"They preach below here, and very well too sometimes,

for I often slide down the rope to peep and listen during service. But, bless you! they don't seem to lay either sermon, psalm or prayer to heart, for while the minister is doing his best, the congregation, tired with the breathless hurry of the week, sleep peacefully, calculate their chances for the morrow, or wonder which of their neighbors will lose or win in the great game. Don't tell me! I've seen them do it, and if I dared I'd have startled every soul of them with a rousing peal. Ah, they don't dream whose eye is on them, they never guess what secrets the telegraph wires tell as the messages fly by, and little know what a report I give to the winds of heaven as I ring out above them morning, noon, and night." And the old spirit shook his head till the tassel on his cap jangled like a little bell.

"There are some, however, whom I love and honor," he said, in a benignant tone, "who honestly earn their bread, who deserve all the success that comes to them, and always keep a warm corner in their noble hearts for those less blest than they. These are the men who serve the city in times of peace, save it in times of war, deserve the highest honors in its gift, and leave behind them a record that keeps their memories green. For such a one we lately tolled a knell, my brothers; and as our united voices pealed over the city, in all grateful hearts, sweeter and more solemn than any chime, rung the words that made him so beloved,—

"'Treat our dead boys tenderly, and send them home to me.'"

He ceased, and all the spirits reverently uncovered their gray heads as a strain of music floated up from the sleeping city and died among the stars.

"Like yours, my report is not satisfactory in all respects," began the second spirit, who wore a very pointed cap and a finely ornamented cloak. But, though his dress was fresh and youthful, his face was old, and he had nodded several times during his brother's speech. "My greatest affliction during the past year has been the terrible extravagance which prevails. My post, as you know, is at the court end of the city, and I see all the fashionable vices and follies. It is a marvel to me how so many of these immortal creatures, with such opportunities for usefulness, self-improvement and genuine happiness can be content to go round and round in one narrow circle of unprofitable and unsatisfactory pursuits. I do my best to warn them; Sunday after Sunday I chime in their ears the beautiful old hymns that sweetly chide or cheer the hearts that truly listen and believe; Sunday after Sunday I look down on them as they pass in, hoping to see that my words have not fallen upon deaf ears; and Sunday after Sunday they listen to words that should teach them much, yet seem to go by them like the wind. They are told to love their neighbor, yet too many hate him because he possesses more of this world's goods or honours than they; they are told that a rich man cannot enter the kingdom of heaven, yet they go on laying up perishable wealth, and though often warned that moth and rust will corrupt, they fail to believe it till the worm that destroys enters and mars their own chapel of ease. Being a spirit, I see below external splendor and find much poverty of heart and soul under the velvet and the ermine which should cover rich and royal natures. Our city saints walk abroad in threadbare suits, and under quiet bonnets shine the eyes that make sunshine in the shady places. Often as I watch the glittering procession passing to and fro below me, I wonder if with all our progress, there is to-day as much real piety as in the times when our fathers, poorly clad, with weapon in one hand and Bible in the other, came weary distances to worship in the wilderness with fervent faith unquenched by danger, suffering and solitude.

"Yet in spite of my fault-finding I love my children, as I call them, for all are not butterflies. Many find wealth no temptation to forgetfulness of duty or hardness of heart. Many give freely of their abundance, pity the poor, comfort the afflicted, and make our city loved and honored in other lands as in our own. They have their cares, losses, and heartaches as well as the poor; it isn't all sunshine with them, and they learn, poor souls, that

> *'Into each life some rain must fall,*
> *Some days must be dark and dreary.'*

"But I've hopes of them, and lately they have had a teacher so genial, so gifted, so well-beloved that all who listen to him must be better for the lessons of charity, goodwill and cheerfulness which he brings home to them by the magic of tears and smiles. We know him, we love him, we always remember him as the year comes round, and the blithest song our brazen tongues utter is a Christmas carol to the Father of 'The Chimes!'"

As the spirit spoke his voice grew cheery, his old face shone, and in a burst of hearty enthusiasm he flung up his cap and cheered like a boy. So did the others, and as the fairy shout echoed through the belfry a troop of shadowy figures, with faces lovely or grotesque, tragical or gay, sailed by on the wings of the wintry wind and waved their hands to the spirits of the bells.

As the excitement subsided and the spirits reseated themselves, looking ten years younger for that burst, another spoke. A venerable brother in a dingy mantel, with a tuneful voice, and eyes that seemed to have grown sad with looking on much misery.

"He loves the poor, the man we've just hurrahed for, and he makes others love and remember them, bless him!" said the spirit. "I hope he'll touch the hearts of those who listen to him here and beguile them to open their hands to my unhappy children over yonder. If I could set some of the forlorn souls in my parish beside the happier creatures who weep over imaginary woes as they are painted by his eloquent lips, that brilliant scene would be better than any sermon. Day and night I look down on lives as full of sin, self-sacrifice and suffering as any in those famous books. Day and night I try to comfort the poor by my cheery voice, and to make their wants known by proclaiming them with all my might. But people seem to be so intent on business, pleasure or home duties that they have no time to hear and answer my appeal. There's a deal of charity in this good city, and when the people do wake up they work with a will; but I can't help thinking that if some of the money lavished on luxuries was spent on necessaries for the poor, there would be fewer tragedies like that which ended yesterday. It's a short story, easy to tell, though long and hard to live; listen to it.

"Down yonder in the garret of one of the squalid houses at the foot of my tower, a little girl has lived for a year, fighting silently and single-handed a good fight against poverty and sin. I saw her when she first came, a hopeful, cheerful, brave-hearted little soul, alone, yet not afraid. She used to sit all day sewing at her window, and her lamp burnt far into the night, for she was very poor, and all she earned would barely give her food and shelter. I watched her feed the doves, who seemed to be her only friends; she never forgot them, and daily gave them the few crumbs that fell from her meagre table. But there was no kind hand to feed and foster the little human dove, and so she starved.

"For a while she worked bravely, but the poor three dollars a week would not clothe and feed and warm her, though the things her busy fingers made sold for enough to keep her comfortably if she had received it. I saw the pretty color fade from her cheeks; her eyes grew hollow, her voice lost its cheery ring, her step its elasticity, and her face began to wear the haggard, anxious look that made its youth doubly pathetic. Her poor little gowns grew shabby, her shawl so thin she shivered when the pitiless wind smote her, and her feet were almost bare. Rain and snow beat on the patient little figure going to and fro, each morning with hope and courage faintly shining, each evening with the shadow of despair gathering darker round her. It was a hard time for all, desperately hard for her, and in her poverty, sin and pleasure tempted her. She resisted, but as another bitter winter came she feared that in her misery she might yield, for body and soul were weakened now by the long struggle. She knew not where to turn for help; there seemed to be no place for her at any safe and happy fireside; life's hard aspect daunted her, and she turned to death, saying confidingly, 'Take me while I'm innocent and not afraid to go.'

"I saw it all! I saw how she sold everything that would bring money and paid her little debts to the utmost penny; how she set her poor room in order for the last time; how she tenderly bade the doves goodby, and lay down on her bed to die. At nine o'clock last night as my bell rang over the city, I tried to tell what was going on in the garret where the light was dying out so fast. I cried to them with all my strength,—

"'Kind souls, below there! a fellow-creature is perishing for lack of charity! Oh, help her before it is too late! Mothers, with little daughters on your knees, stretch out your hands and take her in! Happy women, in the safe shelter of home, think of her desolation! Rich men, who grind the faces of the poor, remember that this soul will one day be required of you! Dear Lord, let not this little sparrow fall to the ground! Help, Christian men and women, in the name of Him whose birthday blessed the world!'

"Ah me! I rang, and clashed, and cried in vain. The passers-by only said, as they hurried home, laden with Christmas cheer: 'The old bell is merry to-night, as it should be at this blithe season, bless it!'

"As the clocks struck ten, the poor child lay down, saying, as she drank the last bitter draught life could give her, 'It's very cold, but soon I shall not feel it;' and with her quiet eyes fixed on the cross that glimmered in the moonlight above me, she lay waiting for the sleep that needs no lullaby.

"As the clock struck eleven, pain and poverty for her were over. It was bitter cold, but she no longer felt it. She lay serenely sleeping, with tired heart and hands, at rest forever. As the clocks struck twelve, the dear Lord remembered her, and with fatherly hand led her into the home where there is room for all. To-day I rung her knell, and though my heart was heavy, yet my soul was glad; for in spite of all her human woe and weakness, I am sure that little girl will keep a joyful Christmas up in heaven."

In the silence which the spirits for a moment kept, a breath of softer air than any from the snowy world below swept through the steeple and seemed to whisper, "Yes!"

"Avast there! fond as I am of salt water, I don't like this kind," cried the breezy voice of the fourth spirit, who had a tiny ship instead of a tassel on his cap, and who wiped his wet eyes with the sleeve of his rough blue cloak. "It won't take me long to spin my yarn; for things are pretty taut and ship-shape aboard our craft. Captain Taylor is an experienced sailor, and has brought many a ship safely into port in spite of wind and tide, and the devil's own whirlpools and hurricanes. If you want to see earnestness, come aboard some Sunday when the Captain's on the quarter-deck, and take an observation. No danger of falling asleep there, no more than there is up aloft, 'when the stormy winds do blow.' Consciences get raked fore and aft, sins are blown clean out of the water, false colors are hauled down and true ones run up to the masthead, and many an immortal soul is warned to steer off in time from the pirates, rocks and quicksands of temptation. He's a regular revolving light, is the Captain,—a beacon always burning and saying plainly, 'Here are life-boats, ready to put off in all weathers and bring the shipwrecked into quiet waters.' He comes but seldom now, being laid up in the home dock, tranquilly waiting till his turn comes to go out with the tide and safely ride at anchor in the great harbor of the Lord. Our crew varies a good deal. Some of 'em have rather rough voyages, and come into port pretty well battered; land-sharks fall foul of a good many, and do a deal of damage; but most of 'em carry brave and tender hearts under the blue jackets, for their rough nurse, the sea, manages to keep something of the child alive in the grayest old tar that makes the world his picture-book. We try to supply 'em with life-preservers while at sea, and make 'em feel sure of a hearty welcome when ashore, and I believe the year '67 will sail away into eternity with a satisfactory cargo. Brother North-End made me pipe my eye; so I'll make him laugh to pay for it, by telling a clerical joke I heard the other day. Bell-ows didn't make it, though he might have done so, as he's a connection of ours, and knows how to use his tongue as well as any of us. Speaking of the bells of a certain town, a reverend gentleman affirmed that each bell uttered an appropriate remark so plainly, that the words were audible to all. The Baptist bell cried, briskly, 'Come up and be dipped! come up and be dipped!' The Episcopal bell slowly said, 'Apostolic suc-cess-ion! apos-tol-ic suc-cess-ion!' The Orthodox bell solemnly pronounced, 'Eternal damnation! eternal damnation!' and the Methodist shouted, invitingly, 'Room for all! room for all!'"

As the spirit imitated the various calls, as only a jovial bell-sprite could, the others gave him a chime of laughter, and vowed they would each adopt some tuneful summons, which should reach human ears and draw human feet more willingly to church.

"Faith, brother, you've kept your word and got the laugh out of us," cried a stout, sleek spirit, with a kindly face, and a row of little saints round his cap and a rosary at his side. "It's very well we are doing this year; the cathedral is full, the flock increasing, and the true faith holding its own entirely. Ye may shake your heads if you will and fear there'll be trouble, but I doubt it. We've warm hearts of our own, and the best of us don't forget that when we were starving, America—the saints bless the jewel!—sent us bread; when we were dying for lack of work, America opened her arms and took us in, and now helps us to build churches, homes and schools by giving us a share of the riches all men work for and win. It's a generous nation ye are, and a brave one, and we showed our gratitude by fighting for ye in the day of trouble and giving ye our Phil, and many another broth of a boy. The land is wide enough for us both, and while we work and fight and grow together, each may learn something from the other. I'm free to confess that your religion looks a bit cold and hard to me, even here in the good city where each man may ride his own hobby to death, and hoot at his neighbors as much as he will. You seem to keep your piety shut up all the week in your bare, white churches, and only let it out on Sundays, just a trifle musty with disuse. You set your rich, warm and soft to the fore, and leave the poor shivering at the door. You give your people bare walls to look upon, common-place music to listen to, dull sermons to put them asleep, and then wonder why they stay away, or take no interest when they come.

"We leave our doors open day and night; our lamps are always burning, and we may come into our Father's house at any hour. We let rich and poor kneel together, all being equal there. With us abroad you'll see prince and peasant side by side, school-boy and bishop, market-woman and noble lady, saint and sinner, praying to the Holy Mary, whose motherly arms are open to high and low. We make our churches inviting with immortal music, pictures by the world's great masters, and rites that are splendid symbols of the faith we hold. Call it mummery if ye like, but let me ask you why so many of your sheep stray into our fold? It's because they miss the warmth, the hearty, the maternal tenderness which all souls love and long for, and fail to find in your stern, Puritanical belief. By Saint Peter! I've seen many a lukewarm worshipper, who for years has nodded in your cushioned pews, wake and glow with something akin to genuine piety while kneeling on the stone pavement of one of our cathedrals, with Raphael's angels before his eyes, with strains of magnificent music in his ears, and all about him, in shapes of power or beauty, the saints and martyrs who have saved the world, and whose presence inspires him to follow their divine example. It's not complaining of ye I am, but just reminding ye that men are but children after all, and need more tempting to virtue than they do to vice, which last comes easy to 'em since the Fall. Do your best in your own ways to get the poor souls into bliss, and good luck to ye. But remember, there's room in the Holy Mother Church for all, and when your own priests send ye to the divil, come straight to us and we'll take ye in."

"A truly Catholic welcome, bull and all," said the sixth spirit, who, in spite of his old-fashioned garments, had a youthful face, earnest, fearless eyes, and an energetic voice that woke the echoes with its vigorous tones. "I've a hopeful report, brothers, for the reforms of the day are wheeling into rank and marching on. The war isn't over nor rebellion conquered yet, but the Old Guard has been 'up and at 'em' through the year. There has been some hard fighting, rivers of ink have flowed, and the Washington dawdlers have signalized themselves by a 'masterly inactivity.' The political campaign has been an anxious one; some of the leaders have deserted; some been mustered out; some have fallen gallantly, and as yet have received no monuments. But at the Grand Review the Cross of the Legion of Honor will surely shine on many a brave breast that won no decoration but its virtue here; for the world's fanatics make heaven's heroes, poets say.

"The flock of Nightingales that flew South during the 'winter of our discontent' are all at home again, some here and some in Heaven. But the music of their womanly heroism still lingers in the nation's memory, and makes a tender minor-chord in the battle-hymn of freedom.

"The reform in literature isn't as vigorous as I could wish; but a sharp attack of mental and moral dyspepsia will soon teach our people that French confectionery and the bad pastry of Wood, Braddon, Yates & Co. is not the best diet for the rising generation.

"Speaking of the rising generation reminds me of the schools. They are doing well; they always are, and we are justly proud of them. There may be a slight tendency toward placing too much value upon book-learning; too little upon home culture. Our girls are acknowledged to be uncommonly pretty, witty and wise, but some of us wish they had more health and less excitement, more domestic accomplishments and fewer ologies and isms, and were contented with simple pleasures and the old-fashioned virtues, and not quite so fond of the fast, frivolous life that makes them old so soon. I am fond of our girls and boys. I love to ring for their christenings and marriages, to toll proudly for the brave lads in blue, and tenderly for the innocent creatures whose seats are empty under my old roof. I want to see them anxious to make Young America a model of virtue, strength and beauty, and I believe they will in time.

"There have been some important revivals in religion; for the world won't stand still, and we must keep pace or be left behind to fossilize. A free nation must have a religion broad enough to embrace all mankind, deep enough to fathom and fill the human soul, high enough to reach the source of all love and wisdom, and pure enough to satisfy the wisest and the best. Alarm bells have been rung, anathemas pronounced, and Christians, forgetful of their creed, have abused one another heartily. But the truth always triumphs in the end, and whoever sincerely believes, works and waits for it, by whatever name he calls it, will surely find his own faith blessed to him in proportion to his charity for the faith of others.

"But look!—the first red streaks of dawn are in the East. Our vigil is over, and we must fly home to welcome in the holidays. Before we part, join with me, brothers, in resolving that through the coming year we will with all our hearts and tongues,—

'Ring out the old, ring in the new,
Ring out the false, ring in the true;
Ring in the valiant man and free,
Ring in the Christ that is to be.'"

Then hand in hand the spirits of the bells floated away, singing in the hush of dawn the sweet song the stars sung over Bethlehem,—"Peace on earth, good will to men."

11

A Hospital Christmas

"MERRY CHRISTMAS!" "Merry Christmas!" "Merry Christmas, and lots of 'em, ma'am!" echoed from every side, as Miss Hale entered her ward in the gray December dawn. No wonder the greetings were hearty, that thin faces brightened, and eyes watched for the coming of this small luminary more eagerly than for the rising of the sun for when they woke that morning, each man found that in the silence of the night some friendly hand had laid a little gift beside his bed. Very humble little gifts they were, but well chosen and thoughtfully bestowed by one who made the blithe anniversary pleasant even in a hospital, and sweetly taught the lesson of the hour—Peace on earth, good will to man.

"I say, ma'am, these are just splendid. I've dreamt about such for a week, but I never thought I'd get 'em," cried one poor fellow, surveying a fine bunch of grapes with as much satisfaction as if he had found a fortune.

"Thank you kindly, Miss, for the paper and the fixings. I hated to keep borrowing, but I hadn't any money," said another, eying his gift with happy anticipations of the home letters with which the generous pages should be filled.

"They are dreadful soft and pretty, but I don't believe I'll ever wear 'em out; my legs are so wimbly there's no go in 'em," whispered a fever patient, looking sorrowfully at the swollen feet ornamented with a pair of carpet slippers gay with roses, and evidently made for his especial need.

"Please hang my posy basket on the gas-burner in the middle of the room, where all the boys can see it. It's too pretty for one alone."

"But then you can't see it yourself, Joe, and you are fonder of such things than the rest," said Miss Hale, taking both the little basket and the hand of her pet patient, a lad of twenty, dying of rapid consumption.

"That's the reason I can spare it for a while, for I shall feel 'em in the room just the same, and they'll do the boys good. You pick out the one you like best, for me to keep, and hang up the rest till by-and-by, please."

She gave him a sprig of mignonette, and he smiled as he took it, for it reminded him of her in her sad-colored gown, as quiet and unobtrusive, but as grateful to the hearts of those about her as was the fresh scent of the flower to the lonely lad who never had known womanly tenderness and care until he found them in a hospital. Joe's prediction was verified; the flowers did do the boys good, for all welcomed them with approving glances, and all felt their refining influence more or less keenly, from cheery Ben, who paused to fill the cup inside with fresher water, to surly Sam, who stopped growling as his eye rested on a geranium very like the one blooming in his sweetheart's window when they parted a long year ago.

"Now, as this is to be a merry day, let us begin to enjoy it at once. Fling up the windows, Ben, and Barney, go for breakfast while I finish washing faces and settling bed-clothes."

With which directions the little woman fell to work with

such infectious energy that in fifteen minutes thirty gentle-men with spandy clean faces and hands were partaking of refreshment with as much appetite as their various condi-tions would permit. Meantime the sun came up, looking bigger, brighter, jollier than usual, as he is apt to do on Christmas days. Not a snow-flake chilled the air that blew in as blandly as if winter had relented, and wished the "boys" the compliments of the season in his mildest mood; while a festival smell pervaded the whole house, and appe-tizing rumors of turkey, mince-pie, and oysters for dinner, circulated through the wards. When breakfast was done, the wounds dressed, directions for the day delivered, and as many of the disagreeables as possible well over, the fun began. In any other place that would have been considered a very quiet morning; but to the weary invalids prisoned in that room, it was quite a whirl of excitement. None were dangerously ill but Joe, and all were easily amused, for weakness, homesickness and *ennui* made every trifle a joke or an event.

In came Ben, looking like a "Jack in the Green," with his load of hemlock and holly. Such of the men as could get about and had a hand to lend, lent it, and soon, under Miss Hale's direction, a green bough hung at the head of each bed, depended from the gas-burners, and nodded over the fireplace, while the finishing effect was given by a cross and crown at the top and bottom of the room. Great was the interest, many were the mishaps, and frequent was the laughter which attended this performance; for wounded men, when convalescent, are particularly jovial. When "Daddy Mills," as one venerable volunteer was irreverently christened, expatiated learnedly upon the difference between "sprewee, hemlock and pine," how they all lis-tened, each thinking of some familiar wood still pleasantly haunted by boyish recollections of stolen gunnings, gum-pickings, and bird-nestings. When quiet Hayward amazed the company by coming out strong in a most unexpected direction, and telling with much effect the story of a certain "fine old gentleman" who supped on hemlock tea and died like a hero, what commendations were bestowed upon the immortal heathen in language more hearty than classical, as a twig of the historical tree was passed round like a new style of refreshment, that inquiring parties might satisfy themselves regarding the flavor of the Socratie draught. When Barney essayed a grand ornament above the door, and relying upon one insufficient nail, descended to survey his success with the proud exclamation, "Look at de neatness of dat job, gen'l'men,"—at which point the whole thing tumbled down about his ears,—how they all shouted but Pneumonia Ned, who, having lost his voice, could only make ecstatic demonstrations with his legs. When Barney cast himself and his hammer despairingly upon the floor, and Miss Hale, stepping into a chair, pounded stoutly at the traitorous nail and performed some miracle with a bit of string which made all fast, what a burst of applause arose from the beds. When gruff Dr. Bangs came in to see what all the noise was about, and the same intrepid lady not only boldly explained, but stuck a bit of holly in his button-hole, and wished him a merry Christmas with such a face full of smiles that the crabbed old doctor felt himself giving in very fast, and bolted out again, calling Christmas a humbug, and exulting over the thirty emetics he would have to prescribe on the morrow, what indignant denials followed him. And when all was done, how everybody agreed with Joe when he said, "I think we are coming Christmas in great style; things look so green and pretty, I feel as I was settin' in a bower."

Pausing to survey her work, Miss Hale saw Sam looking as black as any thunder-cloud. He bounced over on his bed the moment he caught her eye, but she followed him up, and gently covering the cold shoulder he evidently meant to show her, peeped over it, asking, with unabated gentleness,—

"What can I do for you, Sam? I want to have all the faces in my ward bright ones to-day."

"My box ain't come; they said I should have it two, three days ago; why don't they do it, then?" growled Ursur Major.

"It is a busy time, you know, but it will come if they promised, and patience won't delay it, I assure you."

"My patience is used up, and they are a mean set of slow coaches. I'd get it fast enough if I wore shoulder straps; as I don't, I'll bet I sha'n't see it till the things ain't fit to eat; the news is old, and I don't care a hang about it."

"I'll see what I can do; perhaps before the hurry of dinner begins some one will have time to go for it."

"Nobody ever does have time here but folks who would give all they are worth to be stirring round. You can't get it, I know; it's my luck, so don't you worry, ma'am."

Miss Hale did not "worry," but worked, and in time a messenger was found, provided with the necessary money, pass and directions, and despatched to hunt up the missing Christmas-box. Then she paused to see what came next, not that it was necessary to look for a task, but to decide which, out of many, was most important to do first.

"Why, Turner, crying again so soon? What is it now? the light head or the heavy feet?"

"It's my bones, ma'am. They ache so I can't lay easy any way, and I'm so tired I just wish I could die and be out of this misery," sobbed the poor ghost of a once strong and cheery fellow, as the kind hand wiped his tears away, and gently rubbed the weary shoulders.

"Don't wish that, Turner, for the worst is over now, and all you need is to get your strength again. Make an effort to sit up a little; it is quite time you tried; a change of posture will help the ache wonderfully, and make this 'dreadful bed,' as you call it, seem very comfortable when you come back to it."

"I can't, ma'am, my legs ain't a bit of use, and I ain't strong enough even to try."

"You never will be if you don't try. Never mind the poor legs, Ben will carry you. I've got the matron's easy-chair all ready, and can make you very cosy by the fire. It's Christmas-day, you know; why not celebrate it by overcoming the despondency which retards your recovery, and prove that illness has not taken all the man-hood out of you?"

"It has, though, I'll never be the man I was, and may as well lay here till spring, for I shall be no use if I do get up."

If Sam was a growler this man was a whiner, and few hospital wards are without both. But knowing that much suffering had soured the former and pitifully weakened the latter, their nurse had patience with them, and still hoped to bring them round again. As Turner whimpered out his last dismal speech she bethought herself of something which, in the hurry of the morning, had slipped her mind till now.

"By the way, I've got another present for you. The doctor thought I'd better not give it yet, lest it should excite you too much; but I think you need excitement to make you forget yourself, and that when you find how many blessings you have to be grateful for, you will make an effort to enjoy them."

"Blessings, ma'am? I don't see 'em."

"Don't you see one now?" and drawing a letter from her pocket she held it before his eyes. His listless face brightened a little as he took it, but gloomed over again as he said fret-fully,—

"It's from wife, I guess. I like to get her letters, but they are always full of grievings and groanings over me, so they don't do me much good."

"She does not grieve and groan in this one. She is too happy to do that, and so will you be when you read it."

"I don't see why,—hey?—why you don't mean—"

"Yes I do!" cried the little woman, clapping her hands, and laughing so delightedly that the Knight of the Rueful Countenance was betrayed into a broad smile for the first time in many weeks. "Is not a splendid little daughter a present to rejoice over and be grateful for?"

"Hooray! hold on a bit,—it's all right,—I'll be out again in a minute."

After which remarkably spirited burst, Turner vanished under the bed-clothes, letter and all. Whether he read, laughed or cried, in the seclusion of that cotton grotto, was unknown; but his nurse suspected that he did all three, for when he reappeared he looked as if during that pause he had dived into his "sea of troubles," and fished up his old self again.

"What *will* I name her?" was his first remark, delivered with such vivacity that his neighbors began to think he was getting delirious again.

"What is your wife's name?" asked Miss Hale, gladly entering into the domesticities which were producing such a salutary effect.

"Her name's Ann, but neither of us like it. I'd fixed on George, for I wanted my boy called after me; and now you see I ain't a bit prepared for this young woman." Very proud of the young woman he seemed, nevertheless, and perfectly resigned to the loss of the expected son and heir.

"Why not call her Georgiana then? That combines both her parents' names, and is not a bad one in itself."

"Now that's just the brightest thing I ever heard in my life!" cried Turner, sitting bolt upright in his excitement, though half an hour before he would have considered it an utterly impossible feat. "Georgiana Butterfield Turner,—it's a tip-top name, ma'am, and we can call her Georgie just the same. Ann will like that, it's so genteel. Bless 'em both! don't I wish I was at home." And down he lay again, despairing.

"You can be before long, if you choose. Get your strength up, and off you go. Come, begin at once,—drink your beef-tea, and sit up for a few minutes, just in honor of the good news, you know."

"I will, by George!—no, by Georgiana! That's a good one, ain't it?" and the whole ward was electrified by hearing a genuine giggle from the "Blueing-bag."

Down went the detested beef-tea, and up scrambled the determined drinker with many groans, and a curious jumble of chuckles, staggers, and fragmentary repetitions of his first, last, and only joke. But when fairly settled in the great rocking chair, with the gray flannel gown comfortably on, and the new slippers getting their inaugural scorch, Turner forgot his bones, and swung to and fro before the fire, feeling amazingly well, and looking very like a trussed fowl being roasted in the primitive fashion. The languid importance of the man, and the irrepressible satisfaction of the parent, were both laughable and touching things to see, for the happy soul could not keep the glad tidings to himself. A hospital ward is often a small republic, beautifully governed by pity, patience, and the mutual sympathy which lessens mutual suffering. Turner was no favorite; but more than one honest fellow felt his heart warm towards him as they saw his dismal face kindle with fatherly pride, and heard the querulous quaver of his voice soften with fatherly affection, as he said, "My little Georgie, sir."

"He'll do now, ma'am; this has given him the boost he needed, and in a week or two he'll be off our hands."

Big Ben made the remark with a beaming countenance, and Big Ben deserves a word of praise, because he never said one for himself. An ex-patient, promoted to an attendant's place, which he filled so well that he was regarded as a model for all the rest to copy. Patient, strong, and tender, he seemed to combine many of the best traits of both man and woman; for he appeared to know by instinct where the soft spot was to be found in every heart, and how best to help sick body or sad soul. No one would have guessed this to have seen him lounging in the hall during one of the short rests he allowed himself. A brawny, six-foot follow, in red shirt, blue trousers tucked into his boots, an old cap, visor always up, and under it a roughly-bearded, coarsely-featured face, whose prevailing expression was one of great gravity and kindliness, though a humorous twinkle of the eye at times betrayed the man, whose droll sayings often set the boys in a roar. "A good-natured, clumsy body" would have been the verdict passed upon him by a casual observer; but watch him in his ward, and see how great a wrong that hasty judgment would have done him.

Unlike his predecessor, who helped himself generously when the meals came up, and carelessly served out rations for the rest, leaving even the most helpless to bungle for themselves or wait till he was done, shut himself into his pantry, and there,—to borrow a hospital phrase,—gormed, Ben often left nothing for himself, or took cheerfully such cold bits as remained when all the rest were served; so patiently feeding the weak, being hands and feet to the maimed, and a pleasant provider for all that, as one of the boys said,—"It gives a relish to the vittles to have Ben fetch 'em." If one were restless, Ben carried him in his strong arms; if one were undergoing the sharp torture of the surgeon's knife, Ben held him with a touch as firm as kind; if one were homesick, Ben wrote letters for him with great hearty blots and dashes under all the affectionate or important words. More than one poor fellow read his fate in Ben's pitiful eyes, and breathed his last breath away on Ben's broad breast,—always a quiet pillow till its work was done, then it would heave with genuine grief, as his big hand softly closed the tired eyes, and made another comrade ready for the last review. The war shows us many Bens,— for the same power of human pity which makes women brave also makes men tender; and each is the womanlier, the manlier, for these revelations of unsuspected strength and sympathies.

At twelve o'clock dinner was the prevailing idea in ward No. 3, and when the door opened every man sniffed, for savory odors broke loose from the kitchens and went roaming about the house. Now this Christmas dinner had been much talked of; for certain charitable and patriotic persons had endeavored to provide every hospital in Washington with materials for this time-honored feast. Some mistake in the list sent to head-quarters, some unpardonable neglect of orders, or some premeditated robbery, caused the long-expected dinner in this hospital to prove a dead failure; but to which of these causes it was attributable was never known, for the deepest mystery enveloped that sad transaction. The full weight of the dire disappointment was mercifully lightened by premonitions of the impending blow. Barney was often missing; for the attendants were to dine *en masse* after the patients were done, therefore a speedy banquet for the latter parties was ardently desired, and he probably devoted his energies to goading on the cooks. From time to time he appeared in the doorway, flushed and breathless, made some thrilling announcement, and vanished, leaving ever-increasing appetite, impatience and expectation, behind him.

Dinner was to be served at one; at half-past twelve Barney proclaimed, "Dere ain't no vegetables but squash and pitaters." A universal groan arose; and several indignant parties on a short allowance of meat consigned the defaulting cook to a warmer climate than the tropical one he was then enjoying. At twenty minutes to one, Barney increased the excitement by whispering, ominously, "I say, de puddins isn't plummy ones."

"Fling a piller at him and shut the door, Ben," roared one irascible being, while several others *not* fond of puddings received the fact with equanimity. At quarter to one Barney piled up the agony by adding the bitter information, "Dere isn't but two turkeys for dis ward, and dey's little fellers."

Anxiety instantly appeared in every countenance, and intricate calculations were made as to how far the two fowls would go when divided among thirty men; also friendly warnings were administered to several of the feebler gentlemen not to indulge too freely, if at all, for fear of relapses. Once more did the bird of evil omen return, for at ten minutes to one Barney croaked through the key-hole, "Only jes half ob de pies has come, gen'l'-men." That capped the climax, for the masculine palate has a predilection for pastry, and mince-pie was the sheet-anchor to which all had clung when other hopes went down. Even Ben looked dismayed; not that he expected anything but the perfume and pickings for his share, but he had set his heart on having the dinner an honor to the institution and a memorable feast for the men, so far away from home, and all that usually makes the day a festival among the poorest. He looked pathetically grave as Turner began to fret, Sam began to swear under his breath, Hayward to sigh, Joe to wish it was all over, and the rest began to vent their emotions with a freedom which was anything but inspiring. At that moment Miss Hale came in with a great basket of apples and oranges in one hand, and several convivial-looking bottles in the other.

"Here is our dessert, boys! A kind friend remembered us, and we will drink her health in her own currant wine."

A feeble smile circulated round the room, and in some sanguine bosoms hope revived again. Ben briskly emptied the basket, while Miss Hale whispered to Joe,—

"I know you would be glad to get away from the confusion of this next hour, to enjoy a breath of fresh air, and dine quietly with Mrs. Burton round the corner, wouldn't you?"

"Oh, ma'am, so much! the noise, the smells, the fret and flurry, make me sick just to think of! But how can I go? that dreadful ambulance 'most killed me last time, and I'm weaker now."

"My dear boy, I have no thought of trying that again till our ambulances are made fit for the use of weak and wounded men. Mrs. Burton's carriage is at the door, with her motherly self inside, and all you have got to do is to let me bundle you up, and Ben carry you out."

With a long sigh of relief Joe submitted to both these processes, and when his nurse watched his happy face as the carriage slowly rolled away, she felt well repaid for the little sacrifice of rest and pleasure so quietly made; for Mrs. Burton came to carry her, not Joe, away.

"Now, Ben, help me to make this unfortunate dinner go off as well as we can," she whispered. "On many accounts it is a mercy that the men are spared the temptations of a more generous meal; pray don't tell them so, but make the best of it, as you know very well how to do."

"I'll try my best, Miss Hale, but I'm no less disappointed, for some of 'em, being no better than children, have been living on the thoughts of it for a week, and it comes hard to give it up."

If Ben had been an old-time patriarch, and the thirty boys his sons, he could not have spoken with a more paternal regret, or gone to work with a better will. Putting several small tables together in the middle of the room, he left Miss Hale to make a judicious display of plates, knives and forks, while he departed for the banquet. Presently he returned, bearing the youthful turkeys and the vegetables in his tray, followed by Barney, looking unutterable things at a plum-pudding baked in a milk-pan, and six very small pies. Miss Hale played a lively tattoo as the procession approached, and, when the viands were arranged, with the red and yellow fruit prettily heaped up in the middle, it really did look like a dinner.

"Here's richness! here's the delicacies of the season and the comforts of life!" said Ben, falling back to survey the table with as much apparent satisfaction as if it had been a lord mayor's feast.

"Come, hurry up, and give us our dinner, what there is of it!" grumbled Sam.

"Boys," continued Ben, beginning to cut up the turkeys, "these noble birds have been sacrificed for the defenders of their country; they will go as far as ever they can, and, when they can't go any farther, we shall endeavor to supply their deficiencies with soup or ham, oysters having given out unexpectedly. Put it to vote; both have been provided on this joyful occasion, and a word will fetch either."

"Ham! ham!" resounded from all sides. Soup was an every-day affair, and therefore repudiated with scorn; but ham, being a rarity, was accepted as a proper reward of merit and a tacit acknowledgment of their wrongs.

The "noble birds" did go as far as possible, and were handsomely assisted by their fellow martyr. The pudding was not as plummy as could have been desired, but a slight exertion of fancy made the crusty knobs do duty for raisins. The pies were small, yet a laugh added flavor to the mouthful apiece, for, when Miss Hale asked Ben to cut them up, that individual regarded her with an inquiring aspect as he said, in his drollest tone,—

"I wouldn't wish to appear stupid, ma'am, but, when you mention 'pies,' I presume you allude to these trifles. 'Tarts,' or 'patties,' would meet my views better, in speaking of the third course of this lavish dinner. As such I will do my duty by 'em, hoping that the appetites is to match."

Carefully dividing the six pies into twenty-nine diminutive wedges, he placed each in the middle of a large clean plate, and handed them about with the gravity of an undertaker. Dinner had restored good humor to many; this hit at the pies put the finishing touch to it, and from that moment an atmosphere of jollity prevailed. Healths were drunk in currant wine, apples and oranges flew about as an impromptu game of ball was got up, Miss Hale sang a Christmas carol, and Ben gambolled like a sportive giant as he cleared away. Pausing in one of his prances to and fro, he beckoned the nurse out, and, when she followed, handed her a plate heaped up with good things from a better table than she ever sat at now.

"From the matron, ma'am. Come right in here and eat it while it's hot; they are most through in the dining-room, and you'll get nothing half so nice," said Ben, leading the way into his pantry and pointing to a sunny window-seat.

"Are you sure she meant it for me, and not for yourself, Ben?"

"Of course she did! Why, what should I do with it, when I've just been feastin' sumptuous in this very room?"

"I don't exactly see what you have been feasting on," said Miss Hale, glancing round the tidy pantry as she sat down.

"Havin' eat up the food and washed up the dishes, it naturally follows that you don't see, ma'am. But if I go off in a fit by-and-by you'll know what it's owin' to," answered Ben, vainly endeavoring to look like a man suffering from repletion.

"Such kind fibs are not set down against one, Ben, so I will eat your dinner, for if I don't I know you will throw it out of the window to prove that you can't eat it."

"Thankee ma'am, I'm afraid I should; for, at the rate he's going on, Barney wouldn't be equal to it," said Ben, looking very much relieved, as he polished his last pewter fork and hung his towels up to dry.

A pretty general siesta followed the excitement of dinner, but by three o'clock the public mind was ready for amusement, and the arrival of Sam's box provided it. He was asleep when it was brought in and quietly deposited at his bed's foot, ready to surprise him on awaking. The advent of a box was a great event, for the fortunate receiver seldom failed to "stand treat," and next best to getting things from one's own home was the getting them from some other boy's home. This was an unusually large box, and all felt impatient to have it opened, though Sam's exceeding crustiness prevented the indulgence of great expectations. Presently he roused, and the first thing his eye fell upon was the box, with his own name sprawling over it in big black letters. As if it were merely the continuance of his dream, he stared stupidly at it for a moment, then rubbed his eyes and sat up, exclaiming,—

"Hullo! that's mine!"

"Ah! who said it wouldn't come? who hadn't the faith of a grasshopper? and who don't half deserve it for being a Barker by nater as by name?" cried Ben, emphasizing each question with a bang on the box, as he waited, hammer in hand, for the arrival of the ward-master, whose duty it was to oversee the opening of such matters, lest contraband articles should do mischief to the owner or his neighbors.

"Ain't it a jolly big one? Knock it open, and don't wait for anybody or anything!" cried Sam, tumbling off his bed and beating impatiently on the lid with his one hand.

In came the ward-master, off came the cover, and out came a motley collection of apples, socks, dough-nuts, paper, pickles, photographs, pocket-handkerchiefs, ginger-bread, letters, jelly, newspapers, tobacco, and cologne. "All right, glad it's come,—don't kill yourself," said the ward-master, as he took a hasty survey and walked off again. Drawing the box nearer the bed, Ben delicately followed, and Sam was left to brood over his treasures in peace.

At first all the others, following Ben's example, made elaborate pretences of going to sleep, being absorbed in books, or utterly uninterested in the outer world. But very soon curiosity got the better of politeness, and one by one they all turned round and stared. They might have done so from the first, for Sam was perfectly unconscious of everything but his own affairs, and, having read the letters, looked at the pictures, unfolded the bundles, turned everything inside out and upside down, tasted all the eatables and made a spectacle of himself with jelly, he paused to get his breath and find his way out of the confusion he had created. Presently he called out,—

"Miss Hale, will you come and right up my duds for me?" adding, as her woman's hands began to bring matters straight, "I don't know what to do with 'em all, for some won't keep long, and it will take pretty steady eating to get through 'em in time, supposin' appetite holds out."

"How do the others manage with their things?"

"You know they give 'em away; but I'll be hanged if I do, for they are always callin' names and pokin' fun at me. Guess they won't get anything out of me now."

The old morose look came back as he spoke, for it had disappeared while reading the home letters, touching the home gifts. Still busily folding and arranging, Miss Hale asked,—

"You know the story of the Three Cakes; which are you going to be—Harry, Peter, or Billy?"

Sam began to laugh at this sudden application of the nursery legend; and, seeing her advantage, Miss Hale pursued it:

"We all know how much you have suffered, and all respect you for the courage with which you have borne your long confinement and your loss; but don't you think you have given the boys some cause for making fun of you, as you say? You used to be a favorite, and can be again, if you will only put off these crusty ways, which will grow upon you faster than you think. Better lose both arms than cheerfulness and self-control, Sam."

Pausing to see how her little lecture was received, she saw that Sam's better self was waking up, and added yet another word, hoping to help a mental ailment as she had done so many physical ones. Looking up at him with her kind eyes, she said, in a lowered voice,—

"This day, on which the most perfect life began, is a good day for all of us to set about making ourselves readier to follow that divine example. Troubles are helpers if we take them kindly, and the bitterest may sweeten us for all our lives. Believe and try this, Sam, and when you go away from us let those who love you find that two battles have been fought, two victories won."

Sam made no answer, but sat thoughtfully picking at the half-eaten cookie in his hand. Presently he stole a glance about the room, and, as if all helps were waiting for him, his eye met Joe's. From his solitary corner by the fire and the bed he would seldom leave again until he went into his grave, the boy smiled back at him so heartily, so happily, that something gushed warm across Sam's heart as he looked down upon the faces of mother, sister, sweetheart, scattered round him, and remembered how poor his comrade was in all such tender ties, and yet how rich in that beautiful content, which, "having nothing, yet hath all." The man had no words in which to express this feeling, but it came to him and did him good, as he proved in his own way. "Miss Hale," he said, a little awkwardly, "I wish you'd pick out what you think each would like, and give 'em to the boys."

He got a smile in answer that drove him to his cookie as a refuge, for his lips would tremble, and he felt half proud, half ashamed to have earned such bright approval.

"Let Ben help you,—he knows better than I, But you must give them all yourself, it will so surprise and please the boys; and then to-morrow we will write a capital letter home, telling what a jubilee we made over their fine box."

At this proposal Sam half repented; but, as Ben came lumbering up at Miss Hale's summons, he laid hold of his new resolution as if it was a sort of shower-bath and he held the string, one pull of which would finish the baptism. Dividing his most cherished possession, which (alas for romance!) was the tobacco, he bundled the larger half into a paper, whispering to Miss Hale,—

"Ben ain't exactly what you'd call a ministerin' angel to look at, but he is amazin' near one in his ways, so I'm goin' to begin with him."

Up came the "ministering angel," in red flannel and cow-hide boots; and Sam tucked the little parcel into his pocket, saying, as he began to rummage violently in the box,—

"Now jest hold your tongue, and lend a hand here about these things."

Ben was so taken aback by this proceeding that he stared blankly, till a look from Miss Hale enlightened him; and, taking his cue, he played his part as well as could be expected on so short a notice. Clapping Sam on the shoulder,—not the bad one, Ben was always thoughtful of those things,—he exclaimed heartily,—

"I always said you'd come round when this poor arm of yours got a good start, and here you are jollier'n ever. Lend a hand! so I will, a pair of 'em. What's to do? Pack these traps up again?"

"No; I want you to tell what *you'd* do with 'em if they were yours. Free, you know,—as free as if they really was."

Ben held on to the box a minute as if this second surprise rather took him off his legs; but another look from the prime mover in this resolution steadied him, and he fell to work as if Sam had been in the habit of being "free."

"Well, let's see. I think I'd put the clothes and sich into this smaller box that the bottles come in, and stan' it under the table, handy. Here's newspapers—pictures in 'em, too! I should make a circulatin' lib'ry of them; they'll be a real treat. Pickles—well, I guess I should keep them on the winder here as a kind of a relish dinner-times, or to pass along to them as longs for 'em. Cologne—that's a dreadful handsome bottle, ain't it? That, now, would be fust-rate to give away to somebody as was very fond of it,—a kind of a delicate attention, you know,—if you happen to meet such a person anywheres."

Ben nodded towards Miss Hale, who was absorbed in folding pocket-handkerchiefs. Sam winked expressively, and patted the bottle as if congratulating himself that it *was* handsome, and that he *did* know what to do with it. The pantomime was not elegant, but as much real affection and respect went into it as if he had made a set speech, and presented the gift upon his knees.

"The letters and photographs I should probably keep under my piller for a spell; the jelly I'd give to Miss Hale, to use for the sick ones; the cake-stuff and that pot of jam, that's gettin' ready to work, I'd stand treat with for tea, as dinner wasn't all we could have wished. The apples I'd keep to eat, and fling at Joe when he was too bashful to ask for one, and the *tobaccer* I would *not* go lavishin' on folks that have no business to be enjoyin' luxuries when many a poor feller is dyin' of want down to Charlestown. There, sir! that's what I'd do if any one was so clever as to send me a jolly box like this."

Sam was enjoying the full glow of his shower-bath by this time. As Ben designated the various articles, he set them apart; and when the inventory ended, he marched away with the first installment: two of the biggest, rosiest apples for Joe, and all the pictorial papers. Pickles are not usually regarded as tokens of regard, but as Sam dealt them out one at a time,—for he would let nobody help him, and

his single hand being the left, was as awkward as it was
willing,—the boys' faces brightened; for a friendly word
accompanied each, which made the sour gherkins as welcome as sweetmeats. With every trip the donor's spirits
rose; for Ben circulated freely between whiles, and, thanks
to him, not an allusion to the past marred the satisfaction
of the present. Jam, soda-biscuits, and cake were such welcome additions to the usual bill of fare, that when supper
was over a vote of thanks was passed, and speeches were
made; for, being true Americans, the ruling passion found
vent in the usual "Fellow-citizens!" and allusions to the
"Star-spangled Banner." After which Sam subsided, feeling
himself a public benefactor, and a man of mark.

A perfectly easy, pleasant day throughout would be
almost an impossibility in any hospital, and this one was no
exception to the general rule; for, at the usual time, Dr.
Bangs went his rounds, leaving the customary amount of
discomfort, discontent and dismay behind him. A skillful
surgeon and an excellent man was Dr. Bangs, but not a sanguine or conciliatory individual; many cares and crosses
caused him to regard the world as one large hospital, and
his fellow-beings all more or less dangerously wounded
patients in it. He saw life through the bluest of blue spectacles, and seemed to think that the sooner people quitted
it the happier for them. He did his duty by the men, but if
they recovered he looked half disappointed, and congratu-
lated them with cheerful prophecies that there would come
a time when they would wish they hadn't. If one died he
seemed relieved, and surveyed him with pensive satisfaction, saying heartily,—

"He's comfortable, now, poor soul, and well out of this
miserable world, thank God!"

But for Ben the sanitary influences of the doctor's ward would have been small, and Dante's doleful line might have been written on the threshold of the door,—

"Who enters here leaves hope behind."

Ben and the doctor perfectly understood and liked each other, but never agreed, and always skirmished over the boys as if manful cheerfulness and medical despair were fighting for the soul and body of each one.

"Well," began the doctor, looking at Sam's arm, or, rather, all that was left of that member after two amputations, "we shall be ready for another turn at this in a day or two if it don't mend faster. Tetanus sometimes follows such cases, but that is soon over, and I should not object to a case of it, by way of variety." Sam's hopeful face fell, and he set his teeth as if the fatal symptoms were already felt.

"If one kind of lockjaw was more prevailing than 'tis, it wouldn't be a bad thing for some folks I could mention," observed Ben, covering the well-healed stump as carefully as if it were a sleeping baby; adding, as the doctor walked away, "There's a sanguinary old saw-bones for you! Why, bless your buttons, Sam, you are doing splendid, and he goes on that way because there's no chance of his having another cut at you! Now he's squenchin' Turner, jest as we've blowed a spark of spirit into him. If ever there was a born extinguisher it's Bangs!"

Ben rushed to the rescue, and not a minute too soon; for Turner, who now labored under the delusion that his recovery depended solely upon his getting out of bed every fifteen minutes, was sitting by the fire, looking up at the doctor, who pleasantly observed, while feeling his pulse,—

"So you are getting ready for another fever, are you? Well, we've grown rather fond of you, and will keep you six weeks longer if you have set your heart on it."

Turner looked nervous, for the doctor's jokes were always grim ones; but Ben took the other hand in his, and gently rocked the chair as he replied, with great politeness,—

"This robust convalescent of ourn would be happy to oblige you, sir, but he has a pressin' engagement up to Jersey for next week, and couldn't stop on no account. You see Miss Turner wants a careful nuss for little Georgie, and he's a goin' to take the place."

Feeling himself on the brink of a laugh as Turner simpered with a ludicrous mixture of pride in his baby and fear for himself, Dr. Bangs said, with unusual sternness and a glance at Ben,—

"You take the responsibility of this step upon yourself, do you? Very well; then I wash my hands of Turner; only, if that bed is empty in a week, don't lay the blame of it at my door."

"Nothing shall induce me to do it, sir," briskly responded Ben. "Now then, turn in, my boy, and sleep your prettiest, for I wouldn't but disappoint that cheerfulest of men for a month's wages; and that's liberal, as I ain't likely to get it."

"How is this young man after the rash dissipations of the day?" asked the doctor, pausing at the bed in the corner, after he had made a lively progress down the room, hotly followed by Ben.

"I'm first-rate, sir," panted Joe, who always said so, though each day found him feebler than the last. Every one was kind to Joe, even the gruff doctor, whose manner softened, and who was forced to frown heavily to hide the pity in his eyes

"How's the cough?"

"Better, sir; being weaker, I can't fight against it as I used to do, so it comes rather easier."

"Sleep any last night?"

"Not much; but it's very pleasant laying here when the room is still, and no light but the fire. Ben keeps it bright; and, when I fret, he talks to me, and makes the time go telling stories till he gets so sleepy he can hardly speak. Dear old Ben! I hope he'll have some one as kind to him, when he needs it as I do now."

"He will get what he deserves by-and-by, you may be sure of that," said the doctor, as severely as if Ben merited eternal condemnation.

A great drop splashed down upon the hearth as Joe spoke; but Ben put his foot on it, and turned about as if defying any one to say he shed it.

"Of all the perverse and reckless women whom I have known in the course of a forty years' practice, this one is the most perverse and reckless," said the doctor, abruptly addressing Miss Hale, who just then appeared, bringing Joe's "posy-basket" back. "You will oblige me, ma'am, by sitting in this chair with your hands folded for twenty minutes; the clock will then strike nine, and you will go straight up to your bed."

Miss Hale demurely sat down, and the doctor ponderously departed, sighing regretfully as he went through the room, as if disappointed that the whole thirty were not lying at death's door; but on the threshold he turned about, exclaimed "Good-night, boys! God bless you!" and vanished as precipitately as if a trap-door had swallowed him up.

Miss Hale was a perverse woman in some things; for, instead of folding her tired hands, she took a rusty-covered volume from the mantle-piece, and, sitting by Joe's bed, began to read aloud. One by one all other sounds grew still; one by one the men composed themselves to listen; and one by one the words of the sweet old Christmas story came to them, as the woman's quiet voice went reading on. If any wounded spirit needed balm, if any hungry heart asked food, if any upright purpose, new-born aspiration, or sincere repentance wavered for want of human strength, all found help, hope, and consolation in the beautiful and blessed influences of the book, the reader, and the hour.

The bells rung nine, the lights grew dim, the day's work was done; but Miss Hale lingered beside Joe's bed, for his face wore a wistful look, and he seemed loath to have her go.

"What is it, dear?" she said; "what can I do for you before I leave you to Ben's care?"

He drew her nearer, and whispered earnestly,—

"It's something that I know you'll do for me, because I can't do it for myself, not as I want it done, and you can. I'm going pretty fast now, ma'am; and when—when some one else is laying here, I want you to tell the boys,—every one, from Ben to Barney,—how much I thanked 'em, how much I loved 'em, and how glad I was that I had known 'em, even for such a little while."

"Yes, Joe, I'll tell them all. What else can I do, my boy?"

"Only let me say to you what no one else must say for me, that all I want to live for is to try and do something in my poor way to show you how I thank you, ma'am. It isn't what you've said to me, it isn't what you've done for me alone, that makes me grateful; it's because you've learned me many things without knowing it, showed me what I ought to have been before, if I'd had any one to tell me how, and made this such a happy, home-like place, I shall be sorry when I have to go."

Poor Joe! it must have fared hardly with him all those twenty years, if a hospital seemed home-like, and a little sympathy, a little care, could fill him with such earnest gratitude. He stopped a moment to lay his check upon the hand he held in both of his, then hurried on as if he felt his breath beginning to give out:

"I dare say many boys have said this to you, ma'am, better than I can, for I don't say half I feel; but I know that none of 'em ever thanked you as I thank you in my heart, or ever loved you as I'll love you all my life. To-day I hadn't anything to give you, I'm so poor; but I wanted to tell you this, on the last Christmas I shall ever see."

It was a very humble kiss he gave that hand; but the fervor of a first love warmed it, and the sincerity of a great gratitude made it both a precious and pathetic gift to one who, half unconsciously, had made this brief and barren life so rich and happy at its close. Always womanly and tender, Miss Hale's face was doubly so as she leaned over him, whispering,—

"I have had my present, now. Good-night, Joe."

12
How It All Happened

IT WAS A small room, with nothing in it but a bed, two chairs, and a big chest. A few little gowns hung on the wall, and the only picture was the wintry sky, sparkling with stars, framed by the uncurtained window. But the moon, pausing to peep, saw something pretty and heard something pleasant. Two heads in little round night-caps lay on one pillow, two pairs of wide-awake blue eyes stared up at the light, and two tongues were going like mill clappers.

"I'm so glad we got our shirts done in time! It seemed as if we never should, and I don't think six cents is half enough for a great red flannel thing with four button-holes—do you?" said one little voice, rather wearily.

"No; but then we each made four, and fifty cents is a good deal of money. Are you sorry we didn't keep our quarters for ourselves?" asked the other voice, with an under-tone of regret in it.

"Yes, I am, till I think how pleased the children will be with our tree, for they don't expect anything, and will be so surprised. I wish we had more toys to put on it, for it looks so small and mean with only three or four things"

"It won't hold any more, so I wouldn't worry about it. The

toys are very red and yellow, and I guess the babies won't
know how cheap they are, but like them as much as if they
cost heaps of money."

This was a cheery voice, and as it spoke the four blue eyes
turned toward the chest under the window, and the kind
moon did her best to light up the tiny tree standing there. A
very pitiful little tree it was—only a branch of hemlock in an
old flower-pot, propped up with bits of coal, and hung with
a few penny toys earned by the patient fingers of the elder
sisters, that the little ones should not be disappointed.

But in spite of the magical moonlight the broken branch,
with its scanty supply of fruit, looked pathetically poor, and
one pair of eyes filled slowly with tears, while the other pair
lost their happy look, as if a cloud had come over the sunshine.

"Are you crying, Dolly?"

"Not much, Polly."

"What makes you, dear?"

"I didn't know how poor we were till I saw the tree, and
then I couldn't help it," sobbed the elder sister, for at twelve
she already knew something of the cares of poverty, and
missed the happiness that seemed to vanish out of all their
lives when father died.

"It's dreadful! I never thought we'd have to earn our tree,
and only be able to get a broken branch, after all, with nothing on it but three sticks of candy, two squeaking dogs, a
red cow, and an ugly bird with one feather in its tail;" and
overcome by a sudden sense of destitution, Polly sobbed
even more despairingly than Dolly.

"Hush, dear; we must cry softly, or mother will hear, and
come up, and then we shall have to tell. You know we said
we wouldn't seem to mind not having any Christmas, she
felt so sorry about it."

"I *must* cry, but I'll be quiet."

So the two heads went under the pillow for a few minutes, and not a sound betrayed them as the little sisters cried softly in one another's arms, lest mother should discover that they were no longer careless children, but brave young creatures trying to bear their share of the burden cheerfully.

When the shower was over, the faces came out shining like roses after rain, and the voices went on again as before.

"Don't you wish there really was a Santa Claus, who knew what we wanted, and would come and put two silver half-dollars in our stockings, so we could go and see *Puss in Boots* at the Museum to-morrow afternoon?"

"Yes, indeed; but we didn't hang up any stockings, you know, because mother had nothing to put in them. It does seem as if rich people might think of poor people now and then. Such little bits of things would make us happy, and it couldn't be much trouble to take two small girls to the play, and give them candy now and then."

"*I* shall when I'm rich, like Mr. Chrome and Miss Kent. I shall go round every Christmas with a big basket of goodies, and give *all* the poor children some."

"P'r'aps if we sew ever so many flannel shirts we may be rich by-and-by. I should give mother a new bonnet first of all, for I heard Miss Kent say no lady would wear such a shabby one. Mrs. Smith said fine bonnets didn't make real ladies. I like her best, but I do want a locket like Miss Kent's."

"I should give mother some new rubbers, and then I should buy a white apron, with frills like Miss Kent's, and bring home nice bunches of grapes and good things to eat, as Mr. Chrome does. I often smell them, but he never gives *me* any; he only says, 'Hullo, chick!' and I'd rather have oranges any time."

"It will take us a long while to get rich, I'm afraid. It makes me tired to think of it. I guess we'd better go to sleep now, dear."

"Good-night, Dolly."

"Good-night, Polly."

Two soft kisses were heard, a nestling sound followed, and presently the little sisters lay fast asleep cheek against cheek, on the pillow wet with their tears, never dreaming what was going to happen to them to-morrow.

Now Miss Kent's room was next to theirs, and as she sat sewing she could hear the children's talk, for they soon forgot to whisper. At first she smiled, then she looked sober, and when the prattle ceased she said to herself, as she glanced about her pleasant chamber:

"Poor little things! they think I'm rich, and envy me, when I'm only a milliner earning my living. I ought to have taken more notice of them, for their mother has a hard time, I fancy, but never complains. I'm sorry they heard what I said, and if I knew how to do it without offending her, I'd trim a nice bonnet for a Christmas gift, for she *is* a lady, in spite of her old clothes. I can give the children some of the things they want anyhow, and I will. The idea of those mites making a fortune out of shirts at six cents apiece!"

Miss Kent laughed at the innocent delusion, but sympathized with her little neighbors, for she knew all about hard times. She had good wages now, but spent them on herself, and liked to be fine rather than neat. Still, she was a good-hearted girl, and what she had overheard set her to thinking soberly, then to acting kindly, as we shall see.

"If I hadn't spent all my money on my dress for the party to-morrow night, I'd give each of them a half-dollar. As I can not, I'll hunt up the other things they wanted, for it's a shame they shouldn't have a bit of Christmas, when they tried so hard to please the little ones."

As she spoke she stirred about her room, and soon had a white apron, an old carnelian heart on a fresh blue ribbon, and two papers of bonbons ready. As no stockings were hung up, she laid a clean towel on the floor before the door, and spread forth the small gifts to look their best.

Miss Kent was so busy that she did not hear a step come quietly up stairs, and Mr. Chrome, the artist, peeped at her through the balusters, wondering what she was about. He soon saw, and watched her with pleasure, thinking that she never looked prettier than now.

Presently she caught him at it, and hastened to explain, telling what she had heard, and how she was trying to atone for her past neglect of these young neighbors. Then she said good-night, and both went into their rooms, she to sleep happily, and he to smoke as usual.

But his eye kept turning to some of the "nice little bundles" that lay on his table, as if the story he had heard suggested how he might follow Miss Kent's example. I rather think he would not have disturbed himself if he had not heard the story told in such a soft voice, with a pair of bright eyes full of pity looking into his, for little girls were not particularly interesting to him, and he was usually too tired to notice the industrious creatures toiling up and down stairs on various errands, or sewing at the long red seams.

Now that he knew something of their small troubles, he felt as if it would please Miss Kent, and be a good joke, to do his share of the pretty work she had begun.

So presently he jumped up, and, opening his parcels, took out two oranges and two bunches of grapes, then he looked up two silver half-dollars, and stealing into the hall, laid the fruit upon the towel, and the money atop of the oranges. This addition improved the display very much, and Mr. Chrome was stealing back, well pleased, when his eye fell on Miss Kent's door, and he said to himself, "She too shall have a little surprise, for she is a dear, kind-hearted soul."

In his room was a prettily painted plate, and this he filled with green and purple grapes, tucked a sentimental note underneath, and leaving it on her threshold, crept away as stealthily as a burglar.

The house was very quiet when Mrs. Smith, the land-lady, came up to turn off the gas. "Well, upon my word, here's fine doings, to be sure!" she said, when she saw the state of the upper hall. "Now I wouldn't have thought it of Miss Kent, she is such a giddy girl, nor of Mr. Chrome, he is so busy with his own affairs. I meant to give those children each a cake to-morrow, they are such good little things. I'll run down and get them now, as my contribution to this fine set out."

Away trotted Mrs. Smith to her pantry, and picked out a couple of tempting cakes, shaped like hearts and full of plums. There was a goodly array of pies on the shelves, and she took two of them, saying, as she climbed the stairs again, "They remembered the children, so I'll remember them, and have my share of the fun."

So up went the pies, for Mrs. Smith had not much to give, and her spirit was generous, though her pastry was not of the best. It looked very droll to see pies sitting about on the thresholds of closed doors, but the cakes were quite elegant, and filled up the corners of the towel handsomely, for the apron lay in the middle, with the oranges right and left, like two sentinels in yellow uniforms.

It was very late when the flicker of a candle came up stairs, and a pale lady, with a sweet sad face, appeared, bringing a pair of red and a pair of blue mittens for her Dolly and Polly. Poor Mrs. Blake did have a hard time, for she stood all day in a great store that she might earn bread for the poor children who staid at home and took care of one another. Her heart was very heavy that night, because it was the first Christmas she had ever known without gifts and festivity of some sort. But Petkin, the youngest child, had been ill, times were very hard, the little mouths gaped for food like the bills of hungry birds, and there was no tender mate to help fill them.

If any elves had been hovering about the dingy hall just then, they would have seen the mother's tired face brighten beautifully when she discovered the gifts, and found that her little girls had been so kindly remembered. Something more brilliant than the mock diamonds in Miss Kent's best ear-rings fell and glittered on the dusty floor as Mrs. Blake added the mittens to the other things, and went to her lonely room again, smiling as she thought how she could thank them all in a sweet and simple way.

Her windows were full of flowers, for the delicate tastes of the poor lady found great comfort in their beauty. "I have nothing else to give, and these will show how grateful I am," she said, as she rejoiced that the scarlet geraniums were so full of gay clusters, the white chrysanthemum stars were all out, and the pink roses at their loveliest.

They slept now, dreaming of a sunny morrow as they sat safely sheltered from the bitter cold. But that night was their last, for a gentle hand cut them all, and soon three pretty nosegays stood in a glass, waiting for dawn, to be laid

at three doors, with a few grateful words which would surprise and delight the receivers, for flowers were rare in
those hard-working lives, and kind deeds often come back
to the givers in fairer shapes than they go.

Now one would think that there had been gifts enough,
and no more could possibly arrive, since all had added his
or her mite except Betsey, the maid, who was off on a holiday, and the babies fast asleep in their trundle-bed, with
nothing to give but love and kisses. Nobody dreamed that
the old cat would take it into her head that her kittens were
in danger, because Mrs. Smith had said she thought they
were nearly old enough to be given away. But she must have
understood, for when all was dark and still, the anxious
mother went patting up stairs to the children's door, meaning to hide her babies under their bed, sure they would save
them from destruction. Mrs. Blake had shut the door, however, so poor Puss was disappointed; but finding a soft,
clean spot among a variety of curious articles, she laid her
kits there, and kept them warm all night, with her head pil-
lowed on the blue mittens.

In the cold morning Dolly and Polly got up and scrambled into their clothes, not with joyful haste to see what
their stockings held, for they had none, but because they
had the little ones to dress while mother got the breakfast

Dolly opened the door, and started back with a cry of
astonishment at the lovely spectacle before her. The other
people had taken in their gifts, so nothing destroyed the
magnificent effect of the treasures so curiously collected in
the night. Puss had left her kits asleep, and gone down to
get her own breakfast, and there, in the middle of the ruffled apron, as if in a dainty cradle, lay the two Maltese darlings, with white bibs and boots on, and white tips to the
tiny tails curled round their little noses in the sweetest way.

Polly and Dolly could only clasp their hands and look in rapturous silence for a minute; then they went down on their knees and revelled in the unexpected richness before them.

"I do believe there *is* a Santa Claus, and that he heard us, for here is everything we wanted," said Dolly, holding the carnelian heart in one hand and the plummy one in the other.

"It must have been some kind of a fairy, for we didn't mention kittens, but we wanted one, and here are two darlings," cried Polly, almost purring with delight as the downy bunches unrolled and gaped till their bits of pink tongues were visible.

"Mrs. Smith was one fairy, I guess, and Miss Kent was another, for that is her apron. I shouldn't wonder if Mr. Chrome gave us the oranges and the money: men always have lots, and his name is on this bit of paper," said Dolly.

"Oh, I'm *so* glad! Now we shall have a Christmas like other people, and I'll never say again that rich folks don't remember poor folks. Come and show all our treasures to mother and the babies; they must have some," answered Polly, feeling that the world was all right, and life not half as hard as she thought it last night.

Shrieks of delight greeted the sisters, and all that morning there was joy and feasting in Mrs. Blake's room, and in the afternoon Dolly and Polly went to the Museum, and actually saw *Puss in Boots*; for their mother insisted on their going, having discovered how the hard-earned quarters had been spent. This was such unhoped-for bliss that they could hardly believe it, and kept smiling at one another so brightly that people wondered who the happy little girls in shabby cloaks could be who clapped their new mittens so heartily, and laughed till it was better than music to hear them.

This was a very remarkable Christmas-day, and they long remembered it; for while they were absorbed in the fortunes of the Marquis of Carabas and the funny cat, who tucked his tail in his belt, washed his face so awkwardly, and didn't know how to purr, strange things were happening at home, and more surprises were in store for our little friends. You see, when people once begin to do kindnesses, it is so easy and pleasant they find it hard to leave off; and sometimes it beautifies them so that they find they love one another very much—as Mr. Chrome and Miss Kent did, though we have nothing to do with that except to tell how they made the poor little tree grow and blossom.

They were very jolly at dinner, and talked a good deal about the Blakes, who ate in their own rooms. Miss Kent told what the children said, and it touched the soft spot in all their hearts to hear about the red shirts, though they laughed at Polly's lament over the bird with only one feather in its tail.

"I'd give them a better tree if I had any place to put it, and knew how to trim it up," said Mr. Chrome, with a sudden burst of generosity, which so pleased Miss Kent that her eyes shone like Christmas candles.

"Put it in the back parlor. All the Browns are away for a week, and we'll help you trim it—won't we, my dear?" cried Mrs. Smith, warmly; for she saw that he was in a sociable mood, and thought it a pity that the Blakes should not profit by it.

"Yes, indeed; I should like it of all things, and it needn't cost much, for I have some skill in trimmings, as you know." And Miss Kent looked so gay and pretty as she spoke that Mr. Chrome made up his mind that millinery must be a delightful occupation.

"Come on then, ladies, and we'll have a little frolic. I'm

a lonely old bachelor, with nowhere to go to-day, and I'd like some fun."

They had it, I assure you; for they all fell to work as busy as bees, flying and buzzing about with much laughter as they worked their pleasant miracle. Mr. Chrome acted more like the father of a large family than a crusty bachelor, Miss Kent's skillful fingers flew as they never did before, and Mrs. Smith trotted up and down as briskly as if she were sixteen instead of being a stout old woman of sixty.

The children were so full of the play, and telling all about it, that they forgot their tree till after supper; but when they went to look for it they found it gone, and in its place a great paper hand with one finger pointing down stairs, and on it these mysterious words in red ink:

"Look in the Browns' back parlor!"

At the door of that interesting apartment they found their mother with Will and Petkin, for another hand had suddenly appeared to them pointing up. The door flew open quite as if it were a fairy play and they went in to find a pretty tree planted in a red box on the centre table, lighted with candles, hung with gilded nuts, red apples, gay bonbons, and a gift for each.

Mr. Chrome was hidden behind one folding-door, and fat Mrs. Smith squeezed behind the other, and they both thought it a great improvement upon the old-fashioned Santa Claus to have Miss Kent, in the white dress she made for the party, with Mrs. Blake's roses in her hair, step forward as the children gazed in silent rapture, and with a few sweet words welcome them to the little surprise their friends had made.

There were many Christmas trees in the city that night, but none which gave such hearty pleasure as the one which so magically took the place of the broken branch and its few poor toys. They were all there, however, and Dolly and Polly were immensely pleased to see that of all her gifts Petkin chose the forlorn bird to carry to bed with her, the one yellow feather being just to her taste.

Mrs. Blake put on her neat bonnet, and was so gratified that Miss Kent thought it the most successful one she ever trimmed. She was well paid for it by the thanks of one neighbor and the admiration of another; for when she went to her party Mr. Chrome went with her, and said something on the way which made her heart dance more lightly than her feet that night.

Good Mrs. Smith felt that her house had covered itself with glory by this event, and Dolly and Polly declared that it was the most perfect and delightful surprise party ever seen.

It was all over by nine o'clock, and with good-night kisses for every one the little girls climbed up to bed laden with treasures and too happy for many words. But as they tied their round caps Dolly said, thoughtfully:

"On the whole, I think it's rather nice to be poor when people are kind to you."

"Well, I'd *rather* be rich; but if I can't be, it is very good fun to have Christmas trees like this one," answered truthful Polly, never guessing that they had planted the seed from which the little pine-tree grew so quickly and beautifully.

When the moon came to look in at the window on her nightly round; two smiling faces lay on the pillow, which was no longer wet with tears, but rather knobby with the mine of riches hidden underneath,—first fruits of the neighborly friendship which flourished in that house until another and a merrier Christmas came.

13

Tilly's Christmas

"I'M SO GLAD to-morrow is Christmas, because I'm going to have lots of presents."

"So am I glad, though I don't expect any presents but a pair of mittens."

"And so am I; but I shan't have any presents at all."

As the three little girls trudged home from school they said these things, and as Tilly spoke, both the others looked at her with pity and some surprise, for she spoke cheerfully, and they wondered how she could be happy when she was so poor she could have no presents on Christmas.

"Don't you wish you could find a purse full of money right here in the path?" said Kate, the child who was going to have "lots of presents."

"Oh, don't I, if I could keep it honestly!" and Tilly's eyes shone at the very thought.

"What would you buy?" asked Bessy, rubbing her cold hands, and longing for her mittens.

"I'd buy a pair of large, warm blankets, a load of wood, a shawl for mother, and a pair of shoes for me; and if there was enough left, I'd give Bessy a new hat, and then she needn't wear Ben's old felt one," answered Tilly.

The girls laughed at that; but Bessy pulled the funny hat over her ears, and said she was much obliged, but she'd rather have candy.

"Let's look, and may be we *can* find a purse. People are always going about with money at Christmas time, and some one may lose it here," said Kate.

So, as they went along the snowy road, they looked about them, half in earnest, half in fun. Suddenly Tilly sprang forward, exclaiming,—

"I see it! I've found it!"

The others followed, but all stopped disappointed; for it wasn't a purse, it was only a little bird. It lay upon the snow with its wings spread and feebly fluttering, as if too weak to fly. Its little feet were benumbed with cold; its once bright eyes were cold; its once bright eyes were dull with pain, and instead of a blithe song, it could only utter a faint chirp, now and then, as if crying for help.

"Nothing but a stupid old robin; how provoking!" cried Kate, sitting down to rest.

"I shan't touch it. I found one once, and took care of it, and the ungrateful thing flew away the minute it was well," said Bessy, creeping under Kate's shawl, and putting her hands under her chin to warm them.

"Poor little birdie! How pitiful he looks, and how glad he must be to see some one coming to help him! I'll take him up gently, and carry him home to mother. Don't be frightened, dear, I'm your friend;" and Tilly knelt down in the snow, stretching her hand to the bird with the tenderest pity in her face.

Kate and Bessy laughed.

"Don't stop for that thing; it's getting late and cold: let's go on and look for the purse," they said, moving away.

"You wouldn't leave it to die!" cried Tilly. "I'd rather have the bird than the money, so I shan't look any more. The purse wouldn't be mine, and I should only be tempted to keep it; but this poor thing will thank and love me, and I'm *so* glad I came in time."

Gently lifting the bird, Tilly felt its tiny cold claws cling to her hand, and saw its dim eyes brighten as it nestled down with a grateful chirp.

"Now I've got a Christmas present after all," she said, smiling, as they walked on. "I always wanted a bird, and this one will be such a pretty pet for me."

"He'll fly away the first chance he gets, and die anyhow; so you'd better not waste your time over him," said Bessy.

"He can't pay you for taking care of him, and my mother says it isn't worth while to help folks that can't help us," added Kate.

"My mother says, 'Do as you'd be done by;' and I'm sure I'd like any one to help me if I was dying of cold and hunger. 'Love your neighbor as yourself,' is another of her sayings. This bird is my little neighbor, and I'll love him and care for him, as I often wish our rich neighbor would love and care for us," answered Tilly, breathing her warm breath over the benumbed bird, who looked up at her with confiding eyes, quick to feel and know a friend.

"What a funny girl you are," said Kate; "caring for that silly bird, and talking about loving your neighbor in that sober way. Mr. King don't care a bit for you, and never will, though he knows how poor you are; so I don't think your plan amounts to much."

"I believe it, though; and shall do my part, any way. Good-night. I hope you'll have a merry Christmas, and lots of pretty things," answered Tilly, as they parted.

Her eyes were full, and she felt *so* poor as she went on alone toward the little old house where she lived. It would have been so pleasant to know that she was going to have some of the pretty things all children love to find in their full stockings on Christmas morning. And pleasanter still to have been able to give her mother something nice. So many comforts were needed, and there was no hope of getting them; for they could barely get food and fire.

"Never mind, birdie, we'll make the best of what we have, and be merry in spite of every thing. *You* shall have a happy Christmas, any way; and I know. God won't forget us, if every one else does."

She stopped a minute to wipe her eyes, and lean her cheek against the bird's soft breast, finding great comfort in the little creature, though it could only love her, nothing more.

"See, mother, what a nice present I've found," she cried, going in with a cheery face that was like sunshine in the dark room.

"I'm glad of that, dearie; for I haven't been able to get my little girl any thing but a rosy apple. Poor bird! Give it some of your warm bread and milk."

"Why, mother, what a big bowlful! I'm afraid you gave me all the milk," said Tilly, smiling over the nice, steaming supper that stood ready for her.

"I've had plenty, dear. Sit down and dry your wet feet, and put the bird in my basket on this warm flannel."

Tilly peeped into the closet and saw nothing there but dry bread.

"Mother's given me all the milk, and is going without her tea, 'cause she knows I'm hungry. Now I'll surprise her, and she shall have a good supper too. She is going to split wood, and I'll fix it while she's gone."

So Tilly put down the old tea-pot, carefully poured out a part of the milk, and from her pocket produced a great, plummy bun, that one of the school-children had given her, and she had saved for her mother. A slice of the dry bread was nicely toasted, and the bit of butter set by for her put on it. When her mother came in there was the table drawn up in a warm place, a hot cup of tea ready, and Tilly and birdie waiting for her.

Such a poor little supper, and yet such a happy one; for love, charity, and contentment were guests there, and that Christmas eve was a blither one than that up at the great house, where lights shone, fires blazed, a great tree glittered, and music sounded, as the children danced and played.

"We must go to bed early, for we've only wood enough to last over to-morrow. I shall be paid for my work the day after, and then we can get some," said Tilly's mother, as they sat by the fire.

"If my bird was only a fairy bird, and would give us three wishes, how nice it would be! Poor dear, he can't give me any thing; but it's no matter," answered Tilly, looking at the robin, who lay in the basket with his head under his wing, a mere little feathery bunch.

"He can give you one thing, Tilly,—the pleasure of doing good. That is one of the sweetest things in life; and the poor can enjoy it as well as the rich."

As her mother spoke, with her tired hand softly stroking her little daughter's hair, Tilly suddenly started and pointed to the window, saying, in a frightened whisper,—

"I saw a face,—a man's face, looking in! It's gone now; but I truly saw it."

"Some traveller attracted by the light perhaps. I'll go and see." And Tilly's mother went to the door.

No one was there. The wind blew cold, the stars shone,

the snow lay white on field and wood, and the Christmas moon was glittering in the sky.

"What sort of a face was it?" asked Tilly's mother, coming back.

"A pleasant sort of face, I think; but I was so startled I don't quite know what it was like. I wish we had a curtain there," said Tilly.

"I like to have our light shine out in the evening, for the road is dark and lonely just here, and the twinkle of our lamp is pleasant to people's eyes as they go by. We can do so little for our neighbors, I am glad to cheer the way for them. Now put these poor old shoes to dry, and go to bed, dearie; I'll come soon."

Tilly went, taking her bird with her to sleep in his basket near by, lest he should be lonely in the night.

Soon the little house was dark and still, and no one saw the Christmas spirits at their work that night.

When Tilly opened the door next morning, she gave a loud cry, clapped her hands, and then stood still, quite speechless with wonder and delight. There, before the door, lay a great pile of wood, all ready to burn, a big bundle and a basket, with a lovely nosegay of winter roses, holly, and evergreen tied to the handle.

"Oh, mother! did the fairies do it?" cried Tilly, pale with her happiness, as she seized the basket, while her mother took in the bundle.

"Yes, dear, the best and dearest fairy in the world, called 'Charity.' She walks abroad at Christmas time, does beautiful deeds like this, and does not stay to be thanked," answered her mother with full eyes, as she undid the parcel.

There they were,—the warm, thick blankets, the

comfortable shawl, the new shoes, and, best of all, a pretty winter hat for Bessy. The basket was full of good things to eat, and on the flowers lay a paper saying,—

"For the little girl who loves her neighbor as herself."

"Mother, I really think my bird is a fairy bird, and all these splendid things come from him," said Tilly, laughing and crying with joy.

It really did seem so, for as she spoke, the robin flew to the table, hopped to the nosegay, and perching among the roses, began to chirp with all his little might. The sun streamed in on flowers, bird, and happy child, and no one saw a shadow glide away from the window; no one ever knew that Mr. King had seen and heard the little girls the night before, or dreamed that the rich neighbor had learned a lesson from the poor neighbor.

And Tilly's bird *was* a fairy bird; for by her love and tenderness to the helpless thing, she brought good gifts to herself, happiness to the unknown giver of them, and a faithful little friend who did not fly away, but stayed with her till the snow was gone, making summer for her in the winter-time.

14

What Polly Found In Her Stocking

With the first pale glimmer,
Of the morning red,
Polly woke delighted
And flew out of bed.
To the door she hurried,
Never stopped for clothes,
Though Jack Frost's cold fingers
Nipt her little toes.
There it hung! the stocking,
Long and blue and full;
Down it quickly tumbled
With a hasty pull.
Back she capered, laughing,
Happy little Polly;
For from out the stocking
Stared a splendid dolly!
Next, what most she wanted,
In a golden nut,
With a shining thimble,
Scissors that would cut;
Then a book all pictures,

"Children in the Wood."
And some scarlet mittens
Like her scarlet hood.
Next a charming jump-rope,
New and white and strong;
(Little Polly's stocking
Though small was very long,)
In the heel she fumbled,
"Something soft and warm,"
A rainbow ball of worsted
Which could do no harm.
In the foot came bon-bons,
In the toe a ring,
And some seeds of mignonette
Ready for the spring.
There she sat at daylight
Hugging close dear dolly;
Eating, looking, laughing,
Happy little Polly!

15

A Christmas Dream,
and How It Came True

"I'm so tired of Christmas I wish there never would be another one!" exclaimed a discontented-looking little girl, as she sat idly watching her mother arrange a pile of gifts two days before they were to be given.

"Why, Effie, what a dreadful thing to say! You are as bad as old Scrooge; and I'm afraid something will happen to you, as it did to him, if you don't care for dear Christmas," answered mamma, almost dropping the silver horn she was filling with delicious candies.

"Who was Scrooge? What happened to him?" asked Effie, with a glimmer of interest in her listless face, as she picked out the sourest lemon-drop she could find; for nothing sweet suited her just then.

"He was one of Dickens's best people, and you can read the charming story some day. He hated Christmas until a strange dream showed him how dear and beautiful it was, and made a better man of him."

"I shall read it; for I like dreams, and have a great many curious ones myself. But they don't keep me from being tired of Christmas," said Effie, poking discontentedly among the sweeties for something worth eating.

"Why are you tired of what should be the happiest time of all the year?" asked mamma, anxiously.

"Perhaps I shouldn't be if I had something new. But it is always the same, and there isn't any more surprise about it. I always find heaps of goodies in my stocking. Don't like some of them, and soon get tired of those I do like. We always have a great dinner, and I eat too much, and feel ill next day. Then there is a Christmas tree somewhere, with a doll on top, or a stupid old Santa Claus, and children dancing and screaming over bonbons and toys that break, and shiny things that are of no use. Really, mamma, I've had so many Christmases all alike that I don't think I *can* bear another one." And Effie laid herself flat on the sofa, as if the mere idea was too much for her.

Her mother laughed at her despair, but was sorry to see her little girl so discontented, when she had everything to make her happy, and had known but ten Christmas days.

"Suppose we don't give you *any* presents at all,—how would that suit you?" asked mamma, anxious to please her spoiled child.

"I should like one large and splendid one, and one dear little one, to remember some very nice person by," said Effie, who was a fanciful little body, full of odd whims and notions, which her friends loved to gratify, regardless of time, trouble, or money; for she was the last of three little girls, and very dear to all the family.

"Well, my darling, I will see what I can do to please you, and not say a word until all is ready. If I could only get a new idea to start with!" And mamma went on tying up her pretty bundles with a thoughtful face, while Effie strolled to the window to watch the rain that kept her in-doors and made her dismal.

"Seems to me poor children have better times than rich ones. I can't go out, and there is a girl about my age splashing along, without any maid to fuss about rubbers and cloaks and umbrellas and colds. I wish I was a beggar-girl."

"Would you like to be hungry, cold, and ragged, to beg all day, and sleep on an ash-heap at night?" asked mamma, wondering what would come next.

"Cinderella did, and had a nice time in the end. This girl out here has a basket of scraps on her arm, and a big old shawl all round her, and doesn't seem to care a bit, though the water runs out of the toes of her boots. She goes paddling along, laughing at the rain, and eating a cold potato as if it tasted nicer than the chicken and ice-cream I had for dinner. Yes, I do think poor children are happier than rich ones."

"So do I, sometimes. At the Orphan Ashlum to-day I saw two dozen merry little souls who have no parents, no home, and no hope of Christmas beyond a stick of candy or a cake. I wish you had been there to see how happy they were, playing with the old toys some richer children had sent them."

"You may give them all mine; I'm so tired of them I never want to see them again," said Effie, turning from the window to the pretty baby-house full of everything a child's heart could desire.

"I will, and let you begin again with something you will not tire of, if I can only find it." And mamma knit her brows trying to discover some grand surprise for this child who didn't care for Christmas.

Nothing more was said then; and wandering off to the library, Effie found "A Christmas Carol," and curling herself up in the sofa corner, read it all before tea. Some of it she did not understand; but she laughed and cried over many parts of the charming story, and felt better without knowing why.

All the evening she thought of poor Tiny Tim, Mrs. Cratchit with the pudding, and the stout old gentleman who danced so gayly that "his legs twinkled in the air." Presently bed-time arrived.

"Come, now, and toast your feet," said Effie's nurse, "while I do your pretty hair and tell stories."

"I'll have a fairy tale to-night, a very interesting one," commanded Effie, as she put on her blue silk wrapper and little fur-lined slippers to sit before the fire and have her long curls brushed.

So Nursey told her best tales; and when at last the child lay down under her lace curtains, her head was full of a curious jumble of Christmas elves, poor children, snow-storms, sugar-plums, and surprises. So it is no wonder that she dreamed all night; and this was the dream, which she never quite forgot.

She found herself sitting on a stone, in the middle of a great field, all alone. The snow was falling fast, a bitter wind whistled by, and night was coming on. She felt hungry, cold, and tired, and did not know where to go nor what to do.

"I wanted to be a beggar-girl, and now I am one; but I don't like it, and wish somebody would come and take care of me. I don't know who I am, and I think I must be lost," thought Effie, with the curious interest one takes in one's self in dreams.

But the more she thought about it, the more bewildered she felt. Faster fell the snow, colder blew the wind, darker grew the night; and poor Effie made up her mind that she was quite forgotten and left to freeze alone. The tears were chilled on her cheeks, her feet felt like icicles, and her heart died within her, so hungry, frightened, and forlorn was she. Laying her head on her knees, she gave herself up for lost, and sat there with the great flakes fast turning her to a little white mound, when suddenly the sound of music reached her, and starting up, she looked and listened with all her eyes and ears.

Far away a dim light shone, and a voice was heard singing. She tried to run toward the welcome glimmer, but could not stir, and stood like a small statue of expectation while the light drew nearer, and the sweet words of the song grew clearer.

> From our happy home
> Through the world we roam
> One week in all the year,
> Making winter spring
> With the joy we bring,
> For Christmas-tide is here.
>
> Now the eastern star
> Shines from afar
> To light the poorest home;
> Hearts warmer grow,
> Gifts freely flow,
> For Christmas-tide has come.
>
> Now gay trees rise
> Before young eyes,
> Abloom with tempting cheer;
> Blithe voices sing,
> And blithe bells ring,
> For Christmas-tide is here.

Oh, happy chime,
Oh, blessèd time,
That draws us all so near!
"Welcome, dear day,"
All creatures say,
For Christmas-tide is here.

A child's voice sang, a child's hand carried the little candle; and in the circle of soft light it shed, Effie saw a pretty
child coming to her through the night and snow. A rosy,
smiling creature, wrapped in white fur, with a wreath of
green and scarlet holly on its shining hair, the magic candle
in one hand, and the other outstretched as if to shower gifts
and warmly press all other hands.

Effie forgot to speak as this bright vision came nearer,
leaving no trace of footsteps in the snow, only lighting the
way with its little candle, and filling the air with the music
of its song.

"Dear child, you are lost, and I have come to find you,"
said the stranger, taking Effie's cold hands in his, with a
smile like sunshine, while every holly berry glowed like a
little fire.

"Do you know me?" asked Effie, feeling no fear, but a
great gladness, at his coming.

"I know all children, and go to find them; for this is my
holiday, and I gather them from all parts of the world to be
merry with me once a year."

"Are you an angel?" asked Effie, looking for the wings.

"No; I am a Christmas spirit, and alive with my mates in
a pleasant place, getting ready for our holiday, when we are
let out to roam about the world, helping make this a happy
time for all who will let us in. Will you come and see how
we work?"

"I will go anywhere with you. Don't leave me again," cried Effie, gladly.

"First I will make you comfortable. That is what we love to do. You are cold, and you shall be warm; hungry, and I will feed you; sorrowful, and I will make you gay."

With a wave of his candle all three miracles were wrought,—for the snow-flakes turned to a white fur cloak and hood on Effie's head and shoulders; a bowl of hot soup came sailing to her lips, and vanished when she had eagerly drunk the last drop; and suddenly the dismal field changed to a new world so full of wonders that all her troubles were forgotten in a minute.

Bells were ringing so merrily that it was hard to keep from dancing. Green garlands hung on the walls, and every tree was a Christmas tree full of toys, and blazing with candles that never went out.

In one place many little spirits sewed like mad on warm clothes, turning off work faster than any sewing-machine ever invented, and great piles were made ready to be sent to poor people. Other busy creatures packed money into purses, and wrote checks which they sent flying away on the wind,—a lovely kind of snow-storm to fall into a world below full of poverty.

Older and graver spirits were looking over piles of little books, in which the records of the past year were kept, telling how different people had spent it, and what sort of gifts they deserved. Some got peace, some disappointment, some remorse and sorrow, some great joy and hope. The rich had generous thoughts sent them; the poor, gratitude and contentment. Children had more love and duty to parents; and parents renewed patience, wisdom, and satisfaction for and in their children. No one was forgotten.

"Please tell me what splendid place this is?" asked Effie,

as soon as she could collect her wits after the first look at all these astonishing things.

"This is the Christmas world; and here we work all the year round, never tired of getting ready for the happy day. See, these are the saints just setting off; for some have far to go, and the children must not be disappointed."

As he spoke the spirit pointed to four gates, out of which four great sleighs were just driving, laden with toys, while a jolly old Santa Claus sat in the middle of each, drawing on his mittens and tucking up his wraps for a long cold drive.

"Why, I thought there was only one Santa Claus, and even he was a humbug," cried Effie, astonished at the sight.

"Never give up your faith in the sweet old stories, even after you come to see that they are only the pleasant shadow of a lovely truth."

Just then the sleighs went off with a great jingling of bells and pattering of reindeer hoofs, while all the spirits gave a cheer that was heard in the lower world, where people said, "Hear the stars sing."

"I never will say there isn't any Santa Claus again. Now, show me more."

"You will like to see this place, I think, and may learn something here perhaps."

The spirit smiled as he led the way to a little door, through which Effie peeped into a world of dolls. Baby-houses were in full blast, with dolls of all sorts going on like live people. Waxen ladies sat in their parlors elegantly dressed; nurses walked out with the bits of dollies; and the streets were full of tin soldiers marching, wooden horses prancing, express wagons rumbling, and little men hurrying to and fro. Shops were there, and tiny people buying legs of mutton, pounds of tea, mites of clothes, and everything dolls use or wear or want.

But presently she saw that in some ways the dolls improved upon the manners and customs of human beings, and she watched eagerly to learn why they did these things. A fine Paris doll driving in her carriage took up a worsted Dinah who was hobbling along with a basket of clean clothes, and carried her to her journey's end, as if it were the proper thing to do. Another interesting china lady took off her comfortable red cloak and put it round a poor wooden creature done up in a paper shift, and so badly painted that its face would have sent some babies into fits.

"Seems to me I once knew a rich girl who didn't give her things to poor girls. I wish I could remember who she was, and tell her to be as kind as that china doll," said Effie, much touched at the sweet way the pretty creature wrapped up the poor fright, and then ran off in her little gray gown to buy a shiny fowl stuck on a wooden platter for her invalid mother's dinner.

"We recall these things to people's minds by dreams. I think the girl you speak of won't forget this one." And the spirit smiled, as if he enjoyed some joke which she did not see.

A little bell rang as she looked, and away scampered the children into the red-and-green school-house with the roof that lifted up, so one could see how nicely they sat at their desks with mites of books, or drew on the inch-square blackboards with crumbs of chalk.

"They know their lessons very well, and are as still as mice. We make a great racket at our school, and get bad marks every day. I shall tell the girls they had better mind what they do, or their dolls will be better scholars than they are," said Effie, much impressed, as she peeped in and saw no rod in the hand of the little mistress, who looked up and shook her head at the intruder, as if begging her to go away before the order of the school was disturbed.

Effie retired at once, but could not resist one look in at the window of a fine mansion, where the family were at dinner, the children behaved so well at table, and never grumbled a bit when their mamma said they could not have any more fruit.

"Now, show me something else," she said, as they came again to the low door that led out of Doll-land.

"You have seen how we prepare for Christmas; let me show you where we love best to send our good and happy gifts," answered the spirit, giving her his hand again.

"I know. I've seen ever so many," began Effie, thinking of her own Christmases.

"No, you have never seen what I will show you. Come away, and remember what you see to-night."

Like a flash that bright world vanished, and Effie found herself in a part of the city she had never seen before. It was far away from the gayer places, where every store was brilliant with lights and full of pretty things, and every house wore a festival air, while people hurried to and fro with merry greetings. It was down among the dingy streets where the poor lived, and where there was no making ready for Christmas.

Hungry women looked in at the shabby shops, longing to buy meat and bread, but empty pockets forbade. Tipsy men drank up their wages in the bar-rooms; and in many cold dark chambers little children huddled under the thin blankets, trying to forget their misery in sleep.

No nice dinners filled the air with savory smells, no gay trees dropped toys and bonbons into eager hands, no little stockings hung in rows beside the chimney-piece ready to be filled, no happy sounds of music, gay voices, and dancing feet were heard; and there were no signs of Christmas anywhere.

"Don't they have any in this place?" asked Effie, shivering, as she held fast the spirit's hand, following where he led her.

"We come to bring it. Let me show you our best workers." And the spirit pointed to some sweet-faced men and women who came stealing into the poor houses, working such beautiful miracles that Effie could only stand and watch.

Some slipped money into the empty pockets, and sent the happy mothers to buy all the comforts they needed; others led the drunken men out of temptation, and took them home to find safer pleasures there. Fires were kindled on cold hearths, tables spread as if by magic, and warm clothes wrapped round shivering limbs. Flowers suddenly bloomed in the chambers of the sick; old people found themselves remembered; sad hearts were consoled by a tender word, and wicked ones softened by the story of Him who forgave all sin.

But the sweetest work was for the children; and Effie held her breath to watch these human fairies hang up and fill the little stockings without which a child's Christmas is not perfect, putting in things that once she would have thought very humble presents, but which now seemed beautiful and precious because these poor babies had nothing.

"That is so beautiful! I wish I could make merry Christmases as these good people do, and be loved and thanked as they are," said Effie, softly, as she watched the busy men and women do their work and steal away without thinking of any reward but their own satisfaction.

"You can if you will. I have shown you the way. Try it, and

see how happy your own holiday will be hereafter."

As he spoke, the spirit seemed to put his arms about her, and vanished with a kiss.

"Oh, stay and show me more!" cried Effie, trying to hold him fast.

"Darling, wake up, and tell me why you are smiling in your sleep," said a voice in her ear; and opening her eyes, there was mamma bending over her, and morning sunshine streaming into the room.

"Are they all gone? Did you hear the bells? Wasn't it splendid?" she asked, rubbing her eyes, and looking about her for the pretty child who was so real and sweet.

"You have been dreaming at a great rate,—talking in your sleep, laughing, and clapping your hands as if you were cheering some one. Tell me what was so splendid," said mamma, smoothing the tumbled hair and lifting up the sleepy head.

Then, while she was being dressed, Effie told her dream, and Nursey thought it very wonderful; but mamma smiled to see how curiously things the child had thought, read, heard, and seen through the day were mixed up in her sleep.

"The spirit said I could work lovely miracles if I tried; but I don't know how to begin, for I have no magic candle to make feasts appear, and light up groves of Christmas trees, as he did," said Effie, sorrowfully.

"Yes, you have. We will do it! we will do it!" And clapping her hands, mamma suddenly began to dance all over the room as if she had lost her wits.

"How? how? You must tell me, mamma," cried Effie, dancing after her, and ready to believe anything possible when she remembered the adventures of the past night.

"I've got it! I've got it!—the new idea. A splendid one, if

I can only carry it out!" And mamma waltzed the little girl round till her curls flew wildly in the air, while Nursey laughed as if she would die.

"Tell me! tell me!" shrieked Effie.

"No, no; it is a surprise,—a grand surprise for Christmas day!" sung mamma, evidently charmed with her happy thought. "Now, come to breakfast; for we must work like bees if we want to play spirits to-morrow. You and Nursey will go out shopping, and get heaps of things, while I arrange matters behind the scenes."

They were running downstairs as mamma spoke, and Effie called out breathlessly,—

"It won't be a surprise; for I know you are going to ask some poor children here, and have a tree or something. It won't be like my dream; for they had ever so many trees, and more children than we can find anywhere."

"There will be no tree, no party, no dinner, in this house at all, and no presents for you. Won't that be a surprise?" And mamma laughed at Effie's bewildered face.

"Do it. I shall like it, I think; and I won't ask any questions, so it will all burst upon me when the time comes," she said; and she ate her breakfast thoughtfully, for this really would be a new sort of Christmas.

All that morning Effie trotted after Nursey in and out of shops, buying dozens of barking dogs, woolly lambs, and squeaking birds; tiny tea-sets, gay picture-books, mittens and hoods, dolls and candy. Parcel after parcel was sent home; but when Effie returned she saw no trace of them, though she peeped everywhere. Nursey chuckled, but wouldn't give a hint, and went out again in the afternoon with a long list of more things to buy; while Effie wandered forlornly about the house, missing the usual merry stir that went before the Christmas dinner and the evening fun.

As for mamma, she was quite invisible all day, and came in at night so tired that she could only lie on the sofa to rest, smiling as if some very pleasant thought made her happy in spite of weariness.

"Is the surprise going on all right?" asked Effie, anxiously; for it seemed an immense time to wait till another evening came.

"Beautifully! better than I expected; for several of my good friends are helping, or I couldn't have done it as I wish. I know you will like it, dear, and long remember this new way of making Christmas merry."

Mamma gave her a very tender kiss, and Effie went to bed.

THE NEXT DAY was a very strange one; for when she woke there was no stocking to examine, no pile of gifts under her napkin, no one said "Merry Christmas!" to her, and the dinner was just as usual to her. Mamma vanished again, and Nursey kept wiping her eyes and saying: "The dear things! It's the prettiest idea I ever heard of. No one but your blessed ma could have done it."

"Do stop, Nursey, or I shall go crazy because I don't know the secret!" cried Effie, more than once; and she kept her eye on the clock, for at seven in the evening the surprise was to come off.

The longed-for hour arrived at last, and the child was too excited to ask questions when Nurse put on her cloak and hood, led her to the carriage, and they drove away, leaving their house the one dark and silent one in the row.

"I feel like the girls in the fairy tales who are led off to strange places and see fine things," said Effie, in a whisper, as they jingled through the gay streets.

"Ah, my deary, it *is* like a fairy tale, I do assure you, and you *will* see finer things than most children will to-night. Steady, now, and do just as I tell you, and don't say one word whatever you see," answered Nursey, quite quivering with excitement as she patted a large box in her lap, and nodded and laughed with twinkling eyes.

They drove into a dark yard, and Effie was led through a back door to a little room, where Nurse coolly proceeded to take off not only her cloak and hood, but her dress and shoes also. Effie stared and bit her lips, but kept still until out of the box came a little white fur coat and boots, a wreath of holly leaves and berries, and a candle with a frill of gold paper round it. A long "Oh!" escaped her then; and when she was dressed and saw herself in the glass she started back, exclaiming, "Why, Nursey, I look like the spirit in my dream!"

"So you do; and that's the part you are to play, my pretty! Now whist, while I blind your eyes and put you in your place."

"Shall I be afraid?" whispered Effie, full of wonder; for as they went out she heard the sound of many voices, the tramp of many feet, and, in spite of the bandage, was sure a great light shone upon her when she stopped.

"You needn't be; I shall stand close by, and your ma will be there."

After the handkerchief was tied about her eyes, Nurse led Effie up some steps, and placed her on a high platform, where something like leaves touched her head, and the soft snap of lamps seemed to fill the air.

Music began as soon as Nurse clapped her hands, the voices outside sounded nearer, and the tramp was evidently coming up the stairs.

"Now, my precious, look and see how you and your dear

ma have made a merry Christmas for them that needed it!"

Off went the bandage; and for a minute Effie really did think she was asleep again, for she actually stood in "a grove of Christmas trees," all gay and shining as in her vision. Twelve on a side, in two rows down the room, stood the little pines, each on its low table; and behind Effie a taller one rose to the roof, hung with wreaths of popcorn, apples, oranges, horns of candy, and cakes of all sorts, from sugary hearts to gingerbread Jumbos. On the smaller trees she saw many of her own discarded toys and those Nursey bought, as well as heaps that seemed to have rained down straight from that delightful Christmas country where she felt as if she was again.

"How splendid! Who is it for? What is that noise? Where is mamma?" cried Effie[1], pale with pleasure and surprise, as she stood looking down the brilliant little street from her high place.

Before Nurse could answer, the doors at the lower end flew open, and in marched twenty-four little blue-gowned orphan girls, singing sweetly, until amazement changed the song to cries of joy and wonder as the shining spectacle appeared. While they stood staring with round eyes at the wilderness of pretty things about them, mamma stepped up beside Effie, and holding her hand fast to give her courage, told the story of the dream in a few simple words, ending in this way:—

"So my little girl wanted to be a Christmas spirit too, and make this a happy day for those who had not as many pleasures and comforts as she has. She likes surprises, and we planned this for you all. She shall play the good fairy, and give each of you something from this tree, after which every one will find her own name on a small tree, and can go to enjoy it in her own way. March by, my dears, and let us fill your hands."

Nobody told them to do it, but all the hands were clapped heartily before a single child stirred; then one by one they came to look up wonderingly at the pretty giver of the feast as she leaned down to offer them great yellow oranges, red apples, bunches of grapes, bonbons, and cakes, till all were gone, and a double row of smiling faces turned toward her as the children filed back to their places in the orderly way they had been taught.

Then each was led to her own tree by the good ladies who had helped mamma with all their hearts; and the happy hubbub that arose would have satisfied even Santa Claus himself,—shrieks of joy, dances of delight, laughter and tears (for some tender little things could not bear so much pleasure at once, and sobbed with mouths full of candy and hands full of toys). How they ran to show one another the new treasures! how they peeped and tasted, pulled and pinched, until the air was full of queer noises, the floor covered with papers, and the little trees left bare of all but candles!

"I don't think heaven can be any gooder than this," sighed one small girl, as she looked about her in a blissful maze, holding her full apron with one hand, while she luxuriously carried sugar-plums to her mouth with the other.

"Is that a truly angel up there?" asked another, fascinated by the little white figure with the wreath on its shining hair, who in some mysterious way had been the cause of all this merry-making.

"I wish I dared to go and kiss her for this splendid party," said a lame child, leaning on her crutch, as she stood near the steps, wondering how it seemed to sit in a mother's lap, as Effie was doing, while she watched the happy scene before her.

Effie heard her, and remembering Tiny Tim, ran down and put her arms about the pale child, kissing the wistful face, as she said sweetly, "You may; but mamma deserves the thanks. She did it all; I only dreamed about it."

Lame Katy felt as if "a truly angel" was embracing her, and could only stammer out her thanks, while the other children ran to see the pretty spirit, and touch her soft dress, until she stood in a crowd of blue gowns laughing as they held up their gifts for her to see and admire.

Mamma leaned down and whispered one word to the older girls; and suddenly they all took hands to dance round Effie, singing as they skipped.

It was a pretty sight, and the ladies found it hard to break up the happy revel; but it was late for small people, and too much fun is a mistake. So the girls fell into line, and marched before Effie and mamma again, to say good-night with such grateful little faces that the eyes of those who looked grew dim with tears. Mamma kissed every one; and many a hungry childish heart felt as if the touch of those tender lips was their best gift. Effie shook so many small hands that her own tingled; and when Katy came she pressed a small doll into Effie's hand, whispering, "You didn't have a single present, and we had lots. Do keep that; it's the prettiest thing I got."

"I will," answered Effie, and held it fast until the last smiling face was gone, the surprise all over, and she safe in her own bed, too tired and happy for anything but sleep.

"Mamma, it *was* a beautiful surprise, and I thank you so much! I don't see how you did it; but I like it best of all the Christmases I ever had, and mean to make one every year.

I had my splendid big present, and here is the dear little one to keep for love of poor Katy; so even that part of my wish came true."

And Effie fell asleep with a happy smile on her lips, her one humble gift still in her hand, and a new love for Christmas in her heart that never changed through a long life spent in doing good.

16
Kate's Choice

"WELL, WHAT DO you think of her?"

"I think she's a perfect dear, and not a bit stuck up with all her money."

"A real little lady, and ever so pretty."

"She kissed me lots, and doesn't tell me to run away, so I love her."

The group of brothers and sisters standing round the fire laughed as little May finished the chorus of praise with these crowning virtues.

Tall Alf asked the question, and seemed satisfied with the general approval of the new cousin just come from England to live with them. They had often heard of Kate, and rather prided themselves on the fact that she lived in a fine house, was very rich, and sent them charming presents. Now pity was added to the pride, for Kate was an orphan, and all her money could not buy back the parents she had lost. They had watched impatiently for her arrival, had welcomed her cordially, and after a day spent in trying to make her feel at home they were comparing notes in the twilight, while Kate was having a quiet talk with Mamma.

"I hope she will choose to live with us. You know she can go to any of the uncles she likes best," said Alf.

"We are nearer her age than any of the other cousins, and Papa is the oldest uncle, so I guess she will," added Milly, the fourteen-year-old daughter of the house.

"She said she liked America," said quiet Frank.

"Wonder if she will give us a lot of her money?" put in practical Fred, who was always in debt.

"Stop that!" commanded Alf. "Mind now, if you ever ask her for a penny I'll shake you out of your jacket."

"Hush! She's coming," cried Milly, and a dead silence followed the lively chatter.

A fresh-faced bright-eyed girl of fifteen came quietly in, glanced at the group on the rug, and paused as if doubtful whether she was wanted.

"Come on!" said Fred, encouragingly.

"Shall I be in the way?"

"Oh! Dear, no, we were only talking," answered Milly, drawing her cousin nearer with an arm about her waist.

"It sounded like something pleasant," said Kate, not exactly knowing what to say.

"We were talking about you," began little May, when a poke from Frank made her stop to ask, "What's that for? We *were* talking about Kate, and we all said we liked her, so it's no matter if I do tell."

"You are very kind," and Kate looked so pleased that the children forgave May's awkward frankness.

"Yes, and we hoped you'd like us and stay with us," said Alf, in the lofty and polite manner which he thought became the young lord of the house.

"I am going to try all the uncles in turn, and then decide; Papa wished it," answered Kate, with a sudden tremble of the lips, for her father was the only parent she could remember, and had been unusually dear for that reason.

"Can you play billiards?" asked Fred, who had a horror of seeing girls cry.

"Yes, and I'll teach you."

"You had a pony-carriage at your house, didn't you?" added Frank, eager to help on the good work.

"At Grandma's—I had no other home, you know," answered Kate.

"What shall you buy first with your money?" asked May, who *would* ask improper questions.

"I'd buy a grandma if I could," and Kate both smiled and sighed.

"How funny! We've got one somewhere, but we don't care much about her," continued May, with the inconvenient candor of a child.

"Have you? Where is she?" and Kate turned quickly, looking full of interest.

"Papa's mother is very old, and lives ever so far away in the country, so of course we don't see much of her," explained Alf.

"But Papa writes sometimes, and Mamma sends her things every Christmas. We don't remember her much, because we never saw her but once, ever so long ago; but we do care for her, and May mustn't say such rude things," said Milly.

"I shall go and see her. I can't get on without a grandmother," and Kate smiled so brightly that the lads thought her prettier than ever. "Tell me more about her. Is she a dear old lady?"

"Don't know. She is lame, and lives in the old house, and has a maid named Dolly, and—that's all I can tell you about her," and Milly looked a little vexed that she could say no more on the subject that seemed to interest her cousin so much.

Kate looked surprised, but said nothing, and stood looking at the fire as if turning the matter over in her mind, and trying to answer the question she was too polite to ask—how could they live without a grandmother? Here the tea-bell rang, and the flock ran laughing downstairs; but, though she said no more, Kate remembered that conversation, and laid a plan in her resolute little mind which she carried out when the time came.

According to her father's wish she lived for a while in the family of each of the four uncles before she decided with which she would make her home. All were anxious to have her, one because of her money, another because her great-grandfather had been a lord, a third hoped to secure her for his son, while the fourth and best family loved her for herself alone. They were worthy people, as the world goes—busy, ambitious, and prosperous; and everyone, old and young, was fond of bright, pretty, generous Kate. Each family was anxious to keep her, a little jealous of the rest, and very eager to know which she would choose.

But Kate surprised them all by saying decidedly when the time came:

"I must see Grandma before I choose. Perhaps I ought to have visited her first, as she is the oldest. I think Papa would wish me to do it. At any rate, I want to pay my duty to her before I settle anywhere, so please let me go."

Some of the young cousins laughed at the idea, and her old-fashioned, respectful way of putting it, which contrasted strongly with their free-and-easy American speech. The uncles were surprised, but agreed to humor her whim, and Uncle George, the eldest, said softly:

"I ought to have remembered that poor Anna was

Mother's only daughter, and the old lady would naturally love to see the girl. But, my dear, it will be desperately dull. Only two old women and a quiet country town. No fun, no company, you won't stay long."

"I shall not mind the dullness if Grandma likes to have me there. I lived very quietly in England, and was never tired of it. Nursey can take care of me, and I think the sight of me will do the dear old lady good, because they tell me I am like Mamma."

Something in the earnest young face reminded Uncle George of the sister he had almost forgotten, and recalled his own youth so pleasantly that he said, with a caress of the curly head beside him:

"So it would, I'm sure of it, and I've a great mind to go with you and 'pay my duty' to Mother, as you prettily express it."

"Oh, no, please don't, sir; I want to surprise her, and have her all to myself for a little while. Would you mind if I went quite alone with Nursey? You can come later."

"Not a bit; you shall do as you like, and make sunshine for the old lady as you have for us. I haven't seen her for a year, but I know she is well and comfortable, and Dolly guards her like a dragon. Give her my love, Kitty, and tell her I send her something she will value a hundred times more than the very best tea, the finest cap, or the handsomest tabby that ever purred."

So, in spite of the lamentations of her cousins, Kate went gaily away to find the Grandma whom no one else seemed to value as she did.

You see, Grandpa had been a farmer, and lived contentedly on the old place until he died; but his four sons wanted to be something better, so they went away one after the other to make their way in the world. All worked hard, got rich, lived splendidly, and forgot as far as possible the old life and the dull old place they came from. They were good sons in their way, and had each offered his mother a home with him if she cared to come. But Grandma clung to the old home, the simple ways, and quiet life, and, thanking them gratefully, she had remained in the big farmhouse, empty, lonely, and plain though it was, compared to the fine homes of her sons.

Little by little the busy men forgot the quiet, uncomplaining old mother, who spent her years thinking of them, longing to see and know their children, hoping they would one day remember how she loved them all, and how solitary her life must be.

Now and then they wrote or paid her a hasty visit, and all sent gifts of far less value to her than one loving look, one hour of dutiful, affectionate companionship.

"If you ever want me, send and I'll come. Or, if you ever need a home, remember the old place is here always open, and you are always welcome," the good old lady said. But they never seemed to need her, and so seldom came that the old place evidently had no charm for them.

It was hard, but the sweet old woman bore it patiently, and lived her lonely life quietly and usefully, with her faithful maid Dolly to serve and love and support her.

Kate's mother, her one daughter, had married young, gone to England, and, dying early, had left the child to its father and his family. Among them little Kate had grown up, knowing scarcely anything of her American relations until she was left an orphan and went back to her mother's people. She had been the pet of her English grandmother, and, finding all the aunts busy, fashionable women, had longed for the tender fostering she had known, and now felt as if only grandmothers could give.

With a flutter of hope and expectation she approached the old house after the long journey was over. Leaving the luggage at the inn, and accompanied by faithful Nurse, Kate went up the village street, and, pausing at the gate, looked at the home where her mother had been born.

A large, old-fashioned farmhouse, with a hospitable porch and tall trees in front, an orchard behind, and a capital hill for black-berries in summer, and coasting in winter, close by. All the upper windows were curtained, and made the house look as if it was half asleep. At one of the lower windows sat a portly puss, blinking in the sun, and at the other appeared a cap, a regular grandmotherly old cap, with a little black bow perked up behind. Something in the lonely look of the house and the pensive droop of that cap made Katy hurry up the walk and tap eagerly at the antique knocker. A brisk little old woman peered out, as if startled at the sound, and Kate asked, smiling, "Does Madam Coverley live here?"

"She does, dear. Walk right in," and throwing wide the door, the maid trotted down a long, wide hall, and announced in a low tone to her mistress:

"A nice, pretty little girl wants to see you, mum."

"I shall love to see a young face. Who is it, Dolly?" asked a pleasant voice.

"Don't know, mum."

"Grandma must guess," and Kate went straight up to the old lady with both hands out, for the first sight of that sweet old face won her heart.

Lifting her spectacles, Grandma looked silently a minute, then opened her arms without a word, and in the long embrace that followed Kate felt assured that she was welcome to the home she wanted.

"So like my Anna! And this is her little girl? God bless

you, my darling! So good to come and see me!" said the old lady when she could speak.

"Why, Grandma, I couldn't get on without you, and as soon as I knew where to find you I was in a fidget to be off; but had to do my other visits first, because the uncles had planned it so. This is Dolly, I am sure, and that is my good nurse. Go and get my things, please, Nursey. I shall stay here until Grandma sends me away."

"That will never be, dearie. Now tell me everything. It is like an angel coming to see me all of a sudden. Sit close, and let me feel sure it isn't one of the dreams I make to cheer myself when I'm lonesome."

Kate sat on a little stool at Grandma's feet, and, leaning on her knee, told all her little story, while the old lady fed her hungry eyes with the sight of the fresh young face, listened to the music of a loving voice, and felt the happy certainty that someone had remembered her, as she longed to be remembered.

Such a happy day as Kate spent talking and listening, looking at her new home, which she found delightful, and being petted by the two old women, who would hardly let Nursey do anything for her. Kate's quick eyes read the truth of Grandma's lonely life very soon; her warm heart was full of tender pity, and she resolved to devote herself to making the happiness of the dear old lady's few remaining years, for at eighty one should have the prop of loving children, if ever.

To Dolly and madam it really did seem as if an angel had come, a singing, smiling, chattering sprite, who danced all over the old house, making blithe echoes in the silent rooms, and brightening every corner she entered.

Kate opened all the shutters and let in the sun, saying she must see which room she liked best before she settled.

She played on the old piano, that wheezed and jangled, all out of tune; but no one minded, for the girlish voice was as sweet as a lark's. She invaded Dolly's sacred kitchen, and messed to her heart's content, delighting the old soul by praises of her skill, and petitions to be taught all she knew. She pranced to and fro in the long hall, and got acquainted with the lives of painted ancestors hanging there in big wigs or short-waisted gowns. She took possession of Grandma's little parlor, and made it so cozy the old lady felt as if she was bewitched, for cushioned armchairs, fur footstools, soft rugs, and delicate warm shawls appeared like magic. Flowers bloomed in the deep, sunny window-seats, pictures of lovely places seemed to break out on the oaken walls, a dainty work-basket took its place near Grandma's quaint one, and, best of all, the little chair beside her own was seldom empty now.

The first thing in the morning a kiss waked her, and the beloved voice gave her a gay "Good morning, Grandma dear!" All day Anna's child hovered about her with willing hands and feet to serve her, loving heart to return her love, and the tender reverence which is the beautiful tribute the young should pay the old. In the twilight, the bright head always was at her knees; and, in either listening to the stories of the past or making lively plans for the future, Kate whiled away the time that used to be so sad.

Kate never found it lonely, seldom wished for other society, and grew every day more certain that here she could find the cherishing she needed, and do the good she hoped.

Dolly and Nurse got on capitally; each tried which could sing "Little Missy's" praises loudest, and spoil her quickest by unquestioning obedience to every whim or wish. A happy family, and the dull November days went by so fast that Christmas was at hand before they knew it.

All the uncles had written to ask Kate to pass the holidays with them, feeling sure she must be longing for a change. But she had refused them all, saying she should stay with Grandma, who could not go anywhere to join other people's merrymakings, and must have one of her own at home. The uncles urged, the aunts advised, and the cousins teased; but Kate denied them all, yet offended no one, for she was inspired by a grand idea, and carried it out with help from Dolly and Nurse, unsuspected by Grandma.

"We are going to have a little Christmas fun up here among ourselves, and you mustn't know about it until we are ready. So just sit all cozy in your corner, and let me riot about as I like. I know you won't mind, and I think you'll say it is splendid when I've carried out my plan," said Kate, when the old lady wondered what she was thinking about so deeply, with her brows knit and her lips smiling.

"Very well, dear, do anything you like, and I shall enjoy it, only don't get tired, or try to do too much," and with that Grandma became deaf and blind to the mysteries that went on about her.

She was lame, and seldom left her own rooms; so Kate, with her devoted helpers, turned the house topsy-turvy, trimmed up hall and parlors and great dining room with shining holly and evergreen, laid fires ready for kindling on the hearths that had been cold for years, and had beds made up all over the house.

What went on in the kitchen, only Dolly could tell; but such delicious odors as stole out made Grandma sniff the air, and think of merry Christmas revels long ago. Up in her own room Kate wrote lots of letters, and sent orders to the city that made Nursey hold up her hands. More letters came in reply, and Kate had a rapture over every one. Big bundles were left by the express, who came so often that the gates were opened and the lawn soon full of sleigh tracks. The shops in the village were ravaged by Mistress Kate, who laid in stores of gay ribbons, toys, nuts, and all manner of queer things.

"I really think she's lost her mind," said the postmaster as she flew out of the office one day with a handful of letters.

"Pretty critter! I wouldn't say a word against her, not for a mint of money. She's so good to old Mrs. Coverley," answered his fat wife, smiling as she watched Kate ride up the village street on an ox-sled.

If Grandma had thought the girl out of her wits, no one could have blamed her, for on Christmas day she really did behave in the most singular manner.

"You are going to church with me this morning, Grandma. It's all arranged. A closed carriage is coming for us, the sleighing is lovely, the church all trimmed up, and I must have you see it. I shall wrap you in fur, and we will go and say our prayers together, like good girls, won't we?" said Kate, who was in a queer flutter, while her eyes shone, her lips were all smiles, and her feet kept dancing in spite of her.

"Anywhere you like, my darling. I'd start for Australia tomorrow, if you wanted me to go with you," answered Grandma, who obeyed Kate in all things, and seemed to think she could do no wrong.

So they went to church, and Grandma did enjoy it; for she had many blessings to thank God for, chief among them the treasure of a dutiful, loving child. Kate tried to keep herself quiet, but the odd little flutter would not subside, and seemed to get worse and worse as time went on. It increased rapidly as they drove home, and, when Grandma was safe in her little parlor again, Kate's hands trembled so she could hardly tie the strings of the old lady's state and festival cap.

"We must take a look at the big parlor. It is all trimmed up, and I've got my presents in there. Is it ready, Doll?" asked Kate, as the old servant appeared, looking so excited that Grandma said, laughing:

"We have been quiet so long, poor Dolly don't know what to make of a little gaiety."

"Lord bless us, my dear mum! It's all so beautiful and kinder surprisin', I feel as ef merrycles had come to pass agin," answered Dolly, actually wiping away tears with her best white apron.

"Come, Grandma," and Kate offered her arm. "Don't she look sweet and dear?" she added, smoothing the soft, silken shawl about the old lady's shoulders, and kissing the placid old face that beamed at her from under the new cap.

"I always said madam was the finest old lady a-goin', ef folks only knew it. Now, Missy, ef you don't make haste, that parlor door will bust open, and spoil the surprise; for they are just boilin' over in there," with which mysterious remark Dolly vanished, giggling.

Across the hall they went, but at the door Kate paused, and said with a look Grandma never forgot:

"I hope I have done right. I hope you'll like my present, and not find it too much for you. At any rate, remember I meant to please you and give you the thing you need and long for most, my dear old Grandma."

"My good child, don't be afraid. I shall like anything you do, and thank you for your thought of me. What a curious noise! I hope the fire hasn't fallen down."

Without another word, Kate threw open the door and led Grandma in. Only a step or two—for the old lady stopped short and stared about her, as if she didn't know her own best parlor. No wonder she didn't, for it was full of people, and such people! All her sons, their wives and children, rose as she came in, and turned to greet her with smiling faces. Uncle George went up and kissed her, saying, with a choke in his voice, "A merry Christmas, Mother!" and everybody echoed the words in a chorus of goodwill that went straight to the heart.

Poor Grandma could not bear it, and sat down in her big chair, trembling, and sobbing like a little child. Kate hung over her, fearing the surprise had been too much; but joy seldom kills, and presently the old lady was calm enough to look up and welcome them all by stretching out her feeble hands and saying, brokenly yet heartily:

"God bless you, my children! This *is* a merry Christmas, indeed! Now tell me all about it, and who everybody is; for I don't know half the little ones."

Then Uncle George explained that it was Kate's plan, and told how she had made everyone agree to it, pleading so eloquently for Grandma that all other plans were given up. They had arrived while she was at church, and had been with difficulty kept from bursting out before the time.

"Do you like your present?" whispered Kate, quite calm and happy now that the grand surprise was safely over.

Grandma answered with a silent kiss that said more than the warmest words, and then Kate put everyone at ease by leading up the children, one by one, and introducing each with some lively speech. Everybody enjoyed this and got acquainted quickly; for Grandma thought the children the most remarkable she had ever seen, and the little people soon made up their minds that an old lady who had such a very nice, big house, and such a dinner waiting for them (of course they had peeped everywhere), was a most desirable and charming Grandma.

By the time the first raptures were over, Dolly and Nurse and Betsey Jane (a girl hired for the occasion) had got dinner on the table; and the procession, headed by Madam proudly escorted by her eldest son, filed into the dining room where such a party had not met for years.

It would be quite impossible to do justice to that dinner: pen and ink are not equal to it. I can only say that everyone partook copiously of everything; that they laughed and talked, told stories, and sang songs; and when no one could do any more, Uncle George proposed Grandma's health, which was drunk standing, and followed by three cheers. Then up got the old lady, quite rosy and young, excited and gay, and said in a clear strong voice—

"I give you in return the best of grandchildren, little Kate."

I give you my word the cheer they gave Grandma was nothing to the shout that followed these words; for the old lady led off with amazing vigor, and the boys roared so tremendously that the sedate tabby in the kitchen flew off her cushion, nearly frightened into a fit.

After that, the elders sat with Grandma in the parlor, while the younger part of the flock trooped after Kate all over the house. Fires burned everywhere, and the long unused toys of their fathers were brought out for their amusement. The big nursery was full of games, and here Nursey collected the little ones when the larger boys and girls were invited by Kate to go out and coast. Sleds had been provided, and until dusk they kept it up, the city girls getting as gay and rosy as Kate herself in this healthy sport, while the lads frolicked to their hearts' content, building snow forts, pelting one another, and carousing generally without any policeman to interfere or any stupid old ladies to get upset, as at home in the park.

A cozy tea and a dance in the long hall followed, and they were just thinking what they would do next, when Kate's second surprise came.

There were two great fireplaces in the hall: up the chimney of one roared a jolly fire, but the other was closed by a tall fire-board. As they sat about, resting after a brisk contra dance, a queer rustling and tapping was heard behind this fire-board.

"Rats!" suggested the girls, jumping up into the chairs.

"Let's have 'em out!" added the boys, making straight for the spot, intent on fun.

But before they got there, a muffled voice cried, "Stand from under!" and down went the board with a crash, out bounced Santa Claus, startling the lads as much as the rumor of rats had the girls.

A jolly old saint he was, all in fur, with sleigh-bells jingling from his waist and the point of his high cap, big boots, a white beard, and a nose as red as if Jack Frost had had a good tweak at it. Giving himself a shake that set all the bells ringing, he stepped out upon the hearth, saying in a half-gruff, half-merry tone:

"I call this a most inhospitable way to receive me! What do you mean by stopping up my favorite chimney? Never mind, I'll forgive you, for this is an unusual occasion. Here, some of you fellows, lend a hand and help me out with my sack."

A dozen pair of hands had the great bag out in a minute, and, lugging it to the middle of the hall, left it beside St. Nick, while the boys fell back into the eager, laughing crowd that surrounded the newcomer.

"Where's my girl? I want my Kate," said the saint, and when she went to him he took a base advantage of his years, and kissed her in spite of the beard.

"That's not fair," whispered Kate, as rosy as the holly berries in her hair.

"Can't help it—must have some reward for sticking in that horrid chimney so long," answered Santa Claus, looking as roguish as any boy. Then he added aloud, "I've got something for everybody, so make a big ring, and the good fairy will hand round the gifts."

With that he dived into his bag and brought out treasure after treasure, some fine, some funny, many useful, and all appropriate, for the good fairy seemed to have guessed what each one wanted. Shouts of laughter greeted the droll remarks of the jolly saint, for he had a joke about everything, and people were quite exhausted by the time the bottom of the sack was reached.

"Now, then, a rousing good game of blind man's buff, and then this little family must go to bed, for it's past eleven."

As he spoke, the saint cast off his cap and beard, fur coat, and big boots, and proceeded to dance a double shuffle with great vigor and skill; while the little ones, who had been thoroughly mystified, shouted, "Why, it's Alf!" and fell upon him *en masse* as the best way of expressing their delight at his successful performance of that immortal part.

The game of blind man's buff that followed was a "rouser" in every sense of the word, for the gentlemen joined, and the children flew about like a flock of chickens when hawks are abroad. Such peals of laughter, such shouts of fun, and such racing and scrambling that old hall had never seen before. Kate was so hunted that she finally took refuge behind Grandma's chair, and stood there looking at the lively scene, her face full of happiness as she remembered that it was her work.

The going to bed that night was the best joke of all; for, though Kate's arrangements were peculiar, everyone voted that they were capital. There were many rooms, but not enough for all to have one apiece. So the uncles and aunts had the four big chambers, all the boys were ordered into the great playroom, where beds were made on the floor, and a great fire blazing that the camping out might be as comfortable as possible. The nursery was devoted to the girls, and the little ones were sprinkled round wherever a snug corner was found.

How the riotous flock were ever got into their beds no one knows. The lads caroused until long past midnight, and no knocking on the walls of paternal boots, or whispered entreaties of maternal voices through keyholes, had any effect, for it was impossible to resist the present advantages for a grand Christmas rampage.

The girls giggled and gossiped, told secrets, and laid plans more quietly; while the small things tumbled into bed, and went to sleep at once, quite used up with the festivities of this remarkable day.

Grandma, down in her own cozy room, sat listening to the blithe noises with a smile on her face, for the past seemed to have come back again, and her own boys and girls to be frolicking above there, as they used to do forty years ago.

"It's all so beautiful I can't go to bed, Dolly, and lose any of it. They'll go away tomorrow, and I may never see them any more," she said, as Dolly tied on her nightcap and brought her slippers.

"Yes, you will, mum. That dear child has made it so pleasant they can't keep away. You'll see plenty of 'em, if they carry out half the plans they have made. Mrs. George wants to come up and pass the summer here; Mr. Tom says he shall send his boys to school here, and every girl among them has promised Kate to make her a long visit. The thing is done, mum, and you'll never be lonely any more."

"Thank God for that!" and Grandma bent her head as if she had received a great blessing. "Dolly, I want to go and look at those children. It seems so like a dream to have them here, I must be sure of it," said Grandma, folding her wrapper about her, and getting up with great decision.

"Massy on us, mum, you haven't been up them stairs for months. The dears are all right, warm as toasts, and sleepin' like dormice, I'll warrant," answered Dolly, taken aback at this new whim of old madam's.

But Grandma would go, so Dolly gave her an arm, and together the two old friends hobbled up the wide stairs, and peeped in at the precious children. The lads looked like a camp of weary warriors reposing after a victory, and Grandma went laughing away when she had taken a proud survey of this promising portion of the rising generation. The nursery was like a little convent full of rosy nuns sleeping peacefully; while a pictured Saint Agnes, with her lamb, smiled on them from the wall, and the firelight flickered over the white figures and sweet faces, as if the sight were too fair to be lost in darkness. The little ones lay about promiscuously, looking like dissipated Cupids with sugar hearts and faded roses still clutched in their chubby hands.

"My darlings!" whispered Grandma, lingering fondly over them to cover a pair of rosy feet, put back a pile of tumbled curls, or kiss a little mouth still smiling in its sleep.

But when she came to the coldest corner of the room, where Kate lay on the hardest mattress, under the thinnest quilt, the old lady's eyes were full of tender tears; and, forgetting the stiff joints that bent so painfully, she knelt slowly down, and, putting her arms about the girl, blessed her in silence for the happiness she had given one old heart.

Kate woke at once, and started up, exclaiming with a smile:

"Why, Grandma, I was dreaming about an angel, and you look like one with your white gown and silvery hair!"

"No, dear, you are the angel in this house. How can I ever give you up?" answered madam, holding fast the treasure that came to her so late.

"You never need to, Grandma, for I have made my choice."

17

Mrs. Podgers' Teapot

"AH, DEAR ME, dear me, I'm a deal too comfortable!" Judging from appearances, Mrs. Podgers certainly had some cause for that unusual exclamation. To begin with, the room was comfortable. It was tidy, bright, and warm; full of cosy corners and capital contrivances for quiet enjoyment. The chairs seemed to extend their plump arms invitingly; the old-fashioned sofa was so hospitable, that whoever sat down upon it was slow to get up; the pictures, though portraits, did not stare one out of countenance, but surveyed the scene with an air of tranquil enjoyment; and the unshuttered windows allowed the cheery light to shine out into the snowy street through blooming screens of Christmas roses and white chrysanthemums.

The fire was comfortable; for it was neither hidden in a stove nor imprisoned behind bars, but went rollicking up the wide chimney with a jovial roar. It flickered over the supper-table as if curious to discover what savory viands were concealed under the shining covers. It touched up the old portraits till they seemed to wink; it covered the walls with comical shadows, as if the portly chairs had set their arms akimbo and were dancing a jig; it flashed out into the street with a voiceless greeting to every passer-by; it kindled mimic fires in the brass andirons and the teapot simmering on the hob, and, best of all, it shone its brightest on Mrs. Podgers, as if conscious that it couldn't do a better thing.

Mrs. Podgers was comfortable as she sat there, buxom, blooming, and brisk, in spite of her forty years and her widow's cap. Her black gown was illuminated to such an extent that it couldn't look sombre; her cap had given up trying to be prim long ago, and cherry ribbons wouldn't have made it more becoming as it set off her crisp black hair, and met in a coquettish bow under her plump chin; her white apron encircled her trim waist, as if conscious of its advantages; and the mourning-pin upon her bosom actually seemed to twinkle with satisfaction at the enviable post it occupied.

The sleek cat, purring on the hearth, was comfortable, so was the agreeable fragrance of muffins that pervaded the air, so was the drowsy tick of the clock in the corner; and if anything was needed to give a finishing touch to the general comfort of the scene, the figure pausing in the doorway supplied the want most successfully.

Heroes are always expected to be young and comely, also fierce, melancholy, or at least what novel-readers call "interesting"; but I am forced to own that my present hero was none of these. Half the real beauty, virtue, and romance of the world gets put into humble souls, hidden in plain bodies. Mr. Jerusalem Turner was an example of this; and, at the risk of shocking my sentimental readers, I must frankly state that he was fifty, stout, and bald, also that he used bad grammar, had a double chin, and was only the Co. in a prosperous grocery store. A hale and hearty old gentleman, with cheerful brown eyes, a ruddy countenance, and curly gray hair sticking up all round his head, with an air of energy and independence that was pleasant to behold. There he stood, beaming upon the unconscious Mrs. Podgers, softly rubbing his hands, and smiling to himself with the air of a man enjoying the chief satisfaction of his life, as he was.

"Ah, dear me, dear me, I'm a deal too comfortable!" sighed Mrs. Podgers, addressing the teapot.

"Not a bit, mum, not a bit."

In walked the gentleman, and up rose the lady, saying, with a start and an aspect of relief,—

"Bless me, I didn't hear you! I began to think you were never coming to your tea, Mr. 'Rusalem."

Everybody called him Mr. 'Rusalem, and many people were ignorant that he had any other name. He liked it, for it began with the children, and the little voices had endeared it to him, not to mention the sound of it from Mrs Podgers' lips for ten years.

"I know I'm late, mum, but I really couldn't help it. To-night's a busy time, and the lads are just good for nothing with their jokes and spirits, so I stayed to steady 'em, and do a little job that turned up unexpected."

"Sit right down and have your tea while you can, then. I've kept it warm for you, and the muffins are done lovely."

Mrs. Podgers bustled about with an alacrity that seemed to give an added relish to the supper; and when her companion was served, she sat smiling at him with her hand on the teapot, ready to replenish his cup before he could ask for it.

"Have things been fretting of you, mum? You looked down-hearted as I came in, and that ain't accordin' to the time of year, which is merry," said Mr. 'Rusalem, stirring his tea with a sense of solid satisfaction that would have sweetened a far less palatable draught.

"It's the teapot; I don't know what's got into it to-night; but, as I was waiting for you, it set me thinking of one thing and another, till I declare I felt as if it had up and spoke to me, showing me how I wasn't grateful enough for my blessings, but a deal more comfortable than I deserved."

While speaking, Mrs. Podgers' eyes rested on an inscription which encircled the corpulent little silver teapot: *"To our Benefactor.—They who give to the poor lend to the Lord."* Now one wouldn't think there was anything in the speech or the inscription to disturb Mr. 'Rusalem; but there seemed to be, for he fidgeted in his chair, dropped his fork, and glanced at the teapot with a very odd expression. It was a capital little teapot, solid, bright as hands could make it, and ornamented with a robust young cherub perched upon the lid, regardless of the warmth of his seat. With her eyes still fixed upon it, Mrs. Podgers continued meditatively,—

"You know how fond I am of the teapot for poor Podgers' sake. I really feel quite superstitious about it; and when thoughts come to me, as I sit watching it, I have faith in them, because they always remind me of the past."

Here, after vain efforts to restrain himself, Mr. 'Rusalem broke into a sudden laugh, so hearty and infectious that Mrs. Podgers couldn't help smiling, even while she shook her head at him.

"I beg pardon, mum, it's hysterical; I'll never do it again," panted Mr. 'Rusalem, as he got his breath, and went soberly on with his supper.

It was a singular fact that whenever the teapot was particularly alluded to he always behaved in this incomprehensible manner,—laughed, begged pardon, said it was hysterical, and promised never to do it again. It used to trouble Mrs. Podgers very much, but she had grown used to it; and having been obliged to overlook many oddities in the departed Podgers, she easily forgave 'Rusalem his only one. After the laugh there was a pause, during which Mrs. Podgers sat absently polishing up the silver cherub, with the memory of the little son who died two Christmases ago lying heavy at her heart, and Mr. 'Rusalem seemed to be turning something over in his mind as he watched a bit of butter sink luxuriously into the warm bosom of a muffin. Once or twice he paused as if listening, several times he stole a look at Mrs. Podgers, and presently said, in a some-what anxious tone,—

"You was saying just now that you was a deal too comfortable, mum; would you wish to be made uncomfortable in order to realize your blessings?"

"Yes, I should. I'm getting lazy, selfish, and forgetful of other folks. You leave me nothing to do, and make everything so easy for me that I'm growing young and giddy again. Now that isn't as it should be, 'Rusalem."

"It meets my views exactly, mum. You've had your hard times, your worryments and cares, and now it's right to take your rest."

"Then why don't you take yours? I'm sure you've earned it drudging thirty years in the store, with more extra work than holidays for your share."

"Oh well, mum, it's different with me, you know. Business is amusing; and I'm so used to it I shouldn't know myself if I was out of the store for good."

"Well, I hope you are saving up something against the time when business won't be amusing. You are so generous, I'm afraid you forget you can't work for other people all your days."

"Yes, mum, I've put by a little sum in a safe bank that pays good interest, and when I'm past work I'll fall back and enjoy it."

To judge from the cheerful content of the old gentleman's face he was enjoying it already, as he looked about
him with the air of a man who had made a capital invest-
ment, and was in the receipt of generous dividends. Seeing
Mrs. Podgers' bright eye fixed upon him, as if she suspected
something, and would have the truth out of him in two
minutes, he recalled the conversation to the point from
which it had wandered.

"If you would like to try how a little misery suits you,
mum, I can accommodate you if you'll step up-stairs."

"Good gracious, what do you mean? Who's up there?
Why didn't you tell me before?" cried Mrs. Podgers, in a
flutter of interest, curiosity, and surprise, as he knew she
would be.

"You see, mum, I was doubtful how you'd like it. I did it
without stopping to think, and then I was afraid you'd consider it a liberty."

Mr. 'Rusalem spoke with some hesitation; but Mrs.
Podgers didn't wait to hear him, for she was already at the
door, lamp in hand, and would have been off had she
known where to go, "up-stairs" being a somewhat vague
expression. The old gentleman led the way to the room he
had occupied for thirty years, in spite of Mrs. Podgers'
frequent offers of a better and brighter one. He was
attached to it, small and dark as it was, for the joys and
sorrows of more than half his life had come to him in that
little room, and somehow when he was there it brightened
up amazingly. Mrs. Podgers looked well about her, but saw
nothing new, and her conductor said, as he paused beside
the bed,—

"Let me tell you how I found it before I show it. You see,
mum, I had to step down the street just at dark, and passing the windows I give a glance in, as I've a bad habit of

doing when the lamps is lighted and you a setting there alone. Well, mum, what did I see outside but a ragged little chap a flattening his nose against the glass, and staring in with all his eyes. I didn't blame him much for it, and on I goes without a word. When I came back I see him a lying close to the wall, and mistrusting that he was up to some game that might give you a scare, I speaks to him: he don't answer; I touches him: he don't stir; then I picks him up, and seeing that he's gone in a fit or a faint, I makes for the store with a will. He come to rapid; and finding that he was most froze and starved, I fed and warmed and fixed him a trifle, and then tucked him away here, for he's got no folks to worry for him, and was too used up to go out again to-night. That's the story, mum; and now I'll produce the little chap if I can find him."

With that Mr. 'Rusalem began to grope about the bed, chuckling, yet somewhat anxious, for not a vestige of an occupant appeared, till a dive downward produced a sudden agitation of the clothes, a squeak, and the unexpected appearance out at the foot of the bed of a singular figure, that dodged into a corner, with one arm up, as if to ward off a blow, while a sleepy little voice exclaimed beseechingly, "I'm up, I'm up, don't hit me!"

"Lord love the child, who'd think of doing that! Wake up, Joe, and see your friends," said Mr. 'Rusalem, advancing cautiously.

At the sound of his voice down went the arm, and Mrs. Podgers saw a boy of nine or ten, arrayed in a flannel garment that evidently belonged to Mr. 'Rusalem, for though none too long it was immensely broad, and the voluminous sleeves were pinned up, showing a pair of wasted arms, chapped with cold and mottled with bruises. A large blue sock still covered one foot, the other was bound up as if hurt. A tall cotton nightcap, garnished with a red tassel, looked like a big extinguisher on a small candle; and from under it a pair of dark, hollow eyes glanced sharply with a shrewd, suspicious look, that made the little face more pathetic than the marks of suffering, neglect, and abuse, which told the child's story without words. As if quite reassured by 'Rusalem's presence, the boy shuffled out of his corner, saying coolly, as he prepared to climb into his nest again,—

"I thought it was the old one when you grabbed me. Ain't this bed a first-rater, though?"

Mr. 'Rusalem lifted the composed young personage into the middle of the big bed, where he sat bolt upright, surveying the prospect from under the extinguisher with an equanimity that quite took the good lady's breath away. But Mr. 'Rusalem fell back and pointed to him, saying, "There he is, mum," with as much pride and satisfaction as if he had found some rare and valuable treasure; for the little child was very precious in his sight. Mrs. Podgers really didn't know whether to laugh or cry, and settled the matter by plumping down beside the boy, saying cordially, as she took the grimy little hands into her own,—

"He's heartily welcome, 'Rusalem. Now tell me all about it, my poor dear, and don't be afraid."

"Ho, I ain't afraid a you nor he. I ain't got nothin' to tell, only my name's Joe and I'm sleepy."

"Who is your mother, and where do you live, deary?" asked Mrs. Podgers, haunted with the idea that some woman must be anxious for the child.

"Ain't got any, we don't have 'em where I lives. The old one takes care a me."

"Who is the old one?"

"Granny. I works for her, and she lets me stay alonger her."

"Bless the dear! what work can such a mite do?"

"Heaps a things. I sifs ashes, picks rags, goes beggin', runs arrants, and sometimes the big fellers lets me call papers. That's fun, only I gets knocked round, and it hurts, you'd better believe."

"Did you come here begging, and, being afraid to ring, stand outside looking in at me enjoying myself, like a self-ish creeter as I am?"

"I forgot to ask for the cold vittles a lookin' at warm ones, and thinkin' if they was mine what I'd give the little fellers when I has my tree."

"Your what, child?"

"My Christmas-tree. Look a here, I've got it, and all these to put on it to-morrer."

From under his pillow the boy produced a small branch of hemlock, dropped from some tree on its passage to a gayer festival than little Joe's; also an old handkerchief which contained his treasures,—only a few odds and ends picked up in the streets: a gnarly apple, half-a-dozen nuts, two or three dingy bonbons, gleaned from the sweepings of some store, and a bit of cheese, which last possession he evidently prized highly.

"That's for the old one; she likes it, and I kep it for her,— cause she don't hit so hard when I fetch her goodies. You don't mind, do you?" he said, looking inquiringly at Mr. 'Rusalem, who blew his nose like a trumpet, and patted the big nightcap with a fatherly gesture more satisfactory than words.

"What have you kept for yourself, dear?" asked Mrs. Podgers, with an irrepressible sniff, as she looked at the poor little presents, and remembered that they "didn't have mothers" where the child lived.

"Oh, I had my treat alonger him," said the boy, nodding toward 'Rusalem, and adding enthusiastically, "Wasn't that prime! It was real Christmasy a settin' by the fire, eating lots and not bein' hit."

Here Mrs. Podgers broke down; and, taking the boy in her arms, sobbed over him as if she had found her lost Neddy in this sad shape. The little lad regarded her demonstration with some uneasiness at first, but there is a magic about a genuine woman that wins its way everywhere, and soon the outcast nestled to her, feeling that this wonderful night was getting more "Christmassy" every minute.

Mrs. Podgers was herself again directly; and seeing that the child's eyelids were heavy with weakness and weariness, she made him comfortable among the pillows, and began to sing the lullaby that used to hush her little son to sleep. Mr. 'Rusalem took something from his drawer, and was stealing away, when the child opened his eyes and started up, calling out as he nodded, till the tassel danced on this preposterous cap,—

"I say! good night, good night!"

Looking much gratified, Mr. 'Rusalem returned, shook the little hand extended to him, kissed the grateful face, and went away to sit on the stairs with tear after tear dropping off the end of his nose, as he listened to the voice that, after two years of silence, sung the air this simple soul thought the loveliest in the world. At first, it was more sob than song, but soon the soothing music flowed on unbroken, and the wondering child, for the first time within his memory, fell asleep in the sweet shelter of a woman's arms.

When Mrs. Podgers came out, she found Mr. 'Rusalem

intent on stuffing another parcel into a long gray stocking already full to overflowing.

"For the little chap, mum. He let fall that he'd never done this sort of thing in his life, and as he hadn't any stockings of his own, poor dear, I took the liberty of lending him one of mine," explained Mr. 'Rusalem, surveying the knobby article with evident regret that it wasn't bigger.

Mrs. Podgers said nothing, but looked from the stocking to the fatherly old gentleman who held it; and it is my private belief, that if Mrs. Podgers had obeyed the impulse of her heart, she would have forgotten decorum, and kissed him on the spot. She didn't, however, but went briskly into her own room, whence she presently returned with red eyes, and a pile of small garments in her hands. Having nearly exhausted his pincushion in trying to suspend the heavy stocking, Mr. 'Rusalem had just succeeded as she appeared. He saw what she carried, watched her arrange the little shirt, jacket and trousers, the half-worn shoes and tidy socks, beside the bed, with motherly care, and stand looking at the unconscious child, with an expression which caused Mr. 'Rusalem to dart down stairs, and compose himself by rubbing his hair erect, and shaking his fist in the painted face of the late Podgers.

An hour or two later the store was closed, the room cleared, Mrs. Podgers in her arm-chair on one side of the hearth, with her knitting in her hand, Mr. 'Rusalem in his arm-chair on the other side, with his newspaper on his knee, both looking so cosy and comfortable that any one would have pronounced them a Darby and Joan on the spot. Ah, but they weren't, you see, and that spoilt the illusion, to one party at least. Both were rather silent, both looked thoughtfully at the fire, and the fire gave them both excellent counsel, as it seldom fails to do when it finds any kindred warmth and brightness in the hearts and souls of those who study it. Mrs. Podgers kindled first, and broke out suddenly with a nod of great determination.

"'Rusalem, I'm going to keep that boy if it's possible!"

"You shall, mum, whether it's possible or not," he answered, nodding back at her with equal decision.

"I don't know why I never thought of such a thing before. There's a many children suffering for mothers, and heaven knows I'm wearying for some little child to fill my Neddy's place. I wonder if you didn't think of this when you took that boy in; it would be just like you!"

Mr. 'Rusalem shook his head, but looked so guilty, that Mrs. Podgers was satisfied, called him "a thoughtful dear," within herself, and kindled still more.

"Between you, and Joe, and the teapot, I've got another idea into my stupid head, and I know you won't laugh at it. That loving little soul has tried to get a tree for some poor babies who have no one to think of them but him, and even remembered the old one, who must be a wretch to hit that child, and hit hard, too, I know by the looks of his arms. Well, I've a great longing to go and give him a tree,—a right good one, like those Neddy used to have; to get in the 'little fellers' he tells of, give them a good dinner, and then a regular Christmas frolic. Can't it be done?"

"Nothing could be easier, mum;" and Mr. 'Rusalem, who had been taking counsel with the fire till he quite glowed with warmth and emotion, nodded, smiled, and rubbed his hands, as if Mrs. Podgers had invited him to a Lord Mayor's feast, or some equally gorgeous jollification.

"I suppose it's the day, and thinking of how it came to be, that makes me feel as if I wanted to help everybody, and makes this Christmas so bright and happy that I never can forget it," continued the good woman, with a heartiness that made her honest face quite beautiful to behold.

If Mrs. Podgers had only known what was going on under the capacious waistcoat opposite, she would have held her tongue; for the more charitable, earnest, and tender-hearted she grew, the harder it became for Mr. 'Rusalem to restrain the declaration which had been hovering on his lips ever since old Podgers died. As the comely relict sat there talking in that genial way, and glowing with good-will to all mankind, it was too much for Mr. 'Rusalem; and finding it impossible to resist the desire to know his fate, he yielded to it, gave a portentous hem, and said abruptly,—

"Well, mum, have I done it?"

"Done what?" asked Mrs. P., going on with her work.

"Made you uncomfortable, according to promise."

"Oh dear, no, you've made me very happy, and will have to try again," she answered, laughing.

"I will, mum."

As he spoke Mr. 'Rusalem drew his chair nearer, leaned forward, and looking straight at her, said deliberately, though his voice shook a little,—

"Mrs. Podgers, I love you hearty; would you have any objections to marrying of me?"

Not a word said Mrs. Podgers; but her knitting dropped out of her hand, and she looked as uncomfortable as she could desire.

"I thought that would do it," muttered Mr. 'Rusalem; but went on steadily, though his ruddy face got paler and paler, his voice huskier and huskier, and his heart fuller and fuller every word he attempted.

"You see, mum, I have took the liberty of loving you ever since you came, more than ten years ago. I was eager to make it known long before this, but Podgers spoke first and then it was no use. It come hard for a time, but I learned to give you up, though I couldn't learn not to love you, being as it was impossible. Since Podgers died I've turned it over in my mind frequent, but felt as if I was too old, and rough, and poor every way to ask so much. Lately, the wish has growed too strong for me, and to-night it won't be put down. If you want a trial, mum, I should be that I'll warrant, for do my best, I could never be all I'm wishful of being for your sake. Would you give it name, and if not agreeable, we'll let it drop, mum, we'll let it drop."

If it hadn't been for the teapot, Mrs. Podgers would have said Yes at once. The word was on her lips, but as she looked up the fire flashed brightly on the teapot (which always occupied the place of honor on the sideboard, for Mrs. P. was intensely proud of it), and she stopped to think, for it reminded her of something. In order to explain this, we must keep Mr. 'Rusalem waiting for his answer a minute.

Rather more than ten years ago, old Podgers happening to want a housekeeper, invited a poor relation to fill that post in his bachelor establishment. He never would have thought of marrying her, though the young woman was both notable and handsome, if he hadn't discovered that his partner loved her. Whereupon the perverse old fellow immediately proposed, lest he should lose his housekeeper, and was accepted from motives of gratitude. Mrs. Podgers was a dutiful wife, but not a very happy one, for the world said that Mr. P. was a hard, miserly man, and his wife was forced to believe the world in the right, till the teapot changed her opinion. There happened to be much suffering among the poor one year, owing to the burning of the mills, and contributions were solicited for their relief. Old

Podgers, though a rich man, refused to give a penny, but it was afterwards discovered that his private charities exceeded many more ostentations ones, and the word "miserly" was changed to "peculiar." When times grew prosperous again, the workmen, whose families had been so quietly served, clubbed together, got the teapot, and left it at Mr. Podgers' door one Christmas Eve. But the old gentleman never saw it; his dinner had been too much for him, and apoplexy took him off that very afternoon.

In the midst of her grief Mrs. Podgers was surprised, touched and troubled by this revelation, for she had known nothing of the affair till the teapot came. Womanlike, she felt great remorse for what now seemed like blindness and ingratitude; she fancied she owed him some atonement, and remembering how often he had expressed a hope that she wouldn't marry again after he was gone, she resolved to gratify him. The buxom widow had had many opportunities of putting off her weeds, but she had refused all offers without regret till now. The teapot reminded her of Podgers and her vow; and though her heart rebelled, she thought it her duty to check the answer that sprung to her lips, and slowly, but decidedly, replied,—

"I'm truly grateful to you, 'Rusalem, but I couldn't do it. Don't think you'd ever be a trial, for you're the last man to be that to any woman. It's a feeling I have that it wouldn't be kind to Podgers. I can't forget how much I owe him, how much I wronged him, and how much I can please him by staying as I am, for his frequent words were, 'Keep the property together, and don't marry, Jane.'"

"Very well, mum, then we'll let it drop, and fall back into the old ways. Don't fret yourself about it, I shall bear up, and—" there Mr. 'Rusalem's voice gave out, and he sat frowning at the fire, bent on bearing up manfully, though it was very hard to find that Podgers dead as well as Podgers living was to keep from him the happiness he had waited for so long. His altered face and broken voice were almost too much for Mrs. P., and she found it necessary to confirm her resolution by telling it. Laying one hand on his shoulder, she pointed to the teapot with the other, saying gently,—

"The day that came and I found but how good he was, too late to beg his pardon and love him for it, I said to myself, 'I'll be true to Podgers till I die, because that's all I can do now to show my repentance and respect.' But for that feeling and that promise I couldn't say No to you, 'Rusalem, for you've been my best friend all these years, and I'll be yours all my life, though I can't be anything else, my dear."

For the first time since its arrival, the mention of the teapot did not produce the accustomed demonstration from Mr. 'Rusalem. On the contrary, he looked at it with a momentary expression of indignation and disgust, strongly suggestive of an insane desire to cast the precious relic on the floor and trample on it. If any such temptation did assail him, he promptly curbed it, and looked about the room with a forlorn air, that made Mrs. Podgers hate herself, as he meekly answered,—

"I'm obliged to you, mum; the feeling does you honor. Don't mind me, it's rather a blow, but I'll be up again directly."

He retired behind his paper as he spoke, and Mrs. Podgers spoilt her knitting in respectful silence, till Mr. 'Rusalem began to read aloud as usual, to assure her that in spite of the blow he *was* up again.

In the gray dawn the worthy gentleman was roused from

his slumbers, by a strange voice whispering shrilly in his ear,—

"I say, there's two of em. Ain't it jolly?"

Starting up, he beheld a comical little goblin standing at his bedside, with a rapturous expression of countenance, and a pair of long gray stockings in its hands. Both were heaping full, but one was evidently meant for Mr. 'Rusalem, for every wish, whim and fancy of his had been guessed, and gratified in a way that touched him to the heart. If it were not indecorous to invade the privacy of a gentleman's apartment, I could describe how there were two boys in the big bed that morning; how the old boy revelled in the treasures of his stocking as heartily as the young one; how they laughed and exclaimed, pulled each others nightcaps off, and had a regular pillow fight; how little Joe was got into his new clothes, and strutted like a small peacock in them; how Mr. 'Rusalem made himself splendid in his Sunday best, and spent ten good minutes in tying the fine cravat somebody had hemmed for him. But lest it should be thought improper, I will merely say, that nowhere in the city did the sun shine on happier faces than these two showed Mrs. Podgers, as Mr. 'Rusalem came in with Joe on his shoulder, both wishing her a merry Christmas, as heartily as if this were the first the world had ever seen.

Mrs. Podgers was as brisk and blithe as they, though she must have sat up one-half the night making presents for them, and laid awake the other half making plans for the day. As soon as she had hugged Joe, toasted him red, and heaped his plate with everything on the table, she told them the order of performances.

"As soon as ever you can't eat any more you must order home the tree, 'Rusalem, and then go with Joe to invite the party, while I see to dinner, and dress up the pine as well as I can in such a hurry."

"Yes, mum," answered Mr. 'Rusalem with alacrity; though how she was going to do her part was not clear to him. But he believed her capable of working any miracle within the power of mortal woman; and having plans of his own, he soon trudged away with Joe prancing at his side, so like the lost Neddy, in the little cap and coat, that Mrs. Podgers forgot her party to stand watching them down the crowded street, with eyes that saw very dimly when they looked away again.

Never mind how she did it, the miracle was wrought, for Mrs. Podgers and her maid Betsey fell to work with a will, and when women set their hearts on anything it is a known fact that they seldom fail to accomplish it. By noon everything was ready, the tree waiting in the best parlor, the dinner smoking on the table, and Mrs. Podgers at the window to catch the first glimpse of her coming guests. A last thought struck her as she stood waiting. There was but one high chair in the house, and the big ones would be doubtless too low for the little people. Bent on making them as comfortable as her motherly heart could desire, she set about mending the matter by bringing out from Podgers' bookcase several fat old ledgers, and arranging them in the chairs. While busily dusting one of these it slipped from her hands, and as it fell a paper fluttered from among the leaves. She picked it up, looked at it, dropped her duster, and became absorbed. It was a small sheet filled with figures, and here and there short memoranda,—not an interesting looking document in the least; but Mrs. Podgers stood like a statue till she had read it several times; then she caught her breath, clapped her hands, laughed and cried together, and put the climax to her extraordinary behavior by running across the room and embracing the astonished little teapot.

How long she would have gone on in this wild manner it is impossible to say, had not the the jingle of bells, and a shrill, small cheer announced that the party had arrived. Whisking the mysterious paper into her pocket, and dressing her agitated countenance in smiles, she hastened to open the door before chilly fingers could find the bell.

Such a merry load as that was! Such happy faces looking out from under the faded hoods and caps! Such a hearty "Hurrah for Mrs. Podgers!" greeted her straight from the grateful hearts that loved her the instant she appeared! And what a perfect Santa Claus Mr. 'Rusalem made, with his sleigh full of bundles as well as children, his face full of sunshine, his arms full of babies, whom he held up that they too might clap their little hands, while he hurrahed with all his might. I really don't think reindeers, or the immemorial white beard and fur cap, could have improved the picture; and the neighbors were of my opinion, I suspect.

It was good to see Mrs. Podgers welcome them all in a way that gave the shyest courage, made the poorest forget patched jackets or ragged gowns, and caused them all to feel that this indeed was merry Christmas. It was better still to see Mrs. Podgers preside over the table, dealing out turkey and pudding with such a bounteous hand, that the small feasters often paused, in sheer astonishment, at the abundance before them, and then fell to again with renewed energy, as if they feared to wake up presently and find the whole a dream. It was best of all to see Mrs. Podgers gather them about her afterwards, hearing their little stories, learning their many wants, and winning their young hearts by such gentle wiles that they soon regarded her as some beautiful, benignant fairy, who had led them from a cold, dark world into the land of innocent delights they had imagined, longed for, yet never hoped to find.

Then came the tree, hung thick with bonbons, fruit and toys, gay mittens and tippets, comfortable socks and hoods, and, lower down, more substantial but less showy gifts; for Mrs. Podgers had nearly exhausted the Dorcas basket that fortunately chanced to be with her just then. There was no time for candles, but, as if he understood the matter and was bent on supplying all deficiencies, the sun shone gloriously on the little tree, and made it doubly splendid in the children's eyes.

It would have touched the hardest heart to watch the poor little creatures, as they trooped in and stood about the wonderful tree. Some seemed ready to go wild with delight, some folded their hands and sighed with solemn satisfaction, others looked as if bewildered by such unwonted and unexpected good fortune; and when Mr. 'Rusalem told them how this fruitful tree had sprung up from their loving playmate's broken bough, little Joe hid his face in Mrs. Podgers' gown, and could find no vent for his great happiness but tears. It was not a large tree, but it took a long while to strip it; and even when the last gilded nut was gone the children still lingered about it, as if they regarded it with affection as a generous benefactor, and were loath to leave it.

Next they had a splendid round of games. I don't know what will be thought of the worthy souls, but Mr. 'Rusalem and Mrs. Podgers played with all their might. Perhaps the reason why he gave himself up so freely to the spirit of the hour was, that his disappointment was very heavy; and, according to his simple philosophy, it was wiser to soothe his wounded heart and cheer his sad spirit with the sweet society of little children, than to curse fate and reproach a woman. What was Mrs. Podgers' reason it is impossible to tell, but she behaved as if some secret satisfaction filled her heart so full that she was glad to let it bubble over in this harmless fashion. Both tried to be children again, and both succeeded capitally, though now and then their hearts got the better of them. When Mr. 'Rusalem was blinded he tossed all the little lads up to the ceiling when he caught them, kissed all the little girls, and, that no one might feel slighted, kissed Mrs. Podgers also. When they played "Open the gates," and the two grown people stood hand in hand while the mirthful troops marched under the tall arch, Mrs. Podgers never once looked Mr. 'Rusalem in the face, but blushed and kept her eyes on the ground, as if she was a bashful girl playing games with some boyish sweetheart. The children saw nothing of all this, and, bless their innocent little hearts! they wouldn't have understood it if they had; but it was perfectly evident that the gray-headed gentleman and the mature matron had forgotten all about their years, and were in their teens again; for true love is gifted with immortal youth.

When weary with romping, they gathered round the fire, and Mr. 'Rusalem told fairy tales, as if his dull ledgers had preserved these childish romances like flowers between their leaves, and kept them fresh in spite of time. Mrs. Podgers sung to them, and made them sing with her, till passers-by smiled and lingered as the childish voices reached them, and, looking through the screen of roses, they caught glimpses of the happy little group singing in the ruddy circle of that Christmas fire.

It was a very humble festival, but with these poor guests came also Love and Charity, Innocence and Joy,—the strong, sweet spirits who bless and beautify the world; and though eclipsed by many more splendid celebrations, I think the day was the better and the blither for Mrs. Podgers' little party.

When it was all over,—the grateful farewells and riotous cheers as the children were carried home, the twilight raptures of Joe, and the long lullaby before he could extinguish himself enough to go to sleep, the congratulations and clearing up,—then Mr. 'Rusalem and Mrs. Podgers sat down to tea. But no sooner were they alone together than Mrs. P. fell into a curious flutter, and did the oddest things. She gave Mr. 'Rusalem warm water instead of tea, passed the slop-bowl when he asked for the sugar-basin, burnt her fingers, laid her handkerchief on the tray, and tried to put her fork in her pocket, and went on in such a way that Mr. 'Rusalem began to fear the day had been too much for her.

"You're tired, mum," he said presently, hearing her sigh.

"Not a bit," she answered briskly, opening the teapot to add more water, but seemed to forget her purpose, and sat looking into its steamy depths as if in search of something. If it was courage, she certainly found it, for all of a sudden she handed the mysterious paper to Mr. 'Rusalem, saying solemnly,—

"Read that, and tell me if it's true."

He took it readily, put on his glasses, and bent to examine it, but gave a start that caused the spectacles to fly off his nose, as he exclaimed,—

"Lord bless me, he said he'd burnt it!"

"Then it *is* true? Don't deny it, 'Rusalem; it's no use, for I've caught you at last!" and in her excitement Mrs. Podgers slapped down the teapot-lid as if she had got him inside.

"I assure you, mum, he promised to burn it. He made me write down the sums, and so on, to satisfy him that I hadn't took more'n my share of the profits. It was my own; and though he called me a fool he let me do as I liked, but I never thought it would come up again like this, mum."

"Of course you didn't, for it was left in one of the old ledgers we had down for the dears to sit on. I found it, I read it, and I understood it in a minute. It was you who helped the mill-people, and then hid behind Podgers because you didn't want to be thanked. When he died, and the teapot came, you saw how proud I was of it,—how I took comfort in thinking he did the kind things; and for my sake you never told the truth, not even last night, when a word would have done so much. Oh, 'Rusalem, how could you deceive me all these years?"

If Mr. 'Rusalem had desired to answer he would have had no chance; for Mrs. Podgers was too much in earnest to let any one speak but herself, and hurried on, fearing that her emotion would get the better of her before she had had her say.

"It was like you, but it wasn't right, for you've robbed yourself of the love and honor that was your due; you've let people praise Podgers when he didn't deserve it; you've seen me take pride in this because I thought he'd earned it; and you've only laughed at it all as if it was a fine joke to do generous things and never take the credit of 'em. Now I know what bank you've laid up your hard earnings in, and what a blessed interest you'll get by and by. Truly they who give to the poor lend to the Lord,—and you don't need to have the good words written on silver, for you keep 'em always in your heart."

Mrs. Podgers stopped a minute for breath, and felt that she was going very fast; for 'Rusalem sat looking at her with so much humility, love, and longing in his honest face, that she knew it would be all up with her directly.

"You saw how I grieved for Neddy, and gave me this

motherless boy to fill his place; you knew I wanted some one to make the house seem like home again, and you offered me the lovingest heart that ever was. You found I wasn't satisfied to lead such a selfish life, and you showed me how beautiful Charity could make it; you taught me to find my duty waiting for me at my own door; and, putting by your own trouble, you've helped to make this day the happiest Christmas of my life."

If it hadn't been for the teapot Mrs. Podgers would have given out here; but her hand was still on it, and something in the touch gave her steadiness for one more burst.

"I loved the little teapot for Podgers' sake; now I love it a hundred times more for yours, because you've brought its lesson home to me in a way I never can forget, and have been my benefactor as well as theirs, who shall soon know you as well as I do. 'Rusalem, there's only one way in which I can thank you for all this, and I do it with my whole heart. Last night you asked me for something, and I thought I couldn't give it to you. Now I'm sure I can, and if you still want it why—"

Mrs. Podgers never finished that sentence; for, with an impetuosity surprising in one of his age and figure, Mr. 'Rusalem sprang out of his chair and took her in his arms, saying tenderly, in a voice almost inaudible, between a con-flicting choke and chuckle,—

"My dear! my dear! God bless you!"

18

A Country Christmas

"A handful of good life is worth a bushel of learning."

"DEAR EMILY,—*I have a brilliant idea, and at once hasten to share it with you. Three weeks ago I came up here to the wilds of Vermont to visit my old aunt, also to get a little quiet and distance in which to survey certain new prospects which have opened before me, and to decide whether I will marry a millionnaire and become a queen of society, or remain 'the charming Miss Vaughan' and wait till the conquering hero comes.*

"Aunt Plumy begs me to stay over Christmas, and I have consented, as I always dread the formal dinner with which my guardian celebrates the day.

"My brilliant idea is this. I'm going to make it a real old-fashioned frolic, and won't you come and help me? You will enjoy it immensely I am sure, for Aunt is a character, Cousin Saul worth seeing, and Ruth a far prettier girl than any of the city rosebuds coming out this season. Bring Leonard Randal along with you to take notes for his new book; then it will be fresher and truer than the last,

clever as it was.

"The air is delicious up here, society amusing, this old farmhouse full of treasures, and your bosom friend pining to embrace you. Just telegraph yes or no, and we will expect you on Tuesday.

"Ever yours,
SOPHIE VAUGHAN.*"*

"They will both come, for they are as tired of city life and as fond of change as I am," said the writer of the above, as she folded her letter and went to get it posted without delay.

Aunt Plumy was in the great kitchen making pies; a jolly old soul, with a face as ruddy as a winter apple, a cheery voice, and the kindest heart that ever beat under a gingham gown. Pretty Ruth was chopping the mince, and singing so gaily as she worked that the four-and-twenty immortal blackbirds could not have put more music into a pie than she did. Saul was piling wood into the big oven, and Sophie paused a moment on the threshold to look at him, for she always enjoyed the sight of this stalwart cousin, whom she likened to a Norse viking, with his fair hair and beard, keen blue eyes, and six feet of manly height, with shoulders that looked broad and strong enough to bear any burden.

His back was toward her, but he saw her first, and turned his flushed face to meet her, with the sudden lighting up it always showed when she approached.

"I've done it, Aunt; and now I want Saul to post the letter, so we can get a speedy answer."

"Just as soon as I can hitch up, cousin;" and Saul pitched in his last log, looking ready to put a girdle round the earth in less than forty minutes.

"Well, dear, I ain't the least mite of objection, as long as it pleases you. I guess we can stan' it ef your city folks can.

I presume to say things will look kind of sing'lar to 'em, but I s'pose that's what they come for. Idle folks do dreadful queer things to amuse 'em;" and Aunt Plumy leaned on the rolling pin to smile and nod with a shrewd twinkle of her eye, as if she enjoyed the prospect as much as Sophie did.

"I shall be afraid of 'em, but I'll try not to make you ashamed of me," said Ruth, who loved her charming cousin even more than she admired her.

"No fear of that, dear. They will be the awkward ones, and you must set them at ease by just being your simple selves, and treating them as if they were everyday people. Nell is very nice and jolly when she drops her city ways, as she must here. She will enter into the spirit of the fun at once, and I know you'll all like her. Mr. Randal is rather the worse for too much praise and petting, as successful people are apt to be, so a little plain talk and rough work will do him good. He is a true gentleman in spite of his airs and elegance, and he will take it all in good part, if you treat him like a man and not a lion."

"I'll see to him," said Saul, who had listened with great interest to the latter part of Sophie's speech, evidently suspecting a lover, and enjoying the idea of supplying him with a liberal amount of "plain talk and rough work."

"I'll keep 'em busy if that's what they need, for there will be a sight to do, and we can't get help easy up here. Our darters don't hire out much. Work to home till they marry, and don't go gaddin' 'round gettin' their heads full of foolish notions, and forgettin' all the useful things their mothers taught 'em."

Aunt Plumy glanced at Ruth as she spoke, and a sudden color in the girl's cheeks proved that the words hit certain ambitious fancies of this pretty daughter of the house of Basset.

"They shall do their parts and not be a trouble; I'll see to that, for you certainly are the dearest aunt in the world to let me take possession of you and yours in this way," cried Sophie, embracing the old lady with warmth.

Saul wished the embrace could be returned by proxy, as his mother's hands were too floury to do more than hover affectionately round the delicate face that looked so fresh and young beside her wrinkled one. As it could not be done, he fled temptation and "hitched up" without delay.

The three women laid their heads together in his absence, and Sophie's plan grew apace, for Ruth longed to see a real novelist and a fine lady, and Aunt Plumy, having plans of her own to further, said "Yes, dear," to every suggestion.

Great was the arranging and adorning that went on that day in the old farmhouse, for Sophie wanted her friends to enjoy this taste of country pleasures, and knew just what additions would be indispensable to their comfort; what simple ornaments would be in keeping with the rustic stage on which she meant to play the part of prima donna.

Next day a telegram arrived accepting the invitation, for both the lady and the lion. They would arrive that afternoon, as little preparation was needed for this impromptu journey, the novelty of which was its chief charm to these *blasé* people.

Saul wanted to get out the double sleigh and span, for he prided himself on his horses, and a fall of snow came most opportunely to beautify the landscape and add a new pleasure to Christmas festivities.

But Sophie declared that the old yellow sleigh, with Punch, the farm-horse, must be used, as she wished everything to be in keeping; and Saul obeyed, thinking he had never seen anything prettier than his cousin when she appeared in his mother's old-fashioned camlet cloak and blue silk pumpkin hood. He looked remarkably well himself in his fur coat, with hair and beard brushed till they shone like spun gold, a fresh color in his cheek, and the sparkle of amusement in his eyes, while excitement gave his usually grave face the animation it needed to be handsome.

Away they jogged in the creaking old sleigh, leaving Ruth to make herself pretty, with a fluttering heart, and Aunt Plumy to dish up a late dinner fit to tempt the most fastidious appetite.

"She has not come for us, and there is not even a stage to take us up. There must be some mistake," said Emily Herrick, as she looked about the shabby little station where they were set down.

"That is the never-to-be-forgotten face of our fair friend, but the bonnet of her grandmother, if my eyes do not deceive me," answered Randal, turning to survey the couple approaching in the rear.

"Sophie Vaughan, what do you mean by making such a guy of yourself?" exclaimed Emily, as she kissed the smiling face in the hood and stared at the quaint cloak.

"I'm dressed for my part, and I intend to keep it up. This is our host, my cousin, Saul Basset. Come to the sleigh at once, he will see to your luggage," said Sophie, painfully conscious of the antiquity of her array as her eyes rested on Emily's pretty hat and mantle, and the masculine elegance of Randal's wraps.

They were hardly tucked in when Saul appeared with a valise in one hand and a large trunk on his shoulder, swinging both on to a wood-sled that stood near by as easily as if they had been hand-bags.

"That is your hero, is it? Well, he looks it, calm and comely, taciturn and tall," said Emily, in a tone of approbation.

"He should have been named Samson or Goliath; though I believe it was the small man who slung things about and turned out the hero in the end," added Randal, surveying the performance with interest and a touch of envy, for much pen work had made his own hands as delicate as a woman's.

"Saul doesn't live in a glass house, so stones won't hurt him. Remember sarcasm is forbidden and sincerity the order of the day. You are country folks now, and it will do you good to try their simple, honest ways for a few days."

Sophie had no time to say more, for Saul came up and drove off with the brief remark that the baggage would "be along right away."

Being hungry, cold and tired, the guests were rather silent during the short drive, but Aunt Plumy's hospitable welcome, and the savory fumes of the dinner awaiting them, thawed the ice and won their hearts at once.

"Isn't it nice? Aren't you glad you came?" asked Sophie, as she led her friends into the parlor, which she had redeemed from its primness by putting bright chintz curtains to the windows, hemlock boughs over the old portraits, a china bowl of flowers on the table, and a splendid fire on the wide hearth.

"It is perfectly jolly, and this is the way I begin to enjoy myself," answered Emily, sitting down upon the home-made rug, whose red flannel roses bloomed in a blue list basket.

"If I may add a little smoke to your glorious fire, it will be quite perfect. Won't Samson join me?" asked Randal, waiting for permission, cigar case in hand.

"He has no small vices, but you may indulge yours,"

answered Sophie, from the depths of a grandmotherly chair.

Emily glanced up at her friend as if she caught a new tone in her voice, then turned to the fire again with a wise little nod, as if confiding some secret to the reflection of herself in the bright brass andiron.

"His Delilah does not take this form. I wait with interest to discover if he has one. What a daisy the sister is. Does she ever speak?" asked Randal, trying to lounge on the hair-cloth sofa, where he was slipping uncomfortably about.

"Oh yes, and sings like a bird. You shall hear her when she gets over her shyness. But no trifling, mind you, for it is a jealously guarded daisy and not to be picked by any idle hand," said Sophie warningly, as she recalled Ruth's blushes and Randal's compliments at dinner.

"I should expect to be annihilated by the big brother if I attempted any but the 'sincerest' admiration and respect. Have no fears on that score, but tell us what is to follow this superb dinner. An apple bee, spinning match, husking party, or primitive pastime of some sort, I have no doubt."

"As you are new to our ways I am going to let you rest this evening. We will sit about the fire and tell stories. Aunt is a master hand at that, and Saul has reminiscences of the war that are well worth hearing if we can only get him to tell them."

"Ah, he was there, was he?"

"Yes, all through it, and is Major Basset, though he likes his plain name best. He fought splendidly and had several wounds, though only a mere boy when he earned his scars and bars. I'm very proud of him for that," and Sophie looked so as she glanced at the photograph of a stripling in uniform set in the place of honor on the high mantel-piece.

"We must stir him up and hear these martial memories.

I want some new incidents, and shall book all I can get, if I may."

Here Randal was interrupted by Saul himself, who came in with an armful of wood for the fire.

"Anything more I can do for you, cousin?" he asked, surveying the scene with a rather wistful look.

"Only come and sit with us and talk over war times with Mr. Randal."

"When I've foddered the cattle and done my chores I'd be pleased to. What regiment were you in?" asked Saul, looking down from his lofty height upon the slender gentleman, who answered briefly,—

"In none. I was abroad at the time."

"Sick?"

"No, busy with a novel."

"Took four years to write it?"

"I was obliged to travel and study before I could finish it. These things take more time to work up than outsiders would believe."

"Seems to me our war was a finer story than any you could find in Europe, and the best way to study it would be to fight it out. If you want heroes and heroines you'd have found plenty of 'em there."

"I have no doubt of it, and shall be glad to atone for my seeming neglect of them by hearing about your own exploits, Major."

Randal hoped to turn the conversation gracefully; but Saul was not to be caught, and left the room, saying, with a gleam of fun in his eye,—

"I can't stop now; heroes can wait, pigs can't."

The girls laughed at this sudden descent from the sublime to the ridiculous, and Randal joined them, feeling his condescension had not been unobserved.

As if drawn by the merry sound Aunt Plumy appeared, and being established in the rocking-chair fell to talking as easily as if she had known her guests for years.

"Laugh away, young folks, that's better for digestion than any of the messes people use. Are you troubled with dyspepsy, dear? You didn't seem to take your vittles very hearty, so I mistrusted you was delicate," she said, looking at Emily, whose pale cheeks and weary eyes told the story of late hours and a gay life.

"I haven't eaten so much for years, I assure you, Mrs. Basset; but it was impossible to taste all your good things. I am not dyspeptic, thank you, but a little seedy and tired, for I've been working rather hard lately."

"Be you a teacher? or have you a 'perfessun,' as they call a trade nowadays?" asked the old lady in a tone of kindly interest, which prevented a laugh at the idea of Emily's being anything but a beauty and a belle. The others kept their countenances with difficulty, and she answered demurely,—

"I have no trade as yet, but I dare say I should be happier if I had."

"Not a doubt on't, my dear."

"What would you recommend, ma'am?"

"I should say dressmakin' was rather in your line, ain't it. Your clothes is dreadful tasty, and do you credit if you made 'em yourself," and Aunt Plumy surveyed with feminine interest the simple elegance of the travelling dress which was the masterpiece of a French modiste.

"No, ma'am, I don't make my own things, I'm too lazy. It takes so much time and trouble to select them that I have only strength left to wear them."

"Housekeepin' used to be the favorite perfessun in my day. It ain't fashionable now, but it needs a sight of trainin' to be perfeet in all that's required, and I've an idee it would be a sight healthier and usefuller than the paintin' and music and fancy work young women do nowadays."

"But every one wants some beauty in their lives, and each one has a different sphere to fill, if one can only find it."

"'Pears to me there's no call for so much art when nater is full of beauty for them that can see and love it. As for 'spears' and so on, I've a notion if each of us did up our own little chores smart and thorough we needn't go wanderin' round to set the world to rights. That's the Lord's job, and I presume to say He can do it without any advice of ourn."

Something in the homely but true words seemed to rebuke the three listeners for wasted lives, and for a moment there was no sound but the crackle of the fire, the brisk click of the old lady's knitting needles, and Ruth's voice singing overhead as she made ready to join the party below.

"To judge by that sweet sound you have done one of your 'chores' very beautifully, Mrs. Basset, and in spite of the follies of our day, succeeded in keeping one girl healthy, happy and unspoiled," said Emily, looking up into the peaceful old face with her own lovely one full of respect and envy.

"I do hope so, for she's my ewe lamb, the last of four dear little girls; all the rest are in the burying ground 'side of father. I don't expect to keep her long, and don't ought to regret when I lose her, for Saul is the best of sons; but daughters is more to mothers somehow, and I always yearn over girls that is left without a broodin' wing to keep 'em safe and warm in this world of tribulation."

Aunt Plumy laid her hand on Sophie's head as she spoke,

with such a motherly look that both girls drew nearer, and Randal resolved to put her in a book without delay.

Presently Saul returned with little Ruth hanging on his arm and shyly nestling near him as he took the three-cornered leathern chair in the chimney nook, while she sat on a stool close by.

"Now the circle is complete and the picture perfect. Don't light the lamps yet, please, but talk away and let me make a mental study of you. I seldom find so charming a scene to paint," said Randal, beginning to enjoy himself immensely, with a true artist's taste for novelty and effect.

"Tell us about your book, for we have been reading it as it comes out in the magazine, and are much exercised about how it's going to end," began Saul, gallantly throwing himself into the breach, for a momentary embarrassment fell upon the women at the idea of sitting for their portraits before they were ready.

"Do you really read my poor serial up here, and do me the honor to like it?" asked the novelist, both flattered and amused, for his work was of the aesthetic sort, microscopic studies of character, and careful pictures of modern life.

"Sakes alive, why shouldn't we," cried Aunt Plumy. "We have some eddication, though we ain't very genteel. We've got a town libry, kep up by the women mostly, with fairs and tea parties and so on. We have all the magazines reg'lar, and Saul reads out the pieces while Ruth sews and I knit, my eyes bein' poor. Our winter is long and evenings would be kinder lonesome if we didn't have novils and newspapers to cheer 'em up."

"I am very glad I can help to beguile them for you. Now tell me what you honestly think of my work? Criticism is always valuable, and I should really like yours, Mrs. Basset," said Randal, wondering what the good woman would make of the delicate analysis and worldly wisdom on which he prided himself.

Short work, as Aunt Plumy soon showed him, for she rather enjoyed freeing her mind at all times, and decidedly resented the insinuation that country folk could not appreciate light literature as well as city people.

"I ain't no great of a jedge about anything but nat'ralness of books, and it really does seem as if some of your men and women was dreadful uncomfortable creaters. 'Pears to me it ain't wise to be always pickin' ourselves to pieces and pryin' into things that ought to come gradual by way of experience and the visitations of Providence. Flowers won't blow worth a cent ef you pull 'em open. Better wait and see what they can do alone. I do relish the smart sayins, the odd ways of furrin parts, and the sarcastic slaps at folkses weak spots. But, massy knows, we can't live on spice-cake and Charlotte Ruche, and I do feel as if books was more sustainin' ef they was full of everyday people and things, like good bread and butter. Them that goes to the heart and ain't soon forgotten is the kind I hanker for. Mis Terry's books now, and Mis Stowe's, and Dickens's Christmas pieces,—them is real sweet and cheerin', to my mind."

As the blunt old lady paused it was evident she had produced a sensation, for Saul smiled at the fire, Ruth looked dismayed at this assault upon one of her idols, and the young ladies were both astonished and amused at the keenness of the new critic who dared express what they had often felt. Randal, however, was quite composed and laughed good-naturedly, though secretly feeling as if a pail of cold water had been poured over him.

"Many thanks, madam; you have discovered my weak point with surprising accuracy. But you see I cannot help 'picking folks to pieces,' as you have expressed it; that is my gift, and it has its attractions, as the sale of my books will testify. People like the 'spice-bread,' and as that is the only sort my oven will bake, I must keep on in order to make my living."

"So rum sellers say, but it ain't a good trade to foller, and I'd chop wood 'fore I'd earn my livin' harmin' my feller man. 'Pears to me I'd let my oven cool a spell, and hunt up some homely, happy folks to write about; folks that don't borrer trouble and go lookin' for holes in their neighbors' coats, but take their lives brave and cheerful; and rememberin' we are all human, have pity on the weak, and try to be as full of mercy, patience and lovin' kindness as Him who made us. That sort of a book would do a heap of good; be real warmin' and strengthenin', and make them that read it love the man that wrote it, and remember him when he was dead and gone."

"I wish I could!" and Randal meant what he said, for he was as tired of his own style, as a watch-maker might be of the magnifying glass through which he strains his eyes all day. He knew that the heart was left out of his work, and that both mind and soul were growing morbid with dwelling on the faulty, absurd and metaphysical phases of life and character. He often threw down his pen and vowed he would write no more; but he loved ease and the books brought money readily; he was accustomed to the stimulant of praise and missed it as the toper misses his wine, so that which had once been a pleasure to himself and others was fast becoming a burden and a disappointment.

The brief pause which followed his involuntary betrayal of discontent was broken by Ruth, who exclaimed, with a girlish enthusiasm that overpowered girlish bashfulness,—

"*I* think all the novels are splendid! I hope you will write hundreds more, and I shall live to read 'em."

"Bravo, my gentle champion! I promise that I will write one more at least, and have a heroine in it whom your mother will both admire and love," answered Randal, surprised to find how grateful he was for the girl's approval, and how rapidly his trained fancy began to paint the background on which he hoped to copy this fresh, human daisy.

Abashed by her involuntary outburst, Ruth tried to efface herself behind Saul's broad shoulder, and he brought the conversation back to its starting point by saying in a tone of the most sincere interest,—

"Speaking of the serial, I am very anxious to know how your hero comes out. He is a fine fellow, and I can't decide whether he is going to spoil his life marrying that silly woman, or do something grand and generous, and not be made a fool of."

"Upon my soul, I don't know myself. It is very hard to find new finales. Can't you suggest something, Major? then I shall not be obliged to leave my story without an end, as people complain I am rather fond of doing."

"Well, no, I don't think I've anything to offer. Seems to me it isn't the sensational exploits that show the hero best, but some great sacrifice quietly made by a common sort of man who is noble without knowing it. I saw a good many such during the war, and often wish I could write them down, for it is surprising how much courage, goodness and real piety is stowed away in common folks ready to show when the right time comes."

"Tell us one of them, and I'll bless you for a hint. No one knows the anguish of an author's spirit when he can't ring down the curtain on an effective tableau," said Randal, with a glance at his friends to ask their aid in eliciting an anecdote or reminiscence.

"Tell about the splendid fellow who held the bridge, like Horatius, till help came up. That was a thrilling story, I assure you," answered Sophie, with an inviting smile.

But Saul would not be his own hero, and said briefly:

"Any man can be brave when the battle-fever is on him, and it only takes a little physical courage to dash ahead." He paused a moment, with his eyes on the snowy landscape without, where twilight was deepening; then, as if constrained by the memory that winter scene evoked, he slowly continued,—

"One of the bravest things I ever knew was done by a poor fellow who has been a hero to me ever since, though I only met him that night. It was after one of the big battles of that last winter, and I was knocked over with a broken leg and two or three bullets here and there. Night was coming on, snow falling, and a sharp wind blew over the field where a lot of us lay, dead and alive, waiting for the ambulance to come and pick us up. There was skirmishing going on not far off, and our prospects were rather poor between frost and fire. I was calculating how I'd manage, when I found two poor chaps close by who were worse off, so I braced up and did what I could for them. One had an arm blown away, and kept up a dreadful groaning. The other was shot bad, and bleeding to death for want of help, but never complained. He was nearest, and I liked his pluck, for he spoke cheerful and made me ashamed to growl. Such times make dreadful brutes of men if they haven't something to hold on to, and all three of us were most wild with pain and cold and hunger, for we'd fought all day fasting, when we heard a rumble in the road below, and saw lanterns bobbing round. That meant life to us, and we all tried to holler; two of us were pretty faint, but I managed a good yell, and they heard it.

"'Room for one more. Hard luck, old boys, but we are full and must save the worst wounded first. Take a drink, and hold on till we come back,' says one of them with the stretcher.

"'Here's the one to go,' I says, pointin' out my man, for I saw by the light that he was hard hit.

"'No, that one. He's got more chances than I, or this one; he's young and got a mother; I'll wait,' said the good feller, touchin' my arm, for he'd heard me mutterin' to myself about this dear old lady. We always want mother when we are down, you know."

Saul's eyes turned to the beloved face with a glance of tenderest affection, and Aunt Plumy answered with a dismal groan at the recollection of his need that night, and her absence.

"Well, to be short, the groaning chap was taken, and my man left. I was mad, but there was no time for talk, and the selfish one went off and left that poor feller to run his one chance. I had my rifle, and guessed I could hobble up to use it if need be; so we settled back to wait without much hope of help, everything being in a muddle. And wait we did till morning, for that ambulance did not come back till next day, when most of us were past needing it.

"I'll never forget that night. I dream it all over again as plain as if it was real. Snow, cold, darkness, hunger, thirst, pain, and all round us cries and cursing growing less and less, till at last only the wind went moaning over that meadow. It was awful! so lone-some, helpless, and seemingly god-forsaken. Hour after hour we lay there side by side under one coat, waiting to be saved or die, for the wind grew strong and we grew weak."

Saul drew a long breath, and held his hands to the fire as if he felt again the sharp suffering of that night.

"And the man?" asked Emily, softly, as if reluctant to break the silence.

"He *was* a man! In times like that men talk like brothers and show what they are. Lying there, slowly freezing, Joe Cummings told me about his wife and babies, his old folks waiting for him, all depending on him, yet all ready to give him up when he was needed. A plain man, but honest and true, and loving as a woman; I soon saw that as he went on talking, half to me and half to himself, for sometimes he wandered a little toward the end. I've read books, heard sermons, and seen good folks, but nothing ever came so close or did me so much good as seeing this man die. He had one chance and gave it cheerfully. He longed for those he loved, and let 'em go with a good-by they couldn't hear. He suffered all the pains we most shrink from without a murmur, and kept my heart warm while his own was growing cold. It's no use trying to tell that part of it; but I heard prayers that night that meant something, and I saw how faith could hold a soul up when everything was gone but God."

Saul stopped there with a sudden huskiness in his deep voice, and when he went on it was in the tone of one who speaks of a dear friend.

"Joe grew still by and by, and I thought he was asleep, for I felt his breath when I tucked him up, and his hand held on to mine. The cold sort of numbed me, and I dropped off, too weak and stupid to think or feel. I never should have waked up if it hadn't been for Joe. When I came to, it was morning, and I thought I was dead, for all I could see was that great field of white mounds, like graves, and a splendid sky above. Then I looked for Joe, remembering; but he had put my coat back over me, and lay stiff and still under the snow that covered him like a shroud, all except his face. A bit of my cape had blown over it, and when I took it off and the sun shone on his dead face, I declare to you it was so full of heavenly peace I felt as if that common man had been glorified by God's light, and rewarded by God's 'Well done.' That's all."

No one spoke for a moment, while the women wiped their eyes, and Saul dropped his as if to hide something softer than tears.

"It was very noble, very touching. And you? how did you get off at last?" asked Randal, with real admiration and respect in his usually languid face.

"Crawled off," answered Saul, relapsing into his former brevity of speech.

"Why not before, and save yourself all that misery?"

"Couldn't leave Joe."

"Ah, I see; there were two heroes that night."

"Dozens, I've no doubt. Those were times that made heroes of men, and women, too."

"Tell us more;" begged Emily, looking up with an expression none of her admirers ever brought to her face by their softest compliments or wiliest gossip.

"I've done my part. It's Mr. Randal's turn now;" and Saul drew himself out of the ruddy circle of firelight, as if ashamed of the prominent part he was playing.

Sophie and her friend had often heard Randal talk, for he was an accomplished *raconteur,* but that night he exerted himself, and was unusually brilliant and entertaining, as if upon his mettle. The Bassets were charmed. They sat late and were very merry, for Aunt Plumy got up a little supper for them, and her cider was as exhilarating as champagne.

When they parted for the night and Sophie kissed her aunt, Emily did the same, saying heartily,—

"It seems as if I'd known you all my life, and this is certainly the most enchanting old place that ever was."

"Glad you like it, dear. But it ain't all fun, as you'll find out to-morrow when you go to work, for Sophie says you must," answered Mrs. Basset, as her guests trooped away, rashly promising to like everything.

They found it difficult to keep their word when they were called at half past six next morning. Their rooms were warm, however, and they managed to scramble down in time for breakfast, guided by the fragrance of coffee and Aunt Plumy's shrill voice singing the good old hymn—

> "Lord, in the morning Thou shalt hear
> My voice ascending high."

An open fire blazed on the hearth, for the cooking was done in the lean-to, and the spacious, sunny kitchen was kept in all its old-fashioned perfection, with the wooden settle in a warm nook, the tall clock behind the door, copper and pewter utensils shining on the dresser, old china in the corner closet and a little spinning wheel rescued from the garret by Sophie to adorn the deep window, full of scarlet geraniums, Christmas roses, and white chrysanthemums.

The young lady, in a checked apron and mob-cap, greeted her friends with a dish of buckwheats in one hand, and a pair of cheeks that proved she had been learning to fry these delectable cakes.

"You do 'keep it up' in earnest, upon my word; and very becoming it is, dear. But won't you ruin your complexion and roughen your hands if you do so much of this new fancy-work?" asked Emily, much amazed at this novel freak.

"I like it, and really believe I've found my proper sphere at last. Domestic life seems so pleasant to me that I feel as if I'd better keep it up for the rest of my life," answered Sophie, making a pretty picture of herself as she cut great slices of brown bread, with the early sunshine touching her happy face.

"The charming Miss Vaughan in the role of a farmer's wife. I find it difficult to imagine, and shrink from the thought of the wide-spread dismay such a fate will produce among her adorers," added Randal, as he basked in the glow of the hospitable fire.

"She might do worse; but come to breakfast and do honor to my handiwork," said Sophie, thinking of her worn-out millionnaire, and rather nettled by the satiric smile on Randal's lips.

"What an appetite early rising gives one. I feel equal to almost anything, so let me help wash cups," said Emily, with unusual energy, when the hearty meal was over and Sophie began to pick up the dishes as if it was her usual work.

Ruth went to the window to water the flowers, and Randal followed to make himself agreeable, remembering her defence of him last night. He was used to admiration from feminine eyes, and flattery from soft lips, but found something new and charming in the innocent delight which showed itself at his approach in blushes more eloquent than words, and shy glances from eyes full of hero-worship.

"I hope you are going to spare me a posy for tomorrow night, since I can be fine in no other way to do honor to the dance Miss Sophie proposes for us," he said, leaning in the bay window to look down on the little girl, with the devoted air he usually wore for pretty women.

"Anything you like! I should be so glad to have you wear

my flowers. There will be enough for all, and I've nothing else to give to people who have made me as happy as cousin Sophie and you," answered Ruth, half drowning her great calla as she spoke with grateful warmth.

"You must make her happy by accepting the invitation to go home with her which I heard given last night. A peep at the world would do you good, and be a pleasant change, I think."

"Oh, very pleasant! but would it do me good?" and Ruth looked up with sudden seriousness in her blue eyes, as a child questions an elder, eager, yet wistful.

"Why not?" asked Randal, wondering at the hesitation.

"I might grow discontented with things here if I saw splendid houses and fine people. I am very happy now, and it would break my heart to lose that happiness, or ever learn to be ashamed of home."

"But don't you long for more pleasure, new scenes and other friends than these?" asked the man, touched by the little creature's loyalty to the things she knew and loved.

"Very often, but mother says when I'm ready they will come, so I wait and try not to be impatient." But Ruth's eyes looked out over the green leaves as if the longing was very strong within her to see more of the unknown world lying beyond the mountains that hemmed her in.

"It is natural for birds to hop out of the nest, so I shall expect to see you over there before long, and ask you how you enjoy your first flight," said Randal, in a paternal tone that had a curious effect on Ruth.

To his surprise, she laughed, then blushed like one of her own roses, and answered with a demure dignity that was very pretty to see.

"I intend to hop soon, but it won't be a very long flight or very far from mother. She can't spare me, and nobody in the world can fill her place to me."

"Bless the child, does she think I'm going to make love to her," thought Randal, much amused, but quite mistaken. Wiser women had thought so when he assumed the caressing air with which he beguiled them into the little revelations of character he liked to use, as the south wind makes flowers open their hearts to give up their odor, then leaves them to carry it elsewhere, the more welcome for the stolen sweetness.

"Perhaps you are right. The maternal wing is a safe shelter for confiding little souls like you, Miss Ruth. You will be as comfortable here as your flowers in this sunny window," he said, carelessly pinching geranium leaves, and ruffling the roses till the pink petals of the largest fluttered to the floor.

As if she instinctively felt and resented something in the man which his act symbolized, the girl answered quietly, as she went on with her work, "Yes, if the frost does not touch me, or careless people spoil me too soon."

Before Randal could reply Aunt Plumy approached like a maternal hen who sees her chicken in danger.

"Saul is goin' to haul wood after he's done his chores, mebbe you'd like to go along? The view is good, the roads well broke, and the day uncommon fine."

"Thanks; it will be delightful, I dare say," politely responded the lion, with a secret shudder at the idea of a rural promenade at 8 A.M. in the winter.

"Come on, then; we'll feed the stock, and then I'll show you how to yoke oxen," said Saul, with a twinkle in his eye as he led the way, when his new aide had muffled himself up as if for a polar voyage.

"Now, that's too bad of Saul! He did it on purpose, just to please you, Sophie," cried Ruth presently, and the girls ran to the window to behold Randal bravely following his host with a pail of pigs' food in each hand, and an expression of resigned disgust upon his aristocratic face.

"To what base uses may we come," quoted Emily, as they all nodded and smiled upon the victim as he looked back from the barnyard, where he was clamorously welcomed by his new charges.

"It is rather a shock at first, but it will do him good, and Saul won't be too hard upon him, I'm sure," said Sophie, going back to her work, while Ruth turned her best buds to the sun that they might be ready for a peace offering tomorrow.

There was a merry clatter in the big kitchen for an hour; then Aunt Plumy and her daughter shut themselves up in the pantry to perform some culinary rites, and the young ladies went to inspect certain antique costumes laid forth in Sophie's room.

"You see, Em, I thought it would be appropriate to the house and season to have an old-fashioned dance. Aunt has quantities of ancient finery stowed away, for great-grandfather Basset was a fine old gentleman and his family lived in state. Take your choice of the crimson, blue or silver-gray damask. Ruth is to wear the worked muslin and quilted white satin skirt, with that coquettish hat."

"Being dark, I'll take the red and trim it up with this fine lace. You must wear the blue and primrose, with the distracting high-heeled shoes. Have you any suits for the men?" asked Emily, throwing herself at once into the all-absorbing matter of costume.

"A claret velvet coat and vest, silk stockings, cocked hat and snuff-box for Randal. Nothing large enough for Saul, so he must wear his uniform. Won't Aunt Plumy be superb in this plum-colored satin and immense cap?"

A delightful morning was spent in adapting the faded finery of the past to the blooming beauty of the present, and time and tongues flew till the toot of a horn called them down to dinner.

The girls were amazed to see Randal come whistling up the road with his trousers tucked into his boots, blue mittens on his hands, and an unusual amount of energy in his whole figure, as he drove the oxen, while Saul laughed at his vain attempts to guide the bewildered beasts.

"It's immense! The view from the hill is well worth seeing, for the snow glorifies the landscape and reminds one of Switzerland. I'm going to make a sketch of it this afternoon; better come and enjoy the delicious freshness, young ladies."

Randal was eating with such an appetite that he did not see the glances the girls exchanged as they promised to go.

"Bring home some more winter-green, I want things to be real nice, and we haven't enough for the kitchen," said Ruth, dimpling with girlish delight as she imagined herself dancing under the green garlands in her grandmother's wedding gown.

It was very lovely on the hill, for far as the eye could reach lay the wintry landscape sparkling with the brief beauty of sunshine on virgin snow. Pines sighed overhead, hardy birds flitted to and fro, and in all the trodden spots rose the little spires of evergreen ready for its Christmas duty. Deeper in the wood sounded the measured ring of axes, the crash of falling trees, while the red shirts of the men added color to the scene, and a fresh wind brought the aromatic breath of newly cloven hemlock and pine.

"How beautiful it is! I never knew before what winter woods were like. Did you, Sophie?" asked Emily, sitting on a stump to enjoy the novel pleasure at her ease.

"I've found out lately; Saul lets me come as often as I like, and this fine air seems to make a new creature of me," answered Sophie, looking about her with sparkling eyes, as if this was a kingdom where she reigned supreme.

"Something is making a new creature of you, that is very evident. I haven't yet discovered whether it is the air or some magic herb among that green stuff you are gathering so diligently;" and Emily laughed to see the color deepen beautifully in her friend's half-averted face.

"Scarlet is the only wear just now, I find. If we are lost like babes in the woods there are plenty of Redbreasts to cover us with leaves," and Randal joined Emily's laugh, with a glance at Saul, who had just pulled his coat off.

"You wanted to see this tree go down, so stand from under and I'll show you how it's done," said the farmer, taking up his axe, not unwilling to gratify his guests and display his manly accomplishments at the same time.

It was a fine sight, the stalwart man swinging his axe with magnificent strength and skill, each blow sending a thrill through the stately tree, till its heart was reached and it tottered to its fall. Never pausing for breath Saul shook his yellow mane out of his eyes, and hewed away, while the drops stood on his forehead and his arm ached, as bent on distinguishing himself as if he had been a knight tilting against his rival for his lady's favor.

"I don't know which to admire most, the man or his muscle. One doesn't often see such vigor, size and comeliness in these degenerate days," said Randal, mentally booking the fine figure in the red shirt.

"I think we have discovered a rough diamond. I only wonder if Sophie is going to try and polish it," answered Emily, glancing at her friend, who stood a little apart, watching the rise and fall of the axe as intently as if her fate depended on it.

Down rushed the tree at last, and, leaving them to examine a crow's nest in its branches, Saul went off to his men, as if he found the praises of his prowess rather too much for him.

Randal fell to sketching, the girls to their garland-making, and for a little while the sunny woodland nook was full of lively chat and pleasant laughter, for the air exhilarated them all like wine. Suddenly a man came running from the wood, pale and anxious, saying, as he hastened by for help, "Blasted tree fell on him! Bleed to death before the doctor comes!"

"Who? who?" cried the startled trio.

But the man ran on, with some breathless reply, in which only a name was audible—"Basset."

"The deuce it is!" and Randal dropped his pencil, while the girls sprang up in dismay. Then, with one impulse, they hastened to the distant group, half visible behind the fallen trees and corded wood.

Sophie was there first, and forcing her way through the little crowd of men, saw a red-shirted figure on the ground, crushed and bleeding, and threw herself down beside it with a cry that pierced the hearts of those who heard it. In the act she saw it was not Saul, and covered her bewildered face as if to hide its joy. A strong arm lifted her, and the familiar voice said cheeringly,—

"I'm all right, dear. Poor Bruce is hurt, but we've sent for help. Better go right home and forget all about it."

"Yes, I will, if I can do nothing;" and Sophie meekly returned to her friends who stood outside the circle over which Saul's head towered, assuring them of his safety.

Hoping they had not seen her agitation, she led Emily away, leaving Randal to give what aid he could and bring them news of the poor wood-chopper's state.

Aunt Plumy produced the "camphire" the moment she saw Sophie's pale face, and made her lie down, while the brave old lady trudged briskly off with bandages and brandy to the scene of action. On her return she brought comfortable news of the man, so the little flurry blew over and was forgotten by all but Sophie, who remained pale and quiet all the evening, tying evergreen as if her life depended on it.

"A good night's sleep will set her up. She ain't used to such things, dear child, and needs cossetin'," said Aunt Plumy, purring over her until she was in her bed, with a hot stone at her feet and a bowl of herb tea to quiet her nerves.

An hour later, when Emily went up, she peeped in to see if Sophie was sleeping nicely, and was surprised to find the invalid wrapped in a dressing-gown writing busily.

"Last will and testament, or sudden inspiration, dear? How are you? faint or feverish, delirious or in the dumps! Saul looks so anxious, and Mrs. Basset hushes us all up so, I came to bed, leaving Randal to entertain Ruth."

As she spoke Emily saw the papers disappear in a portfolio, and Sophie rose with a yawn.

"I was writing letters, but I'm sleepy now. Quite over my foolish fright, thank you. Go and get your beauty sleep that you may dazzle the natives to-morrow."

"So glad, good night;" and Emily went away, saying to herself, "Something is going on, and I must find out what it is before I leave. Sophie can't blind me."

But Sophie did all the next day, being delightfully gay at the dinner, and devoting herself to the young minister who was invited to meet the distinguished novelist, and evidently being afraid of him, gladly basked in the smiles of his charming neighbor. A dashing sleigh-ride occupied the afternoon, and then great was the fun and excitement over the costumes.

Aunt Plumy laughed till the tears rolled down her cheeks as the girls compressed her into the plum-colored gown with its short waist, leg-of-mutton sleeves, and narrow skirt. But a worked scarf hid all deficiencies, and the towering cap struck awe into the soul of the most frivolous observer.

"Keep an eye on me, girls, for I shall certainly split somewheres or lose my head-piece off when I'm trottin' round. What would my blessed mother say if she could see me rigged out in her best things?" and with a smile and a sigh the old lady departed to look after "the boys," and see that the supper was all right.

Three prettier damsels never tripped down the wise staircase than the brilliant brunette in crimson brocade, the pensive blonde in blue, or the rosy little bride in old muslin and white satin.

A gallant court gentleman met them in the hall with a superb bow, and escorted them to the parlor, where Grandma Basset's ghost was discovered dancing with a modern major in full uniform.

Mutual admiration and many compliments followed, till other ancient ladies and gentlemen arrived in all manner of queer costumes, and the old house seemed to wake from its humdrum quietude to sudden music and merriment, as if a past generation had returned to keep its Christmas there.

The village fiddler soon struck up the good old tunes, and then the strangers saw dancing that filled them with mingled mirth and envy; it was so droll, yet so hearty. The young men, unusually awkward in their grandfathers' knee-breeches, flapping vests, and swallow tail coats, footed it bravely with the buxom girls who were the prettier for their quaintness, and danced with such vigor that their high combs stood awry, their furbelows waved wildly, and their cheeks were as red as their breast-knots, or hose.

It was impossible to stand still, and one after the other the city folk yielded to the spell, Randal leading off with Ruth, Sophie swept away by Saul, and Emily being taken possession of by a young giant of eighteen, who spun her around with a boyish impetuosity that took her breath away. Even Aunt Plumy was discovered jigging it alone in the pantry, as if the music was too much for her, and the plates and glasses jingled gaily on the shelves in time to Money Musk and Fishers' Hornpipe.

A pause came at last, however, and fans fluttered, heated brows were wiped, jokes were made, lovers exchanged confidences, and every nook and corner held a man and maid carrying on the sweet game which is never out of fashion. There was a glitter of gold lace in the back entry, and a train of blue and primrose shone in the dim light. There was a richer crimson than that of the geraniums in the deep window, and a dainty shoe tapped the bare floor impatiently as the brilliant black eyes looked everywhere for the court gentleman, while their owner listened to the gruff prattle of an enamored boy. But in the upper hall walked a little white ghost as if waiting for some shadowy companion, and when a dark form appeared ran to take its arm, saying, in a tone of soft satisfaction,—

"I was so afraid you wouldn't come!"

"Why did you leave me, Ruth?" answered a manly voice in a tone of surprise, though the small hand slipping from the velvet coat sleeve was replaced as if it was pleasant to feel it there.

A pause, and then the other voice answered demurely,—

"Because I was afraid my head would be turned by the fine things you were saying."

"It is impossible to help saying what one feels to such an artless little creature as you are. It does me good to admire anything so fresh and sweet, and won't harm you."

"It might if—"

"If what, my daisy?"

"I believed it," and a laugh seemed to finish the broken sentence better than the words.

"You may, Ruth, for I do sincerely admire the most genuine girl I have seen for a long time. And walking here with you in your bridal white I was just asking myself if I should not be a happier man with a home of my own and a little wife hanging on my arm than drifting about the world as I do now with only myself to care for."

"I know you would!" and Ruth spoke so earnestly that Randal was both touched and startled, fearing he had ventured too far in a mood of unwonted sentiment, born of the romance of the hour and the sweet frankness of his companion.

"Then you don't think it would be rash for some sweet woman to take me in hand and make me happy, since fame is a failure?"

"Oh, no; it would be easy work if she loved you. I know some one—if I only dared to tell her name."

"Upon my soul, this is cool," and Randal looked down, wondering if the audacious lady on his arm could be shy Ruth.

If he had seen the malicious merriment in her eyes he would have been more humiliated still, but they were modestly averted, and the face under the little hat was full of a soft agitation rather dangerous even to a man of the world.

"She is a captivating little creature, but it is too soon for anything but a mild flirtation. I must delay further innocent revelations or I shall do something rash."

While making this excellent resolution Randal had been pressing the hand upon his arm and gently pacing down the dimly lighted hall with the sound of music in his ears, Ruth's sweetest roses in his button-hole, and a loving little girl beside him, as he thought.

"You shall tell me by and by when we are in town. I am sure you will come, and meanwhile don't forget me."

"I am going in the spring, but I shall not be with Sophie," answered Ruth, in a whisper.

"With whom then? I shall long to see you."

"With my husband. I am to be married in May."

"The deuce you are!" escaped Randal, as he stopped short to stare at his companion, sure she was not in earnest.

But she was, for as he looked the sound of steps coming up the back stairs made her whole face flush and brighten with the unmistakable glow of happy love, and she completed Randal's astonishment by running into the arms of the young minister, saying with an irrepressible laugh, "Oh! John, why didn't you come before?"

The court gentleman was all right in a moment, and the coolest of the three as he offered his congratulations and gracefully retired, leaving the lovers to enjoy the tryst he had delayed. But as he went down stairs his brows were knit, and he slapped the broad railing smartly with his cocked hat as if some irritation must find vent in a more energetic way than merely saying, "Confound the little baggage!" under his breath.

Such an amazing supper came from Aunt Plumy's big pantry that the city guests could not eat for laughing at the queer dishes circulating through the rooms, and copiously partaken of by the hearty young folks.

Doughnuts and cheese, pie and pickles, cider and tea, baked beans and custards, cake and cold turkey, bread and butter, plum pudding and French bonbons, Sophie's contribution.

"May I offer you the native delicacies, and share your plate. Both are very good, but the china has run short, and after such vigorous exercise as you have had you must need refreshment. I'm sure I do!" said Randal, bowing before Emily with a great blue platter laden with two doughnuts, two wedges of pumpkin pie and two spoons.

The smile with which she welcomed him, the alacrity with which she made room beside her and seemed to enjoy the supper he brought, was so soothing to his ruffled spirit that he soon began to feel that there is no friend like an old friend, that it would not be difficult to name a sweet woman who would take him in hand and would make him happy if he cared to ask her, and he began to think he would by and by, it was so pleasant to sit in that green corner with waves of crimson brocade flowing over his feet, and a fine face softening beautifully under his eyes.

The supper was not romantic, but the situation was, and Emily found that pie ambrosial food eaten with the man she loved, whose eyes talked more eloquently than the tongue just then busy with a doughnut. Ruth kept away, but glanced at them as she served her company, and her own happy experience helped her to see that all was going well in that quarter. Saul and Sophie emerged from the back entry with shining countenances, but carefully avoided each other for the rest of the evening. No one observed this but Aunt Plumy from the recesses of her pantry, and she folded her hands as if well content, as she murmured fervently over a pan full of crullers, "Bless the dears! Now I can die happy."

Every one thought Sophie's old-fashioned dress immensely becoming, and several of his former men said to Saul with blunt admiration, "Major, you look to-night as you used to after we'd gained a big battle."

"I feel as if I had," answered the splendid Major, with eyes much brighter than his buttons, and a heart under them infinitely prouder than when he was promoted on the field of honor, for his Waterloo was won.

There was more dancing, followed by games, in which Aunt Plumy shone pre-eminent, for the supper was off her mind and she could enjoy herself. There were shouts of merriment as the blithe old lady twirled the platter, hunted the squirrel, and went to Jerusalem like a girl of sixteen; her cap in a ruinous condition, and every seam of the purple dress straining like sails in a gale. It was great fun, but at midnight it came to an end, and the young folks, still bubbling over with innocent jollity, went jingling away along the snowy hills, unanimously pronouncing Mrs. Basset's party the best of the season.

"Never had such a good time in my life!" exclaimed Sophie, as the family stood together in the kitchen where the candles among the wreaths were going out, and the floor was strewn with wrecks of past joy.

"I'm proper glad, dear. Now you all go to bed and lay as late as you like to-morrow. I'm so kinder worked up I couldn't sleep, so Saul and me will put things to rights without a mite of noise to disturb you;" and Aunt Plumy sent them off with a smile that was a benediction, Sophie thought.

"The dear old soul speaks as if midnight was an unheard-of hour for Christians to be up. What would she say if she knew how we seldom go to bed till dawn in the ball season? I'm so wide awake I've half a mind to pack a little. Randal must go at two, he says, and we shall want his escort," said Emily, as the girls laid away their brocades in the great press in Sophie's room.

"I'm not going. Aunt can't spare me, and there is nothing to go for yet," answered Sophie, beginning to take the white chrysanthemums out of her pretty hair.

"My dear child, you will die of ennui up here. Very nice for a week or so, but frightful for a winter. We are going to be very gay, and cannot get on without you," cried Emily, dismayed at the suggestion.

"You will have to, for I'm not coming. I am very happy here, and so tired of the frivolous life I lead in town, that I have decided to try a better one," and Sophie's mirror reflected a face full of the sweetest content.

"Have you lost your mind? experienced religion? or any other dreadful thing? You always were odd, but this last freak is the strangest of all. What will your guardian say, and the world?" added Emily in the awestricken tone of one who stood in fear of the omnipotent Mrs. Grundy.

"Guardy will be glad to be rid of me, and I don't care that for the world," cried Sophie, snapping her fingers with a joyful sort of recklessness which completed Emily's bewilderment.

"But Mr. Hammond? Are you going to throw away millions, lose your chance of making the best match in the city, and driving the girls of our set out of their wits with envy?"

Sophie laughed at her friend's despairing cry, and turning round said quietly,—

"I wrote to Mr. Hammond last night, and this evening received my reward for being an honest girl. Saul and I are to be married in the spring when Ruth is."

Emily fell prone upon the bed as if the announcement was too much for her, but was up again in an instant to declare with prophetic solemnity,—

"I knew something was going on, but hoped to get you away before you were lost. Sophie, you will repent. Be warned, and forget this sad delusion."

"Too late for that. The pang I suffered yesterday when I

thought Saul was dead showed me how well I loved him. To-night he asked me to stay, and no power in the world can part us. Oh! Emily, it is all so sweet, so beautiful, that *everything* is possible, and I know I shall be happy in this dear old home, full of love and peace and honest hearts. I only hope you may find as true and tender a man to live for as my Saul."

Sophie's face was more eloquent than her fervent words, and Emily beautifully illustrated the inconsistency of her sex by suddenly embracing her friend, with the incoherent exclamation, "I think I have, dear! Your brave Saul is worth a dozen old Hammonds, and I do believe you are right."

It is unnecessary to tell how, as if drawn by the irresistible magic of sympathy, Ruth and her mother crept in one by one to join the midnight conference and add their smiles and tears, tender hopes and proud delight to the joys of that memorable hour. Nor how Saul, unable to sleep, mounted guard below, and meeting Randal prowling down to soothe his nerves with a surreptitious cigar found it impossible to help confiding to his attentive ear the happiness that would break bounds and overflow in unusual eloquence.

Peace fell upon the old house at last, and all slept as if some magic herb had touched their eyelids, bringing blissful dreams and a glad awakening.

"Can't we persuade you to come with us, Miss Sophie?" asked Randal the next day, as they made their adieux.

"I'm under orders now, and dare not disobey my superior officer," answered Sophie, handing her Major his driving gloves, with a look which plainly showed that she had joined the great army of devoted women who enlist for life and ask no pay but love.

"I shall depend on being invited to your wedding, then,

and yours, too, Miss Ruth," added Randal, shaking hands with "the little baggage," as if he had quite forgiven her mockery and forgotten his own brief lapse into sentiment.

Before she could reply Aunt Plumy said, in a tone of calm conviction, that made them all laugh, and some of them look conscious,—

"Spring is a good time for weddin's, and I shouldn't wonder ef there was quite a number."

"Nor I;" and Saul and Sophie smiled at one another as they saw how carefully Randal arranged Emily's wraps.

Then with kisses, thanks and all the good wishes that happy hearts could imagine, the guests drove away, to remember long and gratefully that pleasant country Christmas.

19

Cousin Tribulation's Story

DEAR MERRYS:—As a subject appropriate to the season, I want to tell you about a New Year's breakfast which I had when I was a little girl. What do you think it was? A slice of dry bread and an apple. This is how it happened, and it is a true story, every word.

As we came down to breakfast that morning, with very shiny faces and spandy clean aprons, we found father alone in the dining-room.

"Happy New Year, papa! Where is mother?" we cried.

"A little boy came begging and said they were starving at home, so your mother went to see and—ah, here she is."

As papa spoke, in came mamma, looking very cold, rather sad, and very much excited.

"Children, don't begin till you hear what I have to say," she cried; and we sat staring at her, with the breakfast untouched before us.

"Not far away from here, lies a poor woman with a little newborn baby. Six children are huddled into one bed to keep from freezing, for they have no fire. There is nothing to eat over there; and the oldest boy came here to tell me they were starving this bitter cold day. My little girls, will you give them your breakfast, as a New Year's gift?"

We sat silent a minute, and looked at the nice, hot porridge, creamy milk, and good bread and butter; for we were brought up like English children, and never drank tea or coffee, or ate anything but porridge for our breakfast.

"I wish we'd eaten it up," thought I, for I was rather a selfish child, and very hungry.

"I'm so glad you come before we began," said Nan, cheerfully.

"May I go and help carry it to the poor, little children?" asked Beth, who had the tenderest heart that ever beat under a pinafore.

"I can carry the lassy pot," said little May, proudly giving the thing she loved best.

"And I shall take *all* the porridge," I burst in, heartily ashamed of my first feeling.

"You shall put on your things and help me, and when we come back, we'll get something to eat," said mother, beginning to pile the bread and butter into a big basket.

We were soon ready, and the procession set out. First, papa, with a basket of wood on one arm and coal on the other; mamma next, with a bundle of warm things and the teapot; Nan and I carried a pail of hot porridge between us, and each a pitcher of milk; Beth brought some cold meat, May the "lassy pot," and her old hood and boots; and Betsey, the girl, brought up the rear with a bag of potatoes and some meal.

Fortunately it was early, and we went along back streets, so few people saw us, and no one laughed at the funny party.

What a poor, bare, miserable place it was, to be sure,— broken windows, no fire, ragged clothes, wailing baby, sick mother, and a pile of pale, hungry children cuddled under one quilt, trying to keep warm. How the big eyes stared and the blue lips smiled as we came in!

"Ah, mein Gott! it is the good angels that come to us!" cried the poor woman, with tears of joy.

"Funny angels, in woollen hoods and red mittens," said I; and they all laughed.

Then we fell to work, and in fifteen minutes, it really did seem as if fairies had been at work there. Papa made a splendid fire in the old fireplace and stopped up the broken window with his own hat and coat. Mamma set the shivering children round the fire, and wrapped the poor woman in warm things. Betsey and the rest of us spread the table, and fed the starving little ones.

"Das ist gute!" "Oh, nice!" "Der angel—Kinder!" cried the poor things as they ate and smiled and basked in the warm blaze. We had never been called "angel-children" before, and we thought it very charming, especially I who had often been told I was "a regular Sancho." What fun it was! Papa, with a towel for an apron, fed the smallest child; mamma dressed the poor little new-born baby as tenderly as if it had been her own. Betsey gave the mother gruel and tea, and comforted her with assurance of better days for all. Nan, Lu, Beth, and May flew about among the seven children, talking and laughing and trying to understand their funny, broken English. It was a very happy breakfast, though we didn't get any of it; and when we came away, leaving them all so comfortable, and promising to bring clothes and food by and by, I think there were not in all the city four merrier children than the hungry little girls who gave away their breakfast, and contented themselves with a bit of bread and an apple on New Year's day.

Cousin Tribulation.

20
Merry Christmas

In the rush of early morning,
   When the red burns through the gray,
And the wintry world lies waiting
   For the glory of the day,
Then we hear a fitful rustling
   Just without upon the stair,
See two small white phantoms coming,
   Catch the gleam of sunny hair.

Are they Christmas fairies stealing
   Rows of little socks to fill?
Are they angels floating hither
   With their message of good-will?
What sweet spell are these elves weaving,
   As like larks they chirp and sing?
Are these palms of peace from heaven
   That these lovely spirits bring?

Rosy feet upon the threshold,
   Eager faces peeping through,
With the first red ray of sunshine,

Chanting cherubs come in view:
Mistletoe and gleaming holly,
    Symbols of a blessed day,
In their chubby hands they carry,
    Streaming all along the way.

Well we know them, never weary
    Of this innocent surprise;
Waiting, watching, listening always
    With full hearts and tender eyes,
While our little household angels,
    White and golden in the sun,
Greet us with the sweet old welcome,—
    "Merry Christmas, every one!"